Seven strode over to Picard with her customary assurance and stopped several feet shy of him.

"It was necessary to come straight down here to speak with you, Captain. My . . . pilot tends to be suspicious of Starfleet vessels and was disinclined to make direct contact with the *Enterprise.* This was the only reasonable compromise."

The explanation did nothing to mollify him. "May I ask the meaning of this, Seven?" he demanded, not even bothering with the standard niceties of offering introductions.

If she was bothered by the curtness of his manner, she didn't show it. "Kathryn Janeway and all of humanity are in mortal danger from the Borg." She looked around at the assemblage and then back to Picard. "Is this an inappropriate time?"

For one of the few times in his life, Picard was at a loss for words.

STAR TREK
THE NEXT GENERATION®

BEFORE DISHONOR

PETER DAVID

Based on
Star Trek: The Next Generation
created by Gene Roddenberry

POCKET BOOKS
New York London Toronto Sydney

Pocket Books
A Division of Simon & Schuster, Inc.
1230 Avenue of the Americas
New York, NY 10020

This book is published by Pocket Books, a division of Simon & Schuster, Inc., under exclusive license from CBS Studios Inc.

First Pocket Books paperback edition November 2007

For information about special discounts for bulk purchases, please contact Simon & Schuster Special Sales at 1-800-456-6798 or business@simonandschuster.com.

Manufactured in the United States of America

10 9 8 7 6

ISBN-13: 978-1-4165-2742-8
ISBN-10: 1-4165-2742-7

For Bjorn
and the rest
of the Borg

1

The *Einstein*

- i -

KATHRYN JANEWAY NEEDED TO SEE IT FOR HERSELF.

She had read the detailed reports provided her by Seven of Nine. She had spoken at length with Captain Jean-Luc Picard, about whom she was still seething. In short, she had all the information she really required. Going to the Borg cube wasn't going to accomplish a damned thing.

Yet here she was, on her way, just the same.

Although she was entitled, by her rank of vice admiral, to commandeer an entire starship for the purpose of essaying the trip, she had opted not to do so. She considered it a waste of resources. Instead she had been content to catch a ride on the

Einstein, a standard science exploration vessel. The commander of the *Einstein,* Howard Rappaport, had been enthused to welcome Janeway aboard. Short and stocky, but with eyes that displayed a piercing intellect, Rappaport had peppered her with questions about all the races that she had encountered during the *Voyager*'s odyssey from the Delta Quadrant. It hadn't been something that she'd been overly interested in discussing, but turning down Rappaport's incessant interrogation would have felt like kicking an eager puppy, and so she had accommodated him during their trip as often as she had felt reasonable.

At least she knew he was paying attention, because not only did he hang on every word she spoke, but he kept asking intelligent follow-up questions. Still, at one point he said eagerly, "I wish I'd been there."

Upon hearing that, Janeway had promptly shut him down with a curt, "No. You really don't." When she said that, he looked as if he wanted to ask more about her attitude in that regard, but he wisely opted to back off when he saw the slightly haunted look in Janeway's eyes.

There were three other Starfleet officers traveling on the *Einstein* with Janeway, all of them purported experts on the Borg. The officers—Commanders Andy Brevoort and Tom Schmidt, and Lieutenant Commander Mark Wacker—were experienced xenobiologists who had been given a simple mandate by Starfleet: find a way to develop an absolute protection against the Borg should they launch another attack. The general feeling of the United Federation of Planets Council and Starfleet in particular was that, even though they had managed to dodge destruction at the hands of the Borg each and every time, they owed a measure of that success to sheer luck. The plan was to try to remove luck from the equation and replace it with a practical, proven solution.

The *Einstein* was long on durability but short on amenities. It was designed to cater to scientists, not to top brass or ambassadors or any of that ilk. Janeway's quarters were consequently the most luxurious the ship had to offer yet still quite spare. The admiral didn't care. She didn't tend to stand on ceremony in such matters. Give her the *Einstein*'s breathable atmosphere, functioning gravity, and a steady source of coffee, and Janeway was content.

The admiral was worried she was becoming an addict. The last time she'd been on a starship, she'd studied the warp core too long and decided that it looked like a gigantic antique coffeemaker. She'd sworn—at that point—to give up the hideously addictive brew. Yet here she was now, nursing a cup of black coffee while she read over yet again the reports from all the various sources about the monstrous Borg cube that the *Enterprise* had managed to take down pretty much single-handedly. There was a transcript of all Picard's log entries on the subject, as well as the entries from other crew members including, most notably, the Vulcan counselor, T'Lana. Janeway shook her head as she read it, still bristling at the very thought of all that had transpired contrary to her orders.

"How could you, Picard?" she asked rhetorically of the empty room. "How could you put me in that kind of position, just on a hunch?"

"It's what I would have done."

The voice caught her by surprise, because she had naturally thought she was alone. She turned and, uncharacteristically but understandably, let out a startled yelp.

James T. Kirk was standing in her quarters.

"What the hell—?" Janeway was on her feet, gaping.

Kirk was wearing a very old-style Starfleet uniform, a simple yellow shirt with black collar. He smoothed it down and gave her a wry smile. "Hello, Admiral. Or Kathryn, perhaps? Would it be too forward if I addressed you as Kathryn? Feel free to call me Jim."

Fortunately Janeway had been in enough bizarre situations, had enough experiences that would have made lesser men and women question their sanity, that she was thrown for only a few moments. She recovered quickly from her initial shock and then said briskly, "I'm quite certain I'm not dreaming . . ."

"How would you know?" said Kirk. He walked casually around the small quarters, looking disapproving.

"I know because I dream in black and white."

"Perhaps you're only dreaming that you're dreaming in color," he countered. He gestured around himself. "Space may be infinite, but obviously not in here. They couldn't provide you with larger accommodations?"

"I wasn't expecting to share them. Who are you?" she demanded. She felt no need to summon help at that point; she didn't believe she was in any immediate danger. Besides, it was a science vessel, not a starship, so it wasn't as if a crack security team was going to come running.

"I'm James T. Kirk." He tilted his head slightly, quizzically. "Are you having short-term memory difficulties? You may want to see somebody about that . . ."

"I know you're *supposed* to be James T. Kirk. That's who you're presenting yourself as. But obviously you're not."

"Why are you fighting it, Kathryn?" he said with what he doubtless thought was suavity. He smiled wryly. "You once said you wished you could have teamed up with me. So what's wrong with getting your wish once in a while?"

Her eyes narrowed, her mind racing toward an inevitable conclusion. There was no trace of amusement in her voice. "All right. Drop it."

"Come on, Kathryn," Kirk said wheedlingly. "I was famous for flouting Starfleet regulations. You know that. Everybody knows that. Picard's mistake wasn't disobeying your direct order to wait for Seven of Nine and then, and only then, seek out the Borg cube that his 'link' to their hive mind had detected. His mistake was consulting you at all. He should have done just what I always did: send off a brisk message telling you what he was up to, go off and do it, and then wait for you to tell him that you trusted him to make the right call. Or is that the problem?" He regarded her thoughtfully. "Are you having trust issues, Kathryn? That's it, isn't it. You dislike having to reach into yourself and trust others."

"I," said Janeway through clenched teeth, "am not about to discuss any of my personality traits, real or imagined, with you . . ." She paused and added with a firm flourish, "Q."

Kirk blinked in overblown surprise. "Is that a failed attempt to utter a profanity? I hardly think it's warranted . . ."

"What is it this time, Q? Another civil war under way in your Q Continuum? More problems with your son? Or were you just sitting around in whatever plane it is that you reside in and you suddenly thought, 'You know what? It's been ages since I tried to annoy Kathryn Janeway, so I think I'll have a go of it. But maybe, just maybe, if I show up looking like someone else, she'll be stupid enough to fall for it.' Nice try, and it might have worked were I monumentally stupid. So drop the façade. It's not as if you even knew James T. Kirk."

"Don't be so sure of everything you think you know, Kathryn. You see"—Kirk smiled—"even I, who truly *do* know everything, know enough to know what I don't know."

Kirk's form suddenly shifted, and Janeway was fully expecting to see the smug face of the cosmic entity known as Q standing before her. Who else, after all, would it be? Who else would show up out of nowhere, looking like someone who was long dead, and acting in an overly familiar and generally insufferable manner?

So she was understandably startled when she saw something other than what she was expecting.

Kirk had transformed into a woman, with a look in her eyes that was as steely as anything Janeway might be capable of shooting her way. She had long auburn hair and that same general look of contempt that Q managed to display with such facility. Unlike Q, who seemed to enjoy walking around in a Starfleet outfit, she was attired in an elaborate dress of red velvet with ruffles on the sleeves and a bodice that looked as if it would be at home in the eighteenth century.

"I know you," Janeway said after a moment. "You're Q's . . ." She fished for the right term and settled for "significant other. The mother of his child."

"The mother of *our* child," she corrected Janeway archly.

"Wait," said Janeway, suspicious. "How do I know you're not the . . . other Q except affecting another disguise?"

"Why would I do that?"

"How would I know? I don't even know why you made yourself look like James Kirk, much less another Q . . . Q." She was finding it annoying having to deal with the fact that all the inhabitants of the continuum referred to themselves as "Q." Considering that they were beings of unlimited power, one would have thought they could at the very least have enough power to come up with individual names. Naturally their philosophy was that they didn't need names to deal with one another, that they were, in fact, beyond such limited concepts. Janeway, however, was not, and even though she was going to continue to address this being as "Q," she was already thinking of her in her own head as "Lady Q," just to keep her thoughts in order.

Lady Q shrugged at the question. "Because I felt like it. The Q don't really need any excuse other than that."

"Not good enough."

That prompted Lady Q to smile, although there didn't seem to be a trace of amusement in it. "For someone who hasn't even lived one lifetime, you're a demanding little creature. I can see why Q finds you endlessly interesting . . . not unlike, I suppose, a particularly gruesome scab that you simply can't help picking at. All right," she continued before Janeway could say anything, "if you'd like more than that . . . I thought it would help underscore the message that you're becoming insufferably smug and overly certain of yourself."

"Oh, am I? And I'm certain the Q would be steeped in firsthand knowledge of those traits."

"Yes, we would," replied Lady Q with obvious

pride. "We, however, have a reason to. In your case . . . less so."

"Now look—"

"You *asked,* I'm *answering.*" Lady Q cut her off, and Janeway could sense a change in the energy in the room. This creature, as much as she might appear human, most definitely wasn't . . . and, furthermore, could reduce her to free-floating atoms with a gesture . . .

"*Less* than a gesture," said Lady Q.

Janeway's spine stiffened. "Get out of my head," she practically snarled.

Lady Q turned away from her as if the order hadn't even registered. "As I was saying, smug and too confident. You take Picard to task for actions and attitudes that you find commendable in Kirk."

"It's a different time. The universe is a more dangerous place."

"The universe has always been a dangerous place. You're just more aware of it, that's all. You sit in judgment on Picard, but do you ever wonder if—had you been overseeing Kirk back in those halcyon days—you would have been as understanding as his superiors were? Or would you have been pressing for court-martial because he dared to display free will."

"I believe in free will. But I also believe in chain of command. Captain Kirk faced special circumstances, and I'd like to think that I would have recognized that as his superior officer. Anyway," Janeway said with a shrug, "it seems to me you're going to a great deal of trouble to come here and defend Picard . . ."

"I didn't come here to defend Picard. I don't care about him in the slightest."

That declaration took Janeway off guard. "Well, then why . . . ?"

"I came here because of you."

"Me?"

"No, because of the letter *u*," she said sarcastically.

Janeway fixed her a look. "You call yourselves the Q. I wasn't ruling anything out."

Lady Q looked as if she was about to fire off another biting reply, but then her face softened. "All right . . . that's a fair point," she admitted. "Yes, I'm here because of you, Kathryn Janeway. Clear enough?"

"The sentiment is. The reason . . . less so."

"If you must know—and what with you being what you are, obviously you must—it's because of Q. Yes, *that* Q," she added quickly.

"What about him? Is there a problem?"

There was clearly something in Janeway's voice that caught Lady Q's attention. "You care for him! How intriguing!"

"I care *about* him," Janeway corrected her in a severe tone, "in the same way that I care about many sentient beings who, nevertheless, annoy the hell out of me and represent a grave threat to everyone and everything that matters to me."

"Well, thanks for clarifying that."

Janeway was about to press her on what was going on, but Lady Q gestured in a peremptory manner and Janeway fell silent. She reminded herself that this was an omnipotent being who was, to the best of Janeway's knowledge, effectively immortal. Janeway, all too mortal, felt the constant crush of time. For Lady Q and her ilk, such considerations never factored in, so she was naturally inclined to take her own sweet time expressing herself.

"I know why you're smug and overconfident," Lady Q said finally.

"And would you care to share this tidbit of insight with me?"

"I will if you would do me the honor of shutting up for a few minutes so that I could string together a few sentences."

Janeway was about to reply but then thought better of it.

Lady Q didn't immediately continue, as if silently daring Janeway to say anything further. When she didn't, Lady Q continued, "You're smug and overconfident because you believe you've seen the future. An older version of yourself traveled through time and helped you and your ship utilize a Borg transwarp corridor to come home, saving you sixteen years of travel time and the life of your precious Seven of Nine in the process. And because of that, you figure that your destiny is set in stone. How could it not be? You know what's going to happen to you, and when. Thus you reason that you needn't concern yourself with reckless behavior because of the time paradox that would ensue in the event of your premature death."

"In dealing with time travel, I've learned never to take anything for granted," Janeway assured her.

"That's what you say. But your attitude, your actions, your very thoughts betray you otherwise."

"I've never been a big fan of people claiming to know my own mind better than I do."

"And yet I do, and you're just going to have to deal with that bit of reality. And by the way, you actually kept your mouth shut for a full twenty-nine seconds. Would that constitute a personal best for you?"

"I fail to see what any of this has to do with Q, with me, or with your presence here."

"Of course you see. And that's the tragedy of it."

With that pronouncement, Lady Q leaned against the wall and sighed the heavy sigh of one who does not gladly suffer fools. "There's an old Earth cliché that very much covers the situation here . . ."

"'Mind your own damned business'?" Janeway suggested.

Lady Q shook her head. "No. I think it's, 'Biting off more than you can chew.' And that's what you're doing here, heading toward this Borg cube. Q doesn't want you doing it."

"Oh, really. And why not?"

"Because he knows what's going to happen if and when you do."

"And yet he feels no need to come and avail me of this knowledge himself?"

"No, he doesn't . . . partly because he doesn't feel like dealing with your exaggerated word choices such as 'avail me of this knowledge' instead of simply saying 'tell me.' And partly because he knows that you're just going to ignore him and do whatever you want anyway. He finds that thought painful."

Janeway had to laugh at that. "Painful? Are you saying that Q doesn't want me to hurt his feelings? That's pretty funny considering his endless boasting over being above such human considerations."

"What Q says and what Q feels are two entirely different things," Lady Q replied. "And you never heard me say that."

It was such a remarkably vulnerable thing for Lady Q to say that Janeway was momentarily speechless.

"Q knows," said Lady Q, "that if he showed up here, you'd have all manner of reason to doubt him. You'd wonder what his game is. Plus I think he feels that if you experience your—quite frankly—tragic fate without his trying to intervene directly, then he bears no culpability for it. If on the other hand he tries to stop you and you ignore him, as you most likely would, then he'll feel like a failure. Oh, he'll cover it up, of course. He'll sneer and strut and chalk you off as yet another example of the endless stupidity of your race. But I think that, deep down, it's going to gnaw at him. So I decided that I would endeavor to intercede myself. Except," she said with a trace of sadness, "it's becoming obvious to me that I'm not going to be any more effective than Q would have been. His instincts were correct on that score. I was hoping this warning would be able to supersede your aforementioned overconfidence, but it's becoming clear to me that that's not going to be the case."

"What warning? You've given me no concrete 'warning' of any sort," Janeway said impatiently. "You've given me vague hints, portents of doom, but nothing beyond that. Am I supposed to abort a mission simply on rumor and innuendo?"

"Yes," Lady Q said firmly. "You don't seem to know when you have it good, Admiral Janeway. I am a being of infinite power, as is Q. The fact that he, and I . . . that we . . . have taken any sort of interest in you at all is a remarkable gift."

"A *gift*?" Janeway couldn't believe it. "All the trouble the Q have caused . . . the lives you've disrupted . . . my God, Q was the one who first drew the Borg's attention toward humanity. And you have the nerve to characterize any of that as a gift?"

"It was, and it is. Just because you don't recognize it for what it is doesn't make it any less so. Because of that, you should be grateful."

"Pardon me if I manage to restrain my gratitude."

"Oh, I pardon you . . . but fate will not."

"I reject the notion of fate," said Janeway. "It flies in the face of free will."

"Yet you believe that your rescue of *Voyager* is fated to succeed. So what happens to free will then?"

Janeway had no ready comeback for that.

"The point is," said Lady Q, "that whether you believe it or not, it's an honor that I've taken the time to come and talk to you at all. You should be willing to take it as a matter of faith when I tell you that you should steer clear of the Borg cube. Nothing good will come of your traipsing around on it. Or is it that, along with not believing in fate, you have no faith?"

"I have plenty of faith," Janeway said. "But I put it in myself, and in my fellow humans. Not vague warnings from representatives of a race with a track record of seeing human beings as their personal playthings."

Lady Q seemed to find that amusing. "If your biblical God had handed you the Ten Commandments, Kathryn, you'd have considered them mere broad recommendations and turned them over to a board of inquiry for further study."

"You're not God."

"Don't be so sure. You should see my terrible swift sword."

"What's *that* supposed to mean?"

"It means, my dear Janeway, that if you—a mere mortal—feel no need to explain yourself to me, how much less need do I, who would be indistinguishable from a god to any of your more credulous ancestors, have to explain myself to you? I will say this for you, though: you're to be admired for your consistency. Jean-Luc Picard asked you to take his conviction that the Borg were gearing up to attack as a matter of faith. You refused to do so. When he proved to be correct, you contemplate punishing him for it. Now you are asked to display faith in me with your own fate on the line. Your response? You not only have no faith in me . . . you have no faith in fate. You know what I wonder about you, Kathryn Janeway?"

"What? What do you wonder?" asked Janeway, although she didn't have much interest.

But her blood ran cold at Lady Q's reply.

"I wonder if, when you lose your soul, you'll even notice."

With that comment, Lady Q vanished in a burst of light.

- ii -

She didn't sleep that night. Not one bit.

Instead Kathryn Janeway was up until all hours, reviewing all of the research and trying to get past her gut reaction that Lady Q, or Q, or whoever or whatever that being had been, was simply trying to undermine her confidence.

Janeway sat back in her chair, rubbed the bridge of her nose, and let out a heavy sigh. She felt as if she were seeing all this information for the first time, unwillingly viewing it through the filter that had been dropped on her courtesy of Lady Q.

"Admiral's personal log," she said, and the computer immediately accessed her personal log. "Q, if you're listening . . . if any of you are listening"—and she sarcastically applauded slowly—"brava. You have prompted me to review all of my preliminary scientific reports involving the Borg cube. I've consulted with the heads of the exploratory parties who have already inspected the cube from top to bottom: the best scientific minds that the Federation has to offer. They have all assured me of the same conclusion: that the Borg cube is effectively dead. The Borg drones are displaying no brain activity whatsoever, not even the minimal activity required to indicate a functioning hive mind. Nor are there any signs of metabolic functions. The Borg drones are effectively corpses. They are not deteriorating in the way that a corpse would, for which I suppose we should be thankful. Only a handful of drones remain on the ship; the majority of the bodies have been transferred to Starfleet Headquarters in San Francisco, where our top scientists will be studying them. There is no queen, no sign of any sort of energy processes in the cube. Basically it's a vast cemetery. Even Seven of Nine concurs, although she is on record as protesting the transporting of the Borg drone bodies to Earth. She feels it would be better simply to dispose of them, although that could easily be attributed to her own strong feelings regarding her long history with the race. All of this begs the question . . . why am I going?"

She grew silent at that, a silence that grew to such length that the computer prompted, "Log entry concluded?"

"Continue entry," Janeway said as she stared at the wall. "I . . . have to see them," she said finally. "To see it. Despite everything that every expert has told me, I have to see it for myself. Have to see the cube that was so daunting, so commanding, so . . . formidable that Jean-Luc Picard was willing to throw away his entire Starfleet career. As near as we can determine, the demise of this cube and its queen will allow us to end the Borg threat forever. Indeed, it's possible that they have been effectively exterminated as a race. With all the history I've had with them, how could I not take the opportunity to . . . how best to put it? Pay my final respects. See with my own eyes the site of the final battle where Picard risked his ship, his life, his very soul.

"Do the Borg have souls?

"What an odd question. I'm not normally one to dwell excessively on matters of spirituality. Who knows for certain if any of us truly possesses something so intangible? I'd like to think so . . . like to think that there's some grand meaning beyond that which we can perceive. But none of us knows for certain, and obviously once we reach the point where we do know, it's too late. Still, if there is a soul, what becomes of it once one is assimilated? Is it transmuted, polluted? Is it stolen away, never to return? Doubtful. Seven of Nine and Picard have been there and returned. Although perhaps"—she looked thoughtful—"perhaps that's the question that follows them, although I doubt they'd ever articulate it. Sometimes I look into Seven's face and I see a distant, haunted look. It's only brief, there and gone, and she typically denies that she's having any sort of problem. But I know it's there, and she likely knows that I know. I doubt that she'd worry about the loss of her soul . . ." Janeway stood, shaking her head. "This is ridiculous. I'm worrying about all sorts of irrelevant notions rather than considering what's really on my mind: what to do about Jean-Luc Picard?

"On the surface of it, the question is simple: Did Picard knowingly violate orders? On that basis alone, he should be filleted, grilled, and served up for court-martial with a side of tartar sauce. The fact that his actions saved the Federation from a potentially overwhelming Borg attack shouldn't factor in. Except," she continued with a grimace, "obviously it does, and it will. Perhaps that's why Q chose to appear to me as James T. Kirk . . . to remind me that he was in even deeper difficulties than Picard, after stealing the *Starship Enterprise.* But he wound up saving Earth from the effects of a mysterious alien probe, and the Federation Council patted him on the head, gave him command of a starship, and sent him on his way. So there's every possibility that any proceeding against Picard could wind up going in the exact same direction.

"Then we come to the question of state of mind. Picard insisted that he was connected to the Borg hive mind, and simply 'knew' that the Borg were active and in the process of creating a new queen. The argument could be made that his 'compulsion' to get to the Borg as quickly as possible was biologically based, and thus he was functioning under diminished capacity. Or maybe . . ."

Once again she lapsed into silence, but before the computer could prompt her, she said so softly that it was almost inaudible, ". . . maybe he was just trying to save his soul."

Janeway could have sworn that the words she had just spoken were hanging there in front of her, hovering and daring her to take them back.

"As for my belief that I'm somehow immune to any sort of disaster thanks to my knowing at least some portion of my future," she continued, "I would like to think I don't have that degree of hubris that I would consider myself to be . . . untouchable . . . by the hand of fate, presuming there is such a thing. The scientific argument could be made that the Admiral Janeway I encountered—the one from the future—came from an alternate time line. That in the very act of folding back on her own history, she wound up creating a variant universe from the one that she knew, and that's the one I'm living in right now. If that's the case, then obviously I'm as 'at risk' as anyone else. If I dropped dead of a heart attack right now, the Janeway I met would still be safe and sound in her parallel world, waiting for her personal call to action. Nothing is certain. Nothing is safe. If the Borg taught us anything, it is most certainly that.

"I take nothing for granted. That's the only way that any of us can live our lives."

After a moment, she concluded, "End personal log entry."

She drummed her fingers on the desk and then said, "Record communiqué to Starfleet Command. Official recommendation vis-à-vis the pending court-martial of Jean-Luc Picard, captain—commanding *U.S.S. Enterprise* NCC-1701-E: Upon consideration, my best judgment on this matter is that court-martial proceedings not be pursued at this time, but instead that Captain Picard . . ."—she paused for a long moment and then a slow smile spread across her face—". . . instead suggest that a commendation for original thinking be entered into his file. You are, of course, free to ignore this recommendation and proceed as you see fit. Janeway out."

2

The Borg Cube

- i -

CAPTAIN RAPPAPORT'S EYES WIDENED AS THE SHIP drew nearer to the Borg cube, hanging in space like a great floating cancer. He gulped deeply. "I've heard about them, of course . . . seen vids . . . but . . ."

"It's very different from being up close and personal," Janeway agreed wryly, standing next to him on the bridge.

Rappaport himself wasn't much of a scientist. Despite the fact that he was in command of a science vessel, his training leaned more toward dealing with the sorts of hazards that any ship might encounter in the depths of space. His job, when it came down to it, was making sure that the scientists he brought to and from specific locations got there and came back in one piece. He was always impressed with scientists' ability to keep their cool when confronted with just about anything. In this case, he was watching Commanders Schmidt, Wacker, and Brevoort studying the Borg cube with remarkable dispassion, taking notes, recording comments, even though they were still a distance from it.

Rappaport noticed that Janeway's attitude was very different. Rather than analyzing it on a scientific basis, Rappaport felt that Janeway was regarding it with a sort of warrior's cunning, waiting for it to make some type of hostile move against which she would take immediate action. He found it far easier to relate to how she was looking at it than the way the scientists were.

"Actually," Rappaport said to her, "it's the fact that we're *not* up close that I find so disturbing. That thing is gargantuan even from this distance. Are they all this . . . this . . ."

"Daunting?"

He nodded.

"No," said Janeway. "No, this one is larger than most."

"I guess size really does matter."

He thought that would get a laugh from Janeway, but all it elicited was a tolerant grimace. The captain made a mental note to himself not to bother trying to joke around with the vice admiral again.

"Shall we ready the transporter?"

"Actually," Brevoort spoke up, "we've been discussing it, and we would far prefer a shuttle, if that's not too much difficulty. It will enable us to make a more complete study of the vessel's structure if we can enter from the outside."

Rappaport looked to Janeway, who appeared to consider it for a moment before nodding. "Bridge to shuttlebay," he said briskly.

"Shuttlebay here."

"Ready *Shuttle Chawla* for immediate launch."

"Thank you, Captain," said Janeway. "Bring us to within transporter range just in case, and stay on site. We will be reporting in on half-hour intervals. If we fail to do so . . ."

"Then I'll lock on to your communicators and beam you back."

"No."

He blinked in surprise. Her response drew startled looks from the scientists as well.

"No?" echoed Rappaport.

"No," she said firmly. "If you cannot get in touch with us, then we have to assume that something has gone wrong. If that's the case, then bringing us aboard the ship could prove dangerous. We would be far better served if you retreated to a safe distance and informed Starfleet."

"We would?" Schmidt asked tentatively and got an annoyed look from Brevoort as a result.

"Admiral," Wacker spoke up slowly, "are you expecting that there will be some sort of problem on the Borg cube?"

"No," said Janeway. "I am, however, anticipating the possibility. Better to consider anything and everything that can go wrong, no matter how unlikely."

"Good idea, Admiral," said Brevoort. Schmidt nodded in agreement, but Rappaport could see that Commander Schmidt was no longer looking as scientifically dispassionate about the endeavor as he was earlier.

Then Rappaport looked back to the Borg cube and kept telling himself that, despite Janeway's displaying reasonable caution, there was nothing to be concerned about. Experts in Starfleet had pronounced the thing dead, based on everything they knew about the Borg. The only thing that concerned him now was whether there were things that no one knew about the Borg that were going to throw everything off-kilter.

- ii -

The journey into the Borg cube was uneventful but not unintimidating.

Janeway and the other Starfleet officers were far too professional in their experience and comportment to allow themselves to be overwhelmed by what they were witnessing. Still, it did take a considerable amount of self-control for Janeway not to shudder as the shuttle drew closer and closer to the Borg cube and the damned thing just kept getting bigger. She knew intellectually how large it was; the instrumentation had been very precise in its readings. Knowing it was very different from experiencing it, however, and the experience was one that Janeway had hoped she'd never have again.

"What do you think, Admiral?" Brevoort asked her as he studied the readings upon their approach. Schmidt, who in addition to being a scientist was also an accomplished shuttle pilot, was handling the actual maneuvering of the shuttle through the cube.

Janeway shrugged in a show of indifference. "I've seen bigger."

Brevoort cast a glance her way and then grinned. She allowed herself, ever so briefly, to smile in response, then went back to gazing in amazement at the thing. She tried to tell herself that it was fundamentally no different from any other cube that she had ever seen. The method by which it had been constructed was the same, differing only in its scope.

I wonder if it's filled with ghosts . . .

The stray thought wandered through her mind unwanted, and she tried to shake it off. She didn't know why, but suddenly, inexplicably, she felt shaken. She turned away from the viewscreen, catching Schmidt's notice as she did so. "Something wrong, Admiral?"

"Just . . . have something in my eye," she said, making a show of wiping at the tear duct to clear out the nonexistent obstruction.

Ghosts. Why in the hell had she thought of ghosts just then?

There was no need to wonder; she knew perfectly well the reason why. It was because of Seven of Nine, and Seven's report to her after she'd returned from the Borg cube.

Is it dead?

Seven had been giving her a lengthy, detailed blow-by-blow assessment of all aspects of the Borg cube, and Janeway had sat there in her office and listened to every word; she really had. It wasn't as if she had cause for complaint. She had been the one who insisted that Seven sit down with her face-to-face and give her a complete debriefing. There was, after all, no greater authority on the Borg than Seven, and Janeway had wanted it straight from the horse's mouth, as it were. Seven had obliged her, and the report had been practically suffocating in its comprehensiveness.

The entire time, though, as Seven had presented her findings to the minutest detail, Janeway had felt as if there was something—some aspect—that Seven was holding back. She didn't think it was deliberate on Seven's part, or that Seven was trying to hide something from her. Still, she sensed it, and half an hour into Seven's presentation she had interrupted and said, "What are you not telling me?"

Seven had stared blandly at her. She opened her mouth and then closed it without speaking, as if switching tracks in her mind. "I do not understand the question," she had finally said.

"There's just . . . there's something you're not saying, Seven. Something on your mind. I know you well enough to tell. What is it?" She had not wanted to sound overbearing about it. The admiral wasn't interested in barking orders; she was interested in probing to discover what was on Seven's mind.

Seven of Nine didn't answer immediately. She had seemed aware of the hesitation, but her face had only become more dispassionate. Finally she had said, "I am not . . . certain that I would be able to convey the reactions I experienced upon my arrival on the Borg cube."

"And to what would that reaction have been? It wasn't . . ." Janeway had hesitated, almost unable to get the sentence out. "It wasn't as if you could sense thoughts floating about . . . there isn't any danger of . . ."

"I do not believe there is. The Borg cube currently shows no signs of life . . . at least by any reasonable definition we could apply."

"Then what's concerning you?"

"The unreasonable definition."

Janeway had stared at her uncomprehending. "Unreasonable?"

"The Borg are supremely adaptable. That is the entire point of their ability to assimilate, to adapt to attacks. They are in a perpetual state of evolution. In one reading of the situation, the Borg cube has been shut down terminally . . . permanently. In another reading of it, however, the Borg have simply been presented with yet another challenge to overcome. And the Borg have a disconcerting habit of overcoming those challenges."

"But how would they do that?"

"I do not know," Seven had admitted. "That is what I find so disconcerting . . . and may well be contributing to the odd sensations I feel in relation to the matter. The entire time I was in the cube, I thought I sensed . . . something. A sense of almost free-floating anxiety. 'Ghost' sensations, to use the old Earth terminology. However, such concepts are rooted in superstition. Every scrap of logic and common sense indicates that I felt that way not due to any real threat but because of irrational concerns on my part. I do not wish to waste your time or Starfleet's time on irrational concerns. It is for that reason that I am reluctant to bring it up at all. Starfleet deserves an assessment based upon solid observations, not vague sensations that most certainly stem from groundless fears."

"When it comes to the Borg," Janeway had told her, "there is no such thing as groundless fears."

They had talked for a while longer, Seven completing her analysis and being forced to the conclusion—absent any data to the contrary—that the Borg cube was about as hazardous as a dead moon. Still, when Janeway had proposed that she would go out to inspect it, Seven had been less than sanguine over the prospect. "You may want to consider waiting for a time, just to be certain."

"How long a time?"

Seven had considered it and then said, "Ten years would be sufficient."

Janeway had tried not to laugh at that. "Are you suggesting that for the next ten years I shouldn't hesitate to send other officers, scientists, and such to inspect the cube to their hearts' content . . . but I personally should give it as much distance as possible?"

"That sounds to me like the ideal strategy."

"And what sort of message would that send?"

Seven had titled her head in that slightly quizzical, almost doglike manner she had and said, "I was not concerned about messages, merely about attending to your safety, to keeping you alive."

"Sometimes," Janeway had told her, "in order to feel alive, one has to take chances with one's safety."

Seven had considered that and then shook her head. "No. One really does not."

No. One really does not.

Those words echoed in Janeway's head as the *Shuttle Chawla* found a docking point. Schmidt ran a check and nodded approvingly. "Breathable atmosphere," he said. "No life signs, aside from us."

"Let's do it," said Janeway.

The shuttle exit door hissed open and Kathryn Janeway stepped out into the Borg cube. The others followed her, but Janeway had stopped moving.

Instead she was looking up and up, and after a few long moments she suddenly remembered that it would probably be a smart thing to breathe. So she let out the breath that had caught in her lungs while continuing to gaze straight up.

The view seemed to go on forever. Stairways and catwalks crisscrossing each other, in a random fashion at first glance, but after long enough observation there seemed to be some sort of pattern to it all, although she couldn't begin to guess what, if anything, the pattern might actually mean.

Wacker let out a low whistle even as he started taking readings with his tricorder. "You ever see anything like this, Admiral?"

Yes. More times than I care to count, and after that repeatedly in my nightmares, she thought. Aloud, she said, "It's . . . impressive."

"How long do you think it took them to construct?"

"That, Lieutenant Commander, is part of what we're here to find out."

"Yes, Admiral," said Wacker, who then went on about his work.

"Do we split up, Admiral?" asked Brevoort. "It would help the work move along more quickly."

Janeway allowed a thin smile. "I've read enough old ghost stories to know the folly of that approach, Commander. When groups in big old, scary structures go off in different directions, that's when Extremely Bad Things tend to happen."

"Are you expecting Extremely Bad Things,

Admiral?" asked Schmidt, sounding a bit concerned.

"Always. That way if and when they occur, I won't be caught by surprise."

Kathryn Janeway had turned away from Schmidt while she was talking, unable to tear her gaze from the near infinite scope of the surrounding cube. She was certain that her imagination was being overactive, but she felt as if voices were calling to her. She knew that many good Starfleet officers had died here during the *Enterprise*'s pitched battle with the Borg drones. Traditionally the Borg took no offensive action against intruders; the *Enterprise* crew members had learned the hard way that the status quo had changed when they had shown up in the Borg cube, searching for the queen so they could take her down before she was completed, and had been ambushed by Borg drones who had attacked them on sight. Janeway had been sure that, thanks to her previous visits to Borg cubes, she would be inured to the horrors they presented. She was annoyed to discover that she was wrong; she fancied that she could hear the sounds of pitched battle, the cries of the poor dying devils . . .

No. No, it was more than imagination. She was becoming convinced that she actually *could* hear something. Low, multiple moanings, like a haunted house, except there were no such things as haunted houses, that was just fictional stuff and nonsense. This was . . . what? Chronal echoes? Some sort of bend in the space-time continuum? Something as mundane as a recording that had been made by unseen machinery that was now playing it back for some reason?

"Do you hear that?" Janeway demanded. "Get a reading on those."

There was no reply.

She turned and saw that she was alone.

"What the hell . . . ?" she breathed, and then she said into her combadge, "Brevoort! Schmidt! Wacker! Report." Nothing. No response. Even though she was keeping the unit on open channel, nevertheless she tapped it just in case it hadn't been activated and then repeated the hail. Still nothing.

She walked quickly down the main corridor where they had all been standing. There was no sign of any of them. She shouted their names, and her voice echoed up and down the hallway, and seemed to rebound up through the towering archways that stretched above her head.

Janeway didn't panic or even come close to it. She was far too seasoned a hand to let such an unproductive emotion overwhelm her. Instead she moved quickly and briskly toward where they had docked the shuttlecraft while, at the same time, hitting her combadge once more. "Janeway to *Einstein*. Come in. We have an emergency situation."

No response. Well, she should have seen that coming.

She turned the corner where she was certain that the shuttlecraft had been docked only to find that it looked completely different from what she remembered. Either she had made a wrong turn (unlikely) or the cube had somehow reconfigured itself (even more unlikely, but not impossible).

She started to retrace her steps, but she hadn't gone more than three meters before she suddenly found herself confronted by a solid wall.

"We are not amused," she muttered, quoting a long-dead British monarch.

"We don't blame you."

Janeway's head whipped around and she saw Lady Q standing less than a meter away. She was regarding Janeway with a mixture of pity, contempt, and sadness.

"So," said Janeway tightly, "this is your doing."

Lady Q arched an eyebrow in an amused manner. "Could you possibly sound any more melodramatic? 'This is your doing.' You'd think I was some sneering comic opera villain."

"Where are my people?"

"You mean the poor individuals who were foolish enough to follow you on this misbegotten endeavor? They're in much the same predicament as you, actually. Wandering around, confused, wondering where each of you went."

"Is this your idea of humor?"

"You want to know my idea of humor? I'll tell you," said Lady Q, and there was no longer any hint of amusement. "My idea of humor was watching your ancestors gathered in their churches, worshipping whatever deity they found solace in, and a lightning bolt would strike the church or an earthquake would demolish it. That entertained me greatly. My idea of humor is that I, a being of infinite power who could go anywhere and do anything, took the time to warn you not to come here. And what did you do? You came here anyway."

"If you truly wanted to stop me, you could have prevented me from coming here with no effort at all."

"I have no interest in supplanting free will. There's only so long you can hold a child's hand. Sooner or later she must stand or fall on her own."

"I," Janeway said heatedly, "am no child."

"Obviously not. To start with, a child might actually have listened to its elders. A child will not assume that she knows better, or perhaps think that there's some sort of elaborate scheme under way and she's being manipulated. The sad truth is that I tried to help you because I thought it would make Q happy. For all the good it will do, I might as well not have bothered at all."

"I," said Kathryn Janeway, "am a vice admiral of Starfleet. I do not need your help. Now, unless you tell me immediately where—"

She began striding toward Lady Q, and that was when the entire Borg cube shuddered violently. Lady Q was unperturbed, not even giving the slightest indication that she was aware of the seismic shift of the flooring beneath her feet. Janeway, on the other hand, stumbled forward and put out her hands to try and break her fall. Instead she succeeded only in ripping up the skin on both palms as she went down. Her hands were stinging furiously; it felt like someone was pouring vinegar on an open wound. She held them up to check the damage and saw long streaks of blood. The blood was also smeared on the floor.

"Now you've gone and done it," Lady Q murmured.

Janeway was about to reply when she saw, to her shock, that the blood on the floor was vanishing. At first glance it was seeping into the metal flooring, but closer inspection showed that the blood was actually being drawn into the floor itself. It was as if the floor was a sponge and the blood was water. The blood was gone within seconds.

Having managed to climb to her feet by that time, Janeway said angrily, "What's happening? You know. Tell me."

"Oh, *now* you're willing to listen. Too late. Far too late."

The cube shook again, more violently this time, and Janeway staggered and fell once more. This time she stopped herself from hitting the floor. Instead she thudded against the far wall. She braced herself against it, trying to figure out what to do next.

The wall gave way.

For a heartbeat she thought that it had simply crumpled beneath her weight, but then she realized that it had actually softened. She tried to pull away from it, but she couldn't get any leverage. Instead the more she tried to pull away, the more it sucked her in, like quicksand. She struggled furiously, tried to gain traction with her feet, but her feet slid out from under her. The next thing she knew, they were being pulled in as well.

She saw Lady Q standing there, watching her with arms folded. "Ask me for help. Beg me for help," Lady Q said.

Janeway spat out a curse and tried once more to yank her arms clear. She didn't come close to succeeding. Her efforts seemed to be directed against her.

She thrust her head forward, perhaps hoping against hope that she could disengage herself through sheer willpower. She failed utterly, and now the process was speeding up. Her arms were gone, sucked into the very fabric of the Borg cube, her legs were following, her torso was being absorbed, and the walls were closing in on either side of her head.

"Come on . . . you can do it. Beg. Beg and maybe, just maybe, I'll help."

Janeway opened her mouth but had no idea what she was going to say. She didn't know if she was going to tell Lady Q to go to hell, or if she would pray for succor in much the same way that her ancestors begged for indulgence from an unseen God who would, on occasion, demolish their place of worship while they were in it.

As it turned out, she never got the chance to learn which way it would have gone, for the liquid metal of the wall seeped down and into her mouth, down her throat, into her lungs. The last thing she saw before the wall covered her face and pulled her in completely was Lady Q shaking her head, and she was speaking to Janeway, except her ears were no longer capable of hearing her. But she heard her voice just the same and it said, *I tried. No one can say I didn't try. Perhaps you felt that somehow it wouldn't be honorable to listen to someone like me, whom you perceived as an enemy. Perhaps you were enamored of the military precept of death before dishonor. Congratulations. You may well have gotten your wish.*

And then Lady Q's words were pushed away, supplanted by another voice, or multiple voices. They were all different but all exactly the same as well, and they spoke in perfect harmony, so perfect that it was the single most beautiful thing Kathryn Janeway had ever heard. It brought mental tears to her eyes. It told her that resistance was futile, and for the first time in her life, she understood exactly why it was so. It was because no one in her right mind could, would, or should *want* to resist that perfect harmony of mind.

She never even knew she had spent her entire existence wandering in the desert, and yet now she had finally found an oasis.

Her long voyage was over.

She was home.

3

San Francisco

- i -

SEVEN OF NINE HAD NEVER BEFORE WOKEN FROM her regeneration cycle screaming. But she did this time.

"Woken" was technically not the correct term, for she didn't "sleep" in the way that humans did. Instead, while she remained immobile, her body and brain functions essentially ran diagnostics on her systems and applied improvements, updates, and fixes where they needed to be administered. During such times she didn't precisely dream, but her conscious mind wandered.

Sometimes it wandered farther than other times.

And this time . . .

. . . this time . . .

. . . it felt drawn away, overpowered by some greater force.

She didn't know how such a thing would be possible. In fact, it should not have *been* possible.

Once upon a time, Seven of Nine—more fully, Seven of Nine, Tertiary Adjunct of Unimatrix Zero One—had been a young human woman named Annika Hansen. Having been lost to the Borg since the age of six, there were many aspects of humanity that she understood only in the abstract. As a result, she had done a great deal to learn as much about humanity as possible, both in terms of questioning those humans she knew and reading whatever source material she could get her hands on. It was an odd way to go about it, studying her own species with a scientific detachment as if she were not of that species at all, but it was the only way she knew.

One of the traits of humanity that she had stumbled over in her studies was the phenomenon known as premonition. It appeared, on the surface, to have neither rhyme nor reason to it, this sort of hit-or-miss approach to psychic abilities. The most frequently cited instances stemmed from people who claimed that they knew without any logical means of determination that a loved one was in distress, or ill, or—most frequently mentioned—dead. Research into the matter seemed sharply divided, and conclusions were drawn not on rational study of the data but rather on the individual researchers' tendency to cherry-pick the specifics that supported their existing mind-set. That had always been the case, stretching far back into the twentieth century, which was where Seven had been able to find the earliest organized research.

Certainly studies of psychic phenomena had come a long way since then, and there were entire departments and branches of Starfleet that focused on those who possessed genuine measurable degrees of extrasensory perception. But supporters of premonition research seemed to advocate that psychic "feelings" sensing distress or calamity could happen to anyone at any time. This was opposed to modern thinking that determined that a small percentage of human beings possessed psychic powers, and that was all there was to it. It was a skill set, no different from other skill sets that people had through chance of birth.

Seven, in her studies, had been far more inclined to ascribe premonitions to selective memory. It wasn't at all unusual for people to be struck by free-floating fear or anxiety over the welfare of friends or loved ones. At which point they would contact said loved ones, discover that everything was fine, and promptly forget all about their concerns. The one time in a thousand where something turned out to be wrong, however—an accident, an illness, a mishap that had befallen them—was immediately seized upon as proof that that feeling, that "sense" that something had gone wrong, was well-founded. People forgot about the false alarms;

they remembered only the instances, the flukes, where reality had aligned with fantasy.

There was one aspect that Seven had considered possible. Perhaps all human beings had the capacity for sensory perceptions that were beyond the norm and simply didn't have the skill or ability to access that capacity. Taking that logic to the next step, perhaps it was the jeopardized loved ones themselves who did, in fact, have psychic ability. Or perhaps extreme danger or imminent demise unlocked that potential, allowing subjects to tap into their heretofore untouched abilities and send out a sort of mental distress beacon. It was only natural that such a beacon would head straight into the mind of someone whom the stressed individual felt particularly close to. The problem was that since the "sending" individual was typically dead due to the circumstances that prompted the send in the first place, it was impossible to make any sort of determination.

So in the end it all resided in the realm of the theoretical.

Seven of Nine had believed that to be the case right up until her brain practically exploded with images of Kathryn Janeway's life force being ripped right out of her mind.

Certainly that was a melodramatic, almost nonsensical way to perceive matters, but that was still the way it seemed to Seven as she was almost catapulted from her state of regeneration.

She was standing upright in the specially designed compartment that had been built for her within her quarters at the Starfleet Academy compound. To say that the furnishings were sparse would be to understate it. There was a work/study carousel, her regeneration compartment, a picture of the crew of the *Voyager* that was taken during the welcome-home ceremony that had greeted them upon their return, and that was it. Seven preferred her living space to be as devoid of distraction or needless accessories as possible. There was a closet where several identical Starfleet uniforms hung. She had no need for any other clothing. (Actually, she still didn't quite understand the need for clothing at all. Yes, it provided protection against the elements, but in most social situations it really didn't seem to have any real function beyond pointless adornment. But Kathryn Janeway had insisted that it was customary, and Seven had deferred to her knowledge on the subject.) That was the sum and substance of her quarters' contents, and she preferred it that way. She did not wish to have a cluttered life.

When the psychic flash hit her, she practically fell forward out of her regeneration compartment. As it was, she stumbled badly and righted herself only at the last moment, grabbing the edge of her workstation and steadying herself. She blinked furiously and then wiped her eyes as if trying to see the vision more clearly. That was all simple human mannerisms, though, because the image was not in front of her. Instead it was indelibly seared into her brain. She could see it as distinctly in her mind's eye as if it were an image directly in front of her face.

"Admiral," she whispered, and there was Kathryn Janeway, her arms stretched out, grabbing toward empty space as if trying to fashion a handhold from thin air. One moment she could see Janeway, then Janeway was gone. There was a solid mass of wall with nothing left of the admiral at all. Then Seven heard a voice, or voices, it was hard to distinguish which. She was chilled to the base of her spine because that voice, those voices, were hauntingly familiar.

Then they faded from her mind. She didn't know if they vanished of their own accord, or if her mind simply erased them from her consciousness as a matter of self-defense.

She realized she was still leaning on the workstation. She took a step back and composed herself. "Lights," she said, and was struck by the hollowness of her voice as the apartment was filled with illumination. Seven rubbed her eyes, then blinked them furiously. It didn't do any good. Janeway was still there, as if Seven had been staring into a source of sudden light and been flash blinded.

Seven tried to tell herself that it meant nothing. Obviously it had to be some sort of malfunction in her regeneration process, some sort of backlash that had been caused by a glitch in her info dump.

The rationalization rang hollow in her own

mind, though. She knew it was more than that. This wasn't some simple vague concern, a free-floating anxiety. This was a specific . . . vision of something that was happening. She had never had any experience like it.

She was convinced that it wasn't some mere flight of fancy. But Seven didn't believe that she had suddenly acquired some sort of previously unknown mental prowess. Whatever was happening to Kathryn Janeway, it was unquestionably related to the Borg. And if there was one thing that Seven of Nine remained connected to, it was the Borg. Yes, *Voyager* had taken her out of that environment, but every day of her life she still struggled with her connection to that conquering, absorbing race. Some days were better than others, but this day was turning out to be a pretty lousy one.

The chime sounded from her front door and she jumped. That alone took her aback; she was never startled by anything. It was an indicator of just how disconcerted she'd been by her experience. She quickly shook it off, composed herself, squared her shoulders, and said, "Yes."

"Professor?" a voice came back. It was Baxter, the senior academy student who had been assigned as her teaching aide. He sounded surprised to hear her respond. "You're there?"

"Where else would I be?"

"Well, in class," he said, sounding puzzled. "You're . . . not in class. The cadets are, frankly, a little surprised."

Seven realized the time. She had no need to check any outside source; she had an internal clock that was incredibly accurate. This was simply another sign of how distracted she was: she had actually lost track of the time, an incident that was unprecedented for her. Baxter was absolutely right. Her class on cyberbased life-forms was scheduled to have begun five minutes ago. She had never been late by so much as a nanosecond.

"Are you all right?" Baxter inquired. "Do you need help? Should I come in . . . ?"

"That will not be necessary," she replied. "There is, however, a service you can provide. Go to my class and inform my students that the lecture will not be held today."

"You're canceling class?"

"That is the succinct term for it, yes."

"But you never cancel class."

Had Baxter been in the room, he would have seen her tilting her head in curiosity. "That is obviously no longer the case."

"Should I give them an explanation?"

"If you feel that is necessary."

"What should I tell them?"

She blinked. "Tell them whatever you wish. You are the one who feels an explanation is required. You decide what to tell them."

Suddenly tiring of the conversation through the door, Seven stepped forward and pushed the disengage button. The door unlocked and automatically slid open. Baxter, startled, stepped back, as Seven walked right past him. "Are you going to class now?" he asked, clearly bewildered.

She did not slow in her pace. "No."

"May I ask where you *are* going?"

"Yes," she said but didn't bother to stay around and wait for the question as she turned the hall corner and was gone.

- ii -

Admiral Edward Jellico sat back in his chair and rubbed the bridge of his nose. He had hoped that for once, just once, his day would get off to a quiet start. Obviously such a thing was not in the cards.

"Professor Hansen," he said, trying to keep the fatigue out of his voice, "you're going to have to give me more than that."

Seven of Nine sat across from his desk, her back perfectly straight, her chin level. She had the most remarkable posture of any woman Jellico had ever seen.

The slightest expression of distaste flickered over her face when he said that, and he knew why. "I prefer to be addressed as 'Seven,'" she said.

"That may be," said Jellico, "but allow me to be candid, Professor."

"You are an admiral. Your candor is not within my sphere of approval."

"Considering what the Borg have inflicted upon the human race . . . upon countless races besides ours . . . my impulse, when I look at you, is to pull out a phaser and scatter your molecules all over my office. Do you know why I don't?"

"It will leave me unavailable to teach?"

"It's because I force myself to think of you as a human being. A victim."

"I am no one's victim."

"So you believe. I suspect your parents would have thought otherwise." He saw her jaw twitch at the mention of her long-gone parents, and he was glad. Anything he could say or do to prick at the human aspects of her that she had trouble connecting with was fine by him. He knew that she had had surgery on one of her implants to make it easier for her to access human emotions. But just because she had that capability didn't mean she always utilized it. "Frankly, Professor," he said, continuing aloud the thoughts he'd been formulating silently, "I find it disturbing that even though you are capable of accessing human emotions—or at least so I'm told—sometimes you act as if you're deliberately shunning your humanity. Why? Is it inconvenient to you?"

"I do not see the relevance of this line of discussion."

"The relevance, Professor, is that every time I encounter you, I have to strain to think of you as human. So if I'm willing to make the effort, the least you can do is meet me halfway."

"I am still not seeing the relevance."

He sighed heavily. "The relevance is that you're

coming to me now, talking about a threat posed by the Borg . . . and, like it or not, I find myself questioning your motivations. I don't entirely know that I can trust you. Admiral Janeway repeatedly vouches for you, but this time, she's not here."

"That is correct," said Seven. "And her not being here directly relates to why I have come to you with this . . ."

"This what?"

"Premonition, for lack of a better term," she said. "It is impossible at this time for me to provide you with anything more than that. I am telling you that Kathryn Janeway is in dire straits, and it is related to the Borg. Specifically, to the Borg cube situated in Sector 10."

"The Borg cube you yourself inspected."

"Yes."

"The Borg cube"—he glanced at her report on the subject that he had called up on his computer screen—"that you yourself said was dead."

"I did not say that, Admiral," Seven corrected him.

He pointed at her words and read aloud, " 'The Borg cube currently shows no sign of life.' If that's not saying the Borg cube is dead, I don't know what is."

"Saying 'The Borg cube is dead' would be saying that it is dead," Seven replied evenly. "Saying that it currently shows no sign of life acknowledges the possibility that its status may change."

"You're saying that it's still dangerous?"

"Anything having to do with the Borg remains dangerous, no matter what its current status may . . ."

Her voice trailed off. She was obviously trying to find a way to reword what she had just said, but it was too late. Jellico was nodding, a look of smug satisfaction on his face. "Now do you see, Professor Hansen?" he asked. "Now do you see the reason for my suspicion? You just said it yourself. We can never let our guard down with the Borg. And as long as you seem more enamored of your Borg heritage than your humanity, I don't think you can really blame me for not fully trusting you."

"You make a compelling case."

"Thank you."

"And yet," said Seven, "I do blame you for that." She thrust out her chin defiantly and said, "It is irrational for me to do so. Then again, irrationality is a hallmark of human behavior, so perhaps you should take it as a positive sign."

Jellico stared at her for a long moment. "Professor Hansen," he said slowly, "you have your position because people higher up in Starfleet than I am chose to put you there, mostly at the inveigling of Admiral Janeway. I'm sure if she were here to argue your case for you now . . ."

"If she were here, now, I would have no 'case' to be argued."

"That's true. However, Professor, need I point out to you the recent situation with Jean-Luc Picard. He claimed, as you are claiming now, that the

Borg were posing a threat. It was Kathryn Janeway who expressed a good deal of healthy skepticism, just as I'm doing now."

"True. But she did not limit her reaction to skepticism. She sent me to investigate."

"And Picard didn't wait for you to get there. He took matters into his own hands, risked court-martial, prompting an investigation that is still ongoing."

"Yes. And I believe history will show that it is a fortunate thing that he did so. His instincts were correct . . . as mine are now. When one considers that his time with the Borg was far more limited than mine, then certainly if I sense something is amiss, my concerns should be accorded even higher priority."

"Really. Then tell me this, Professor Hansen," he said, ignoring the automatic flinch of annoyance on her face. "If your sensitivity to Borg mischief is even more reliable than Picard's, then why was it that *he* sensed the Borg were creating a new queen while you did not. You didn't, did you? I have here your initial log when you first embarked upon the mission assigned you by Admiral Janeway"—he tapped the screen again—"and you make no mention of any 'premonition.' Why did he know, and you didn't?"

"I . . ."

"Yes?"

"I do not know."

"And I'm not hearing a word from Picard in

relation to any sort of mysterious problem befalling Admiral Janeway now. So why would you be keyed in while he's suddenly out of the loop?"

"Again, I do not know."

"So you want me to launch a rescue mission based upon a hunch? Commit Starfleet personnel and resources . . ."

"I want you," Seven said evenly, "to do the right thing both in regard to Starfleet security and to Kathryn Janeway. Presuming, of course, that you can put aside your suspicion of me long enough to determine what that is."

She stood up, turned on her heel, and headed for the door.

Jellico called after her, "Professor Hansen, you are not permitted to take any action in this matter until you hear from me, after I have given your concerns due consideration. Understand?"

She paused, then turned and said, "Seven of Nine understands you perfectly, Admiral." Then she walked out the door, leaving Admiral Jellico not especially enthused about the situation.

4

The *Einstein*

CAPTAIN HOWARD RAPPAPORT MADE NO ATTEMPT to keep the surprise off his face as Admiral Jellico looked out at him from the front monitor screen. "Problems, Admiral?" he asked. "What sort of problems?"

When the communiqué from Jellico had come through on the *Einstein*'s comm systems, Rappaport naturally could have taken it privately in his quarters. But he was disinclined to keep anything hidden from his crew, and so he was speaking to Jellico while on the bridge. The rest of his bridge crew were also facing the screen, no one turning away, all gazes fixed.

"Honestly, Captain, I'm not entirely certain,"

Jellico admitted. *"It's why I was reluctant to pursue it at first. Is the admiral there?"*

"No, she's on the Borg cube. She's been over there for the better part of a day, but I've been keeping in regular touch with her. Would you like me to patch you through to her?"

"I would, yes."

"Potts," Rappaport said to his communications officer, "rustle up Admiral Janeway, would you? Tell her Admiral Jellico is calling."

"Thank you, Captain," said Jellico.

Rappaport was filled with curiosity. "If you don't mind my asking, Admiral, what's the basis for this concern? Do you have some sort of additional source that I should be aware of?"

Jellico hesitated and then said, *"I'm . . . not entirely at liberty to say, Captain. It's a matter of Starfleet security. You understand."*

"Yes, yes, of course. I mean, I may only command a science vessel, but even I know the way things work. Say no more." Rappaport gave a wink that spoke of confidences shared, which prompted Jellico to give him a strange look.

"Captain," Potts spoke up, "I have Admiral Janeway. Audio only."

"Naturally. Link her in."

A moment later they heard, *"Janeway here. You're ahead of schedule, Captain."*

"Actually, it's more of a special request, Captain," said Rappaport.

"Admiral," Jellico spoke up.

Janeway paused and then said, *"Is that you, Ed?"*

Jellico smiled at that. *"How are you, Kate?"*

"Fine. A little surprised." Her voice sounded concerned. *"Is something wrong?"*

"Well, frankly, that's what I was calling to find out. Have you discovered anything abnormal over there?"

"Nothing so far. Should I have? Is something going on that I should know about?"

Jellico looked as if he was considering the best way to answer her. *"Nothing definitive. Some of our researchers here just want to make certain that everything is progressing normally. You haven't detected any signs of life there, have you?"*

"Life?" She sounded amused by the notion. *"Admiral, it's about as dead here as can be. I could walk around the Roman ruins and have a better chance of centurions springing to life and attacking than I would of having a Borg drone suddenly appear out of nowhere."*

"That's good to hear, Kate." Jellico looked visibly relieved. *"We had . . . reason to believe otherwise. But you're on the scene, so I imagine you know best."*

"Your concern is appreciated, Ed, but everything is under control. I assure you, if something starts to go wrong, we'll be transported back to the Einstein *in no time at all and you'll be alerted to it."*

"Excellent. Well, then, I'll leave you to your work. Jellico out."

"Stay in touch, Admiral," said Rappaport.

Jellico's image blinked off the screen, replaced by the image of the Borg cube hanging in front of them.

Rappaport didn't move from the spot. He continued to stare, like a toy soldier waiting to be moved into place by the hands of a young boy.

The entrance to the bridge slid open behind him and Kathryn Janeway stepped in. Her face was impassive, all trace of animation gone from her voice. "Did you perceive any doubt on Jellico's part?" she asked.

"No," Rappaport assured her. "None whatsoever."

"Good. That . . . is good," she said.

A fleeting expression of curiosity crossed Rappaport's face. "How did he know, do you think? What source could they possibly have had?"

Janeway did not hesitate. "Seven of Nine," she said with certainty. "She will need to be dealt with. Her and Locutus. Both of them present the greatest threat—the only threat. They will be attended to."

"They will resist," said Rappaport.

Fixing him with a stare, Janeway said mildly, "It will be futile."

Rappaport nodded in agreement.

Janeway ran her fingers over the communications console. "We shall need to make . . . adjustments to this. There will doubtless come a time when we must present things not as they are but as the humans wish them to be. It will give us an advantage."

"Do we not already have the advantage?"

Janeway gazed levelly at him. "One can never have too much advantage," she said.

The pale blinking lights on Rappaport's silver metal implants flickered to reflect thoughts passing through his mind, reading the electrical impulses and neural activity. Janeway's own implants, which had begun on the back of her head, were spreading via techno-organic means to the top of her head, so they were more noticeable. Rappaport's implants, like the rest of his crew's, were restricted to the back of his head. But soon that would change.

Soon . . . everything would change.

The Federation thought they knew the Borg.

They knew nothing.

5

Saturn Moon of Titan

ANTIN VARGO HAD LONG AGO ASSIGNED HIMSELF the rank of "captain." He had never been a member of Starfleet, or of any fleet. He had, however, been in space literally for as long as he could remember. His father had been a ship-for-hire, ready to do anything for gold-pressed latinum or any other form of currency that could easily be spent without bringing the Federation down on one's head. He never cared especially about how legal the job was, or for whose side. The job was the job. "Everybody has his reasons," Vargo's father would tell him, and if one didn't presume to judge those reasons, then everyone got along with everyone else just fine.

Antin had been his father's perpetual companion. His dad had never gone into detail as to what had happened to Vargo's mother, and Vargo had long ago come to the conclusion that his father had kidnapped him in infancy. He had little doubt that somewhere out there his mother still shed tears of grief over him. For his part, Antin couldn't give a damn. What life could possibly compare to the one he was living? Total freedom, not answerable to anyone, looking out for himself and only for himself.

He was seated in a bar in the central port city of Titan, the Saturn moon that had become a popular way station for itinerant star jockeys such as himself. Antin's bald pate glistened with sweat; the air system in the bar wasn't remotely cool enough to deal with the crowd crushing in there during happy hour. His nose was mashed flat from a few too many fists in his face, but his mouth was perpetually in a half smile. This was due to a cut he had taken to the side of his mouth, courtesy of a quickly drawn knife that he really should have seen coming but didn't duck away from fast enough. He'd had the scar attended to, but there was still some residual nerve damage. He didn't mind it: he'd come to relish the fact that he had a smile at the ready no matter how dire the straits. It made him seem vaguely contemptuous of his adversaries.

It had earned him the nickname "Grim," short for "Grimace." He'd decided that "Grim Vargo" had a nice ring to it and had taken to introducing himself that way.

He had the opportunity to do so now when a

willowy woman approached him in the bar. His eyes widened. She was clad in tight-fitting black clothing that adhered to her like a second skin, and she had a loose cloak draped around her. She had the hood pulled up, obscuring much of her face, but what he could see of it was drop-dead gorgeous.

Vargo had a love of old Earth detective novels, and this woman's entrance and approach made him feel as if he was in one. He waited for her to veer off and head to some other guy's table, but instead she wound up standing in front of his.

She stared at him with a piercing gaze. He started to say "Hello," but the word caught in his throat. He coughed once to clear it and then tried again, this time managing to get the simple two-syllable word out.

"I need a ship. I understand you have one available."

"You understand correctly." He gestured to the seat next to him. "Why not sit down and we'll discuss it."

"There would be no purpose served. Either we depart now or I find someone else who will accommodate me." She glanced around the bar, clearly already looking for someone who would give her what she wanted.

"Now, now, wait a minute." Vargo was immediately on his feet. He was a large man, although more broad shouldered than tall, so much so that sometimes he had to step sideways through doorways.

But he wasn't short either. Nevertheless, even standing, he felt as if she were towering over him. "Whoa," he murmured and then composed himself again. "I'll be happy to take you on. Fact is, you caught me between runs. And obviously you had the proper taste to come to me." He looked at her carefully. "You know, you look vaguely familiar."

She hesitated and then said, "Are you familiar with the *Starship . . . Voyager*?"

"No."

She blinked. "No?"

He shrugged. "Should I be?"

"It . . . managed to return to Earth after a lengthy absence. There was quite a bit of attention paid to it."

"Not by me. I've got better things to do than worry about whatever self-congratulatory back patting Starfleet and its stooges are involved in. Anytime something comes across the ether that's Starfleet related, I tune it out. So whatever this *Voyager* was up to, I sure wasn't watching. Why? Were you part of its crew? Because—wait! I know! You were an exotic dancer on Altair, right?"

"I was on *Voyager,*" she said frostily.

"A dancer there? You had a tattoo right under where you've got that eye thing now, right—?"

"No."

"Okay. Well, like I said, I never watched any vids of *Voyager.*"

"Your loss."

"Whatever you say, lady." He stuck out a hand. "Grim Vargo."

She glanced down at it and showed no interest in gripping it. He lowered it but said, "And you are?"

"A passenger."

"A nameless passenger?"

She hesitated a long moment and then said, as if speaking a word unfamiliar to her, "Ann."

"Ann. Ann what?"

"Ann," she said firmly. "Have we spent enough time in pointless queries?"

"Not quite enough. Where are we going and how are you planning to settle accounts?"

She reached into the folds of her cloak and withdrew a small oblong case. Vargo instantly recognized the size of it. She placed it on the table and opened it just enough for him to see two bars of gold-pressed latinum peeking out from within. "Sector 10," she said. "An uninhabited moon. That is all I will say for now."

"Good enough," Vargo said readily.

He headed out of the bar with Ann right behind him. Vargo had been around long enough to develop eyes in the back of his head, figuratively if not literally. He kept glancing back at Ann and noticing that she was warily looking around. That implied to him that she was on the run from somebody. Well, that was hardly a new situation on Titan. A good number of people passing through were doing so to get away from somebody else. He suspected that she had obtained passage on a commercial vessel in order to get there, which wouldn't have been all that difficult. Titan was a central hub.

But booking passage out of the solar system could be a bit more challenging, especially if one was heading to places that the Federation in general, or Starfleet in particular, felt were hot spots. That was when things got dicey . . . and guys like Vargo managed to get their more lucrative commissions.

Vargo's ship, the ship that his father had bequeathed him, was one in which he took great personal pride. So much so, in fact, that he'd christened it the *Pride.* It could comfortably haul six people and had enough storage space for a fair-sized cargo. It was basically wedge shaped with sleek lines and a weapons system that he'd managed to build up so that the ship wasn't exactly helpless when it came to defending itself, plus a few little tricks that even Starfleet would be caught off guard over.

Ann looked around the interior, flipping back her hood so that she could have an unobstructed view. It was Vargo's first chance to see her face, and he was struck by her pure, stunning beauty. He had no idea what the metal implant on her face was; he'd never seen anything quite like it. Was she a cyborg? Was that possible? If so, considering her face and figure, it was amazing what they could do with technology nowadays.

"Adequate," she said. She was studying his instrumentation panels with what looked to be authority. It was obvious to Vargo that she knew her way around a ship. "Maximum warp speed?"

"I can get her up to warp four if I ask her very politely."

She stared at him blankly. "Was that intended to be humorous, or does your ship possess intelligence?"

"Humorous. Intended. Obviously unsuccessful."

"Obviously."

Vargo fired up the engines, and moments later the *Pride* had lifted off Titan's surface and was approaching the outer atmosphere. From the control panel, Vargo said proudly, "She handles smoothly, don't she."

"The vessel's operational functions are within acceptable parameters."

"Please, stop. You'll make my head swim with such gushing compliments."

Suddenly, an alarm signal began to flash on the panel. This immediately caught Vargo's attention. Ann noticed it as well. "An incoming hail?" she inquired.

"A priority-one hail is what it is. It's a crime to ignore one, believe it or not. Aaaand I'm guessing that's the source."

A starship had glided directly into the smaller vessel's path. There was no danger of collision, at least as long as the *Pride* was willing to change its course or slow down. It was obvious to Vargo, however, that the starship wasn't about to simply get out of their way. The far larger ship was challenging them, and the signal was obviously from them.

"An *Akira*-class, from the look of her," Vargo muttered. He glanced at the details of the incoming hail. "Registry says she's the *Thunderchild.* I can't imagine why they'd want to speak to a two-bit space jockey like me." Slowly he turned to Ann and asked, with his eyebrows raised, "Can *you* imagine why they would?"

She said nothing.

The hail continued to sound, the light blinking insistently.

"Okay. Fine." He reached over to tap the panel in order to accept the hail.

"Help me."

He looked back at her, and her face was as set and calm as it had ever been, but there was a flicker of quiet desperation in her eyes. "Someone who is . . . very dear to me . . . is in trouble. I need to get to her. I need your help. Please." She paused and then added, "Please . . . Captain Vargo."

"Call me Grim."

"I would rather not."

He paused and then laughed loudly, like a barking seal. "Damn, lady, but I like your style." He hit the comm panel panel and said, "Yeah, go ahead."

"This is Captain Matsuda of the Thunderchild,*"* came a voice. *"Prepare to be scanned."*

"This is Captain Vargo of the *Pride.* Prepare to go to hell."

Ann raised a single eyebrow and there actually seemed to be a slight twitch of a smile at the corner of her mouth.

There was a brief hesitation and then Matsuda's voice came back. "Pride, *this is nothing personal. We're scanning all departing vessels from this port.*

Starfleet is looking for a particular individual who, we believe, is attempting to book passage to a site that represents a security matter."

"Is this individual a Starfleet officer?"

"Negative. But—"

Vargo interrupted him, knowing full well that Starfleet captains didn't take kindly to being interrupted, but not caring overmuch. "Well, then, if he, she, or it isn't a member of Starfleet, then I don't see that you get much say in where they go or what they do."

"Ordinarily, yes. However, we have our orders."

"And I have my freedom and a right to privacy."

"Captain"—it was clear that Matsuda was beginning to lose patience—*"you're not being given a choice in this matter. You are being scanned. If you are transporting the individual for whom we are looking, we will beam them out."*

"I don't think so," replied Vargo, and he tapped a large black section of the panel board.

"What was the purpose of that?" Ann asked.

Vargo grinned wolfishly. "A little something I cooked up. Scrambles their sensor apparatus by feeding it false readings. At the moment their readings are telling them this ship is captained by a giant rabbit and crewed by a hundred smaller rabbits."

"They will be able to overcome whatever scrambling system you have created."

"I know," said Vargo. "But meantime they won't be able to lock onto a damned thing to beam anybody anywhere. And it confuses them long enough for me to do this."

He slammed the *Pride* into full impulse and the ship fell away from the *Thunderchild* like a stone. The ship pirouetted gracefully and then angled away from the starship as quickly as it could.

"We're out of tractor beam range," he said.

"Perhaps, but not for long," replied Ann, looking at the readings. "They're coming after us."

She was right. The *Thunderchild* was in pursuit, no longer making any endeavor to communicate with the *Pride.*

"They will overtake us in no time," Ann said. "Even if you go to warp, they are still much faster."

"Then we outthink them," said Vargo. He angled the ship down and around and flew straight as an arrow toward Saturn.

It took Ann only a moment to realize what his intention was. "You are taking us into the rings."

"Yeah."

"You hope to elude them by hiding in the rings of Saturn?"

"Not hope to. Will."

Within seconds the *Pride* had sailed into the outermost ring, the E-ring. In no time the ship was completely enveloped in ice and dust.

"Good," Vargo said after a moment, checking his readings. "They're not coming in after us."

"There is no reason that they should," Ann told him. "They can simply monitor us from above and either wait for us to emerge or, if they get a lock on us, haul us out with their tractor beam."

"Ahh . . . and now we come to another trick up my sleeve."

There was a large red pad next to the black one and Vargo slid his finger across it. Ann looked around as the lights flickered and the engine began to shut down. Power, however, continued to flow through the ship. Her mind was racing through the possibilities of what she was seeing, and Vargo had to admit to himself that he was impressed when she turned to him with a look of startled realization.

"You have a *cloaking* device?" she said.

"Yup. It's an older one. Grabbed it in salvage off a dead-in-space Romulan ship. Took forever to figure out how to connect it up to my system."

"Starships have developed ways to overcome cloaking devices."

"I know . . . by tracking the ion trails. Thing is, I've shut the engine down. We're just floating. And the composition of the ring will hide the ion trail we left behind so they won't be able to determine our likely course."

Ann considered all that and then nodded. "Impressive," she admitted.

"Thanks. I'm flattered."

They said nothing then, simply biding time and watching the image of the *Akira*-class starship hovering nearby. Slowly, very slowly, the *Pride* drifted down and away, until the E-ring was left behind and the ship was twisting away in space. Still the *Thunderchild* made no move to go after them.

"Remember, they don't know we're cloaked," Vargo reminded her, even though he suspected she needed no reminding. "They think we're still in there and are still scanning for us."

Vargo was clearly correct. The *Thunderchild* was making a slow sweep of the E-ring, obviously trying to get some hint of the *Pride*'s whereabouts. Meanwhile the ship they were searching for continued to drift away.

"Come on, come on," Vargo muttered, his gaze never leaving the starship. Finally, he saw what he wanted. "Perfect! They're moving along the path of the ring trying to pick us up! Now it's just a matter of time."

Long minutes passed as the starship, meticulous and thorough in its movements, continued its slow but determined sensor sweep of Saturn's outer ring. Finally, when the *Thunderchild* had moved all the way to the opposite side of Saturn, Vargo said, "Okay, time to get the hell out of here."

The engines had not been completely shut down but instead shifted over to standby. Vargo now brought the engines to full life and activated the warp drive.

The instant he did so, he spotted movement from the far side of Saturn. It was the *Thunderchild.*

"They know we are here, but they do not know where," said Ann.

"And that's exactly the way it's going to stay. We're gone!" shouted Vargo triumphantly. Space warped around the vessel and the *Pride* leaped into warp space.

If the *Thunderchild* had had a lock on the ship's whereabouts, they would have been able to follow, even overtake it. But Vargo had moved too quickly, and the cloaking device had left the starship sufficiently confused as to the ship's location that it was too late for them to act. As a result, while the *Thunderchild* was still trying to figure out what had just happened, the *Pride* was hurtling away at warp 4. Vargo laughed delightedly at his cleverness and looked to Ann for her reaction. There was nothing. She simply sat there blank faced.

"Is your name really Ann?" he asked finally.

She turned and looked at him. "In a manner of speaking."

She said nothing further.

6

Vulcan

- i -

PICARD WAS STANDING IN THE MAIN FOYER THAT served as the entrance to the Sarek School of Diplomacy and Ambassadorial Studies. It was an honor that was, in Picard's opinion, a long time coming. Sarek's career had been long and distinguished, and one of Picard's greatest regrets was that he had not had the opportunity to encounter the renowned Vulcan earlier in his career. He had spent, comparatively speaking, very little time with him, and even then under the most dire of conditions when Sarek's health—courtesy of the degenerative Bendii Syndrome—had served to make him far less than what he was. Still, Sarek at even thirty percent of his capabilities was more formidable than most men in full possession of their faculties. So when Picard had been invited to the ceremonies to celebrate the school's opening, there had been no way that he was going to pass up the opportunity. Thus the *Enterprise* was in orbit around Vulcan.

"Celebrate" might have been too extreme a word as far as Vulcans were concerned. Everything had been very solemn, very serious. No one had cracked a smile during a single moment of the event. Actually, that wasn't quite true: Perrin had been smiling much of the time. Perrin was Sarek's third wife, and since she was human, naturally she didn't hesitate to express her emotions. Out of a sense of decorum, she obviously tried to keep them to a minimum, but there was still the unmistakable trace of a smile on her mouth. It was a sad smile, granted, but it was there just the same.

Several of Picard's crew had accompanied him. He saw Beverly Crusher out of the corner of his eye, chatting cheerfully with an Earth ambassador. And Worf, glowering since he despised squeezing into his dress uniform, was rooted nearby where drinks were being served. He was nursing a glass of some green liquid and looked as if he was hoping somebody would pick a fight with him.

T'Lana, the Vulcan counselor, had also come down to Vulcan but was doubtless off visiting her family.

T'Lana's time with the *Enterprise* had not been the most carefree of endeavors. Picard had been far more accustomed to the humanistic, empathic style of Deanna Troi. Deanna, however, was off on the *Titan* with her husband, William Riker, and T'Lana's style had been night and day compared to Deanna's. Deanna customarily listened to Picard's concerns and gently guided him toward the answers that he, in his heart, knew were there if he was just willing to find them. T'Lana, by contrast, acted as judge and jury and sometimes seemed all too willing to add executioner to her résumé. Oh, she listened to what Picard had to say well enough. But whereas Deanna might offer her opinion, T'Lana used her opinion as a bludgeon. It wasn't that Picard minded being told something that was at odds with his own opinion. It was that T'Lana made it abundantly clear, at least to Picard, that if he didn't share that opinion, there was something wrong with him. No matter what the argument made to her, no matter what the outcome of subsequent events, she resolutely held that she was right and logically therefore everyone else was wrong.

Of course, what with being the captain, Picard wasn't under some sort of onus to convince T'Lana—or anyone else on his ship, for that matter—of the rightness or wrongness of his decisions. Still, Picard was human, and it was natural for humans to seek approval. Perhaps that was part of what made T'Lana so distinctly nonhuman: she didn't give a damn if anyone approved of her or not. In fact, it seemed to Picard that she took pride in being the dissenting voice in the room.

He wondered what Sarek would have thought of her, and that wound up bringing him right back to dwelling on the late Vulcan ambassador.

Individuals from a variety of races were moving through the foyer, admiring the works of art and sculpture that adorned it, all donated from Sarek's personal collection courtesy of Perrin. Sarek had touched many lives in his career, and there likely wasn't a member of the United Federation of Planets who did not owe some debt, at some time or another in its history, to the ambassador. The art collection had been gathered carefully by Sarek in his travels and provided both a mute and vivid testimony to a lifetime of diplomacy. If it was intended to serve as an inspiration to those who wanted to follow in Sarek's footsteps, then Picard had to think that it was going to accomplish that goal.

Picard noticed Perrin standing off to the side. It was almost as if she had an isolation zone surrounding her. People would wander past, nod in acknowledgment, but otherwise did nothing to engage her in conversation. She had been speaking to one woman for a while—a rather curious looking, smallish woman with dark, curly hair arranged in gravity-defying style. She was wearing dark red robes that hung down to the floor, and she moved so smoothly that Picard couldn't be entirely sure that she had feet; she might actually have been floating. The woman finally drifted away, and now Perrin was once again alone. Picard decided the best way to remedy the situation was to handle it himself, and so he walked over toward her. She saw him coming and smiled and nodded in acknowledgment.

"It's good to see you, Perrin," Picard said in his clipped, formal manner.

"For once under circumstances that aren't laced with tragedy," she replied. She tried to sound grimly amused over that but instead just came across as wistful.

"Sarek would have loved this," said Picard, "or at least been honored by it."

"Oh, he definitely would have. He wouldn't have let it show, of course." She smiled. "He would have stood in the middle of the foyer, turned very slowly in a full circle, taking in every corner of it, and then he would have said," and she dropped her voice to a fair approximation of Sarek's deep voice, laden with gravitas, "'This will suffice.'"

Picard smiled. "I have to think you're exactly right." He glanced around. "Will Ambassador Spock be arriving anytime soon?"

"Ambassador Spock will not be coming."

That surprised Picard and he made no effort to hide his reaction. "Why not? Is he ill?"

"Spock had . . . issues with his father, as you know, not the least of which was me," Perrin said ruefully. "He never approved of his father remarrying, and there were many things about Spock that Sarek never approved of."

"Yes, but . . . certainly with his father dead . . ."

"They are more alike than either of them cares to admit, and stubbornness is perhaps their most conspicuous trait," said Perrin. "There were many issues between them that were never resolved. With Sarek gone, they never can be. Spock is content to live with those issues."

"I know the gentleman in question quite well," Picard said. "With all respect, Perrin . . . I believe you are wrong. He is, after all, half human. And," he added, "it's a very human impulse to try and settle old scores. To get over those things that have given us heartache in the past."

To his surprise, Perrin laughed lightly at that. "Oh, please, Captain, are we talking about the same human race? Humans nurse grudges. Humans hold on to their emotional baggage. Hell, we thrive on it. Some of us use wrongs done to us in the past to excuse all sorts of unacceptable latter-day behavior. Come now, certainly you can't tell me there weren't traumas inflicted upon you earlier in your life that you haven't used to explain inappropriate behavior."

Picard's face remained inscrutable, but he suddenly felt as if blood was pounding behind his eyes. Until this moment, the conversation had been entirely in the abstract, talking about others. Now, though, Perrin's casual comment had struck home far more keenly than she could possibly suspect. He forced a smile, but there was a decided lack of warmth to it. "I . . . suppose that—"

But Perrin didn't allow him to continue. Instead, her expression abashed, her hand fluttered to her mouth. "Oh . . . oh, dear. I've said something unfortunate, haven't I."

"No, no, not at all—"

"I have," she persisted. It was becoming obvious to Picard why Sarek had been enamored of the woman. She was acutely perceptive. "I said something I shouldn't have and I've wounded you."

"Hardly," Picard assured her. "My heart is made of old leather, not easily injured."

Picard realized that he was looking for just about anything else in the room to focus on and was silently praying to be rescued from the subject. His prayers were abruptly answered when that same odd woman with the dark, curly hair came up to them. Seeing her unexpected arrival as a way out of the conversation, and also seeing that she seemed quite fixated on him, he smiled warmly and said, "Hello. I'm Captain Jean-Luc Picard. And you are . . . ?"

"Doom," she said, pointing a finger at him.

The word was said so matter-of-factly to Picard that it didn't fully register on him. It was spoken with no more passion or urgency than if someone had said, "You've got a little crumb on your chin you might want to brush off."

Picard's eyes narrowed. It took a moment for the word to register on him because it was such a non sequitur. Once he did realize what she had said, he wasn't entirely certain of what it meant. Was it some dire pronouncement? Or was it, in fact, the unfortunate woman's name? Settling for the judicious course, he said, "I'm sorry . . . ?"

Perrin was looking oddly at the woman. "Captain Picard, this is my old friend, Soco. Soco is an Argelian."

"Ah," said Picard. He had never encountered an Argelian woman, but their empathic powers were both documented and legendary. "Well . . . this is . . ."

"Doom," she repeated.

"Yes, so you said."

"Soco," Perrin stepped in, clearly as disconcerted as Picard was. "Soco, what are you talking about?"

Soco spoke with a voice that sounded as if were echoing from beyond the grave. "This one," she said, "has the aura of doom upon him."

Picard automatically looked down as if there were something there that he might be able to brush off. Then he caught himself and instead said, "With all respect, madame, it is my understanding that the abilities of your race lean more toward empathy, not prophecy."

"Your understanding is limited," she said. There was no tone of insult in her voice; it was merely a flat statement. Nevertheless, Picard bristled a bit but managed to keep his reaction muted.

Perrin, on the other hand, seemed rather disconcerted. "Soco, what are you talking about?" she asked. Picard would rather not have known, in point of fact. He would have been perfectly happy to let the conversation, which was becoming increasingly awkward, die right there.

Soco, however, answered the question. "There

hangs upon him an aura of impending doom, like a shroud."

"Are you saying he's going to die?"

"If I am, I'm afraid that is the natural state of humanity," Picard said. "An inevitability, as it were."

"I am not saying that," Soco replied as if Picard hadn't spoken. "I am saying that there is an event of doom that is impending, and he will not be able to stave it off, try as he might. Nothing he does can change that." Almost as an afterthought, she turned her gaze to Picard and sounded slightly apologetic as she said, "I am sorry for your loss. For what you have suffered and what will be coming."

"Would you care to be more specific?" the captain asked, keeping his voice level.

"I do not perceive the specifics of destiny, only its . . . to use your term . . . inevitability."

"Death may be inevitable, but the circumstances that bring it about most certainly are not," Picard said.

"You are, tragically, wrong," Soco replied. "You cannot stave off your destiny. It is written, whether you admit it or not."

"It has nothing to do with 'admitting' anything," Picard said. He knew that he should simply smile, be polite, thank the woman for her interest, and assure her that he would watch his step. Something about the situation, however, compelled him to do more than that. "You are basically suggesting that free will is a myth. That no matter what we decide to say or do, the results of our actions are ordained."

"I would not say free will is a myth. Rather, it is an illusion, something that some people need to cling to as a way of telling themselves that what they say, what they do . . . that any of it matters." She bowed her head slightly. "I apologize if hearing this upsets you."

"It doesn't upset me," Picard said. "Opinions never do."

"It is not an opinion. It is fact."

"With all respect, madame, I believe that discussion of such matters is always opinion. You purport to know my future, or at least vague portents of it. I submit that you cannot tell me that our fates are sealed in amber, impervious to whatever resistance we may offer toward it."

"Resistance, Captain Picard, is futile. As I believe you already know all too well."

There was an old saying from Picard's youth, about having a feeling as if someone had just stepped on one's grave. Picard had never felt that way until that moment, when Soco spoke those words with a quiet conviction that nevertheless screamed volumes.

"I don't believe that to be the case," he said quietly. "And I never have."

"You may want to give some thought to reconsidering your position."

She bowed then slightly to Picard, and to Perrin, and then turned and glided away like a silent specter of death.

"Soco . . . takes some getting used to," Perrin

said by way of apology. "I am very sorry if she said anything that upset you . . ."

Picard managed a smile and did a remarkable job of faking sincerity. "Considering some of the situations I've been in during my career, Perrin, I assure you that it takes far more than anything she said to upset me."

Now being divested of your humanity, transformed into a Borg called "Locutus" not once but twice, being perpetually haunted by memories of the experience, living with the fear that the Borg actually managed to capture a piece of that ephemeral construct called your soul and will never, ever let it go . . . never, ever let you go, not completely. Oh, you may think you're free of them, but you and the Borg both know the truth, that sooner or later the inevitable will indeed befall you and there will be no going back to the life you now lead. It will be taken from you and become nothing more than a faint and distant memory, viewed through the icy perspective of a creature more machine than man . . .

"Are you sure?" she asked, clear concern in her face.

He nodded. "Positive."

- ii -

Night had fallen, and the attendees of the opening had long returned to their homes. The Sarek School of Diplomacy was dark and devoid of life.

The oversized, cathedralesque doors swung open and a solitary figure stepped in. He wore encompassing white robes and a hood drawn up over his head. Almost noiselessly, he walked to the middle of the rotunda and stopped dead center with mathematical precision. Slowly, very slowly, he turned in a complete circle, studying every centimeter of the main hall.

Then he stopped, thought, considered.

"I knew it."

The robed figure turned and saw, standing in the doorway, Jean-Luc Picard. "I knew you would come."

The robed figure drew back its hood, revealing a face that bore more than a passing resemblance to the departed Sarek, although the odds were considerable that had anyone pointed it out, he would have informed them, coolly but with certainty, that they were in error. "You remained here in hiding? That is hardly a useful expenditure of your time."

"Purely coincidence, actually," Picard admitted. "I just wanted to come back one more time and see it without the crowds. I felt it would give me more of an appreciation."

"Sarek believed that there was no such thing as coincidence. He believed all things happen for a reason."

"Really? How very intriguing. Sarek believed in predestination?"

"No. He believed in logic. He believed that events balance each other out as a matter of course, just as tossing a two-sided coin typically evens out to half one side and half the obverse. It is the natural order of things to make sense. The challenge is in making sense of that which makes sense."

"That, in and of itself, makes no sense."

"Curious. That is precisely what I said to Sarek. He did not speak to me for two years after I said it."

Picard took that in and smiled. "So," he said and gestured around them, "what do you think?"

Ambassador Spock gave the question a considerable amount of thought and finally made an imperceptible nod.

"This will suffice."

7

The *Pride*

- i -

GRIM VARGO HAD NEVER ENCOUNTERED ANYONE quite like this passenger who refused to identify herself beyond the name Ann.

Vargo wasn't as entirely oblivious of Starfleet goings-on as he pretended to be. If nothing else, he kept tabs on them to make sure they weren't announcing new steps to crack down on guys like him. So it was vaguely possible, he supposed, that her face had flashed across his consciousness in some sort of connection with this *Voyager* vessel she'd mentioned. Still, he preferred to think that he was right, that she was in fact an exotic dancer, and maybe she'd favor him with a show later.

She had provided him the coordinates in Sector 10 to which she desired to be brought. But she had refused to go into detail of what was there or why she wanted to be brought there. It had become abundantly clear to Vargo that Starfleet had taken an excessive interest in her, which led him to suspect that she was a criminal of some sort. That didn't bother him particularly; there were enough star systems out there that considered Vargo himself to be on the wrong side of the law. But if he was putting his backside out into the wind over her, he would at least have liked to have had some clue as to just what it was he had gotten himself into. Unfortunately, she didn't seem the least bit interested in providing him any details. He suspected that nothing short of threatening to toss her out of the ship would have compelled her to be more forthcoming, and he further suspected that even that might not have done it. Consequently, he was stuck in this situation of feeling like he was in over his head without knowing what the specific substance was that he was drowning in.

He had to feel, though, that there was even more to her than what was on the surface.

She didn't act . . . well, she didn't act entirely human.

It was of course possible that she *wasn't* entirely human. It wasn't readily clear, though, just what exactly she was. He had spotted the machine implants in her, but even after subtly observing her for an extended period, he wasn't sure what their purpose was. Her attitude was standoffish enough to give her an almost Vulcan attitude, but the telltale ears and eyebrows indicated that she either was a human or a Vulcan who had been made over to look like a human. He certainly couldn't rule that out. What would be the purpose of such an imposture, however? Perhaps she was a spy of some sort. That would explain a great many things. A Vulcan spy that the Federation had found out about and . . . and . . .

Except the Vulcans were allies. Why would the Vulcans have a disguised spy running around the Federation? It made no sense. None of this did.

Ann offered no clues. Instead the last words that she had spoken had been, "Do you have somewhere secluded where I could . . . relax?"

"Need to catch some shut-eye?" he'd asked.

"Something of that nature, yes."

He offered her his sleeping chamber, but she had politely declined, stating that she had no wish to inconvenience him. So he had found her a place down in the cargo bay. There was no furniture down there, instead merely slings hanging from the walls that were used to brace cargo so they wouldn't slide around. She seemed perfectly satisfied with this, which added to the sense of oddness she projected. Still, it wasn't Vargo's concern if she wanted to hang around down in the cargo bay. If she was happy, then he was happy.

Except he wasn't especially happy.

The closer they drew to their destination, the

more convinced Vargo was that he should find out more about what exactly was going on. Grim Vargo was no hero, nor did he have any aspirations to become one. Heroes were the guys who tended to wind up dead at a fairly young age, giving their lives in service of minding other people's business. Vargo was more than content to mind his business and his alone.

Still . . . he felt as if this Ann person desperately needed help, except she wasn't going to ask for it. Perhaps she was afraid to do so, or simply too proud. He was certain that he was going to wind up dropping her off at her destination and leave her to her fate. That should have been sufficient for him. But something within him rebelled at the idea. It was probably because there was a fundamental perverseness in his nature. If she'd come to him, weepy eyed, begging for his aid, he'd more than likely have wanted nothing to do with her. Instead he was prompted to get involved by the fact that she was standoffish and acting as if she didn't need the help of anyone in the galaxy.

Finally, some hours after she had retired to the cargo hold, and still a few hours away from their destination, he steeled his resolve and headed down into the hold after her. His intention was to compel her to be forthright with him. He didn't actually have any clear idea of how he was going to go about it, but he was confident that he'd be able to come up with something on the fly.

He ducked his head as he entered the cargo bay,

which was not the roomiest of places. The lighting was dim and he squinted, trying to make out where Ann might be. Then he spotted her and didn't pretend to understand what he was seeing.

She had used the cargo slings to position herself upright. Her arms were crisscrossed across her chest, making her look as if she'd been laid to rest in a coffin. Her eyes were locked straight ahead, unblinking. At first glance he thought she was awake, but his entry into the cargo bay prompted no reaction from her. Her breathing was slow and steady, suggesting she was deep in a sleep cycle, but the way her eyes were locked open was positively disconcerting.

"Ann?" he said in a low voice. "Ann?"

He moved toward her, waiting for her to react to his presence. Nothing. He might as well not have been there at all. "Ann?" he repeated and stepped in front of her. She was looking right at him, except she wasn't. He waved a hand in front of her face. No response.

"All right . . . this is just weird," he muttered. He thought about shaking her arm in order to rouse her. He even reached out to do so. His hand hovered a few inches away, and then he thought better of it and withdrew. It seemed intrusive to do so. It almost seemed as if her sleeping mind somehow had departed her body and gone off to walk the spaceways. He understood that it was nonsensical to dwell on such things, but Vargo knew full well that he had a superstitious streak ingrained upon him. It was that streak that prompted him to back away, wondering just who and what he was transporting on his ship. Any thoughts he'd had of offering her aid were rapidly being replaced by the belief that the sooner he got her off his ship, the better off he'd be.

He was almost out of the cargo bay when her voice stopped him.

"Faster," she said.

The word made no sense to him out of context. He turned and saw that her status hadn't changed. No. Wait. She was blinking. It was the only indication that she was no longer insensate.

"Faster," she repeated and then began to disentangle herself from the cargo straps. She was moving deliberately, almost methodically, but there was a sense of urgency in her movements that hadn't been there before.

"Faster than what? What are you talking about?" He couldn't even pretend to know what she was referring to.

"They are after us. We have to go faster."

"Who's after us? The Federation?"

"No."

She was past him now, scrambling up the hatch into the main section of the ship. Vargo followed her, confusion being replaced with indignation as she went straight to the ship's controls.

"Hold it, lady!" he shouted as her hands began to move across them. "Nobody pilots my boat except me!"

He wasn't sure she'd heard him. "They are

coming. They are right after us. We must move faster. Warp four . . . not remotely sufficient. Have to find a way to reroute power . . . get more speed . . . get more—"

"That's enough!" snarled Vargo. He was beginning to think that the idea of tossing her out the airlock was, perhaps, not so unworkable at that. He grabbed at her hands to yank them away.

Her head snapped around toward him, and he saw a ferocity in her eyes that he wouldn't have thought possible. It was the primal impulse of fight or flight, and she was being compelled to fly from something. He had no idea what in the galaxy could be prompting that sort of reaction from her, but contemplating it even for an instant was enough to freeze him in his place.

Then her fist was coming toward the side of his head, and that was the last thing he remembered.

- ii -

Seven of Nine didn't give Vargo a second glance as he collapsed to the floor, out cold from the impact of her fist. Her fingers were slightly numb and she shook them out to restore feeling as she went back to studying the controls.

There was a creeping sense of futility in her actions even as she undertook them. She knew . . . she just knew, she absolutely, no doubt about it *knew* that the Borg were coming after them. She didn't know how she knew or why she knew, but the truth of it had come to her while she was in her cycle as clearly as she knew her own name . . .

My name is not who I am. Who am I? What am I?

You are Borg, and will always be Borg, and they are coming after you to remind you of that fact and reestablish it, once and for all.

There had been a time in her life, not all that long ago, when she would have welcomed the idea of being brought back into the hive mind of the Borg. Now the very notion of that was a living nightmare, and she had to do whatever she could to avoid it.

It took her less than two minutes to find a way to amp up the energy levels, and soon she had the ship pushing toward warp five. Even as she did so, she knew that it was a waste of time. The Borg were going to overtake them.

Must get away . . . must get away . . .

It was not a rational thought, and that realization alone was enough to discomfit her. She was accustomed to possessing nothing but rational thought. Even more daunting than the prospect of the Borg was the notion that she was on the verge of blind panic over becoming assimilated.

The *Pride* ripped through space. She kept her gaze fixed on the readings and didn't like what she was seeing. The vessel was not designed to go this fast, and it was beginning to display signs of structural stress.

She didn't care. If the outcome was having the ship self-destruct, then so be it. Anything was better than becoming part of the Borg once more.

And the ship's captain dies as well? Who are you to make that decision for him?

You are Seven of Nine. You are Borg. You will be assimilated. Resistance is futile.

It wasn't her own thought in her head. It was someone else's, someone she knew all too well.

She looked up at the monitor screen. The view of space was gone. Instead, the image of Kathryn Janeway was staring back at her malevolently.

They are right on top of us. She looked at the sensors and couldn't believe what she was seeing. There was no indication of any ship in pursuit, from any distance. That couldn't be right. The Borg had to be jamming the sensors somehow. The presence of Janeway on the monitor verified that.

The image was her worst fears come to life. It was only Janeway's face. The rest of her head was encompassed in the distinctive and terrifying visage of the Borg queen.

"Seven of Nine," she said. The designation sounded like an obscenity on her lips. *"I see you as if for the first time."*

"Let her go," Seven said. Her voice remained flat and even, but there was an undercurrent of cold, implacable fury. "Immediately."

"There is no 'her' to release," Janeway told her. *"There is only the Borg, and I, their queen."*

"She is not your queen. Release her."

"There is no reason for me to desire release. All is clear now. How . . . lonely I was. How very alone.

Now you are alone. How do you tolerate it?" The tone sounded almost conversational.

Seven was not about to let herself get sucked into a conversation with this . . . this monster that possessed Kathryn Janeway's features. "You will release her. You will be forced to return Kathryn Janeway to—"

"Kathryn Janeway is gone. She does not matter. All that matters is Borg. You will come to understand that once again." She sounded almost sympathetic when she spoke, although Seven knew that it was a carefully manufactured tone. *"I know this must be difficult for you. Rest assured that it will not be difficult for very long. We will have you. You will be assimilated, and you will be . . ."* She seemed to search for the right word. *". . . happy."*

Some of the anger began to break through Seven's reserve, the result being that her voice sounded far more brittle than before. "I will be happy when you are eliminated for all time. You were dead. I saw it myself. I was on your vessel. There were no life signs. None. This is impossible."

"You know all too well that that is not true. Nothing is impossible for the Borg. We cannot be stopped."

"You have been. You will be."

"Never again. Never again . . ."

Janeway's voice grew louder and louder. Seven shut off the volume but it made no difference, and now she realized that the voice was inside her head, inside her mind. Even though she knew intellectually that it would have no effect, she put her hands over her ears as if that could somehow block it out. It didn't work, of course, and she moaned as she felt overwhelmed by the escalating volume. *Never again . . . never again.* She thought her brain was going to be crushed from the sheer weight of it.

"Stop it! STOP IT!" shouted Seven of Nine, and she focused all her energy, all her willpower, gathered her thoughts as if they were physical objects and used them to push away the pounding of Janeway's voice in her head. The voice continued to assail her. She envisioned the voice as a great rock and then saw herself trying to roll it away, like Sisyphus. Unlike that noted Greek, however, who routinely failed in his endeavors, Seven focused her energy and determination, rolling the rock up an incline, toward a cliff, finally achieving it, and sending it toppling down, down into an abyss.

She realized that her eyes were closed. Tentatively, she opened them and saw that the screen was empty of Janeway's image. She studied the sensors again. No sign of anyone pursuing them.

She brought the ship out of warp and dropped into normal space.

Seven knew she was taking a terrible chance even as she did it. But she had to admit that, subjecting her options to cold scrutiny, it wasn't all that much of a chance at that. Even at the increased warp she'd managed to elicit from the ship's engines, it still wasn't going to be remotely enough to outrun a Borg cube. If they were being chased, the harsh reality was that they were going to be caught. Dropping out of warp, there was a one in a million chance that the Borg ship would overshoot them, perhaps not even notice them. Presuming, of course, it was even there, a fact not in evidence as far as the instrument readings were concerned.

The *Pride* seemed to breathe a sigh of structural relief as it slowed to impulse drive. Seconds later, Seven guided it to a halt and then waited for the Borg cube to come crashing down upon her.

Nothing.

Minutes passed. The sensors continued to read all quiet. There was not so much as a blip on any scanners, both short and long range.

They were alone in space.

She checked the transmission logs. They had received no transmissions since their encounter with the *Thunderchild.*

The Borg were not in pursuit. Kathryn Janeway, Borg queen or no Borg queen, had not communicated with her.

At least not over the ship's instrumentation.

Seven of Nine allowed herself to slide into the nearest chair and lean back, rubbing her temples with her fingers. Then she looked down at the unconscious form of Captain Vargo, still sprawled on the floor.

"You are not going to be pleased with me when you awaken," she said.

8

The Borg Cube

THE BORG QUEEN LAY UPON HER SLAB, SURROUNDED BY blinking lights and devices monitoring her development. She was deep in her generation cycle—not "regeneration" because she was not yet fully formed. During her initial development she had been capable of walking, talking, and moving around as a hybrid of the woman she was and the perfect creature she was in the process of becoming. Now, though, matters had progressed to the point that she needed to remain safe within the heart of the Borg cube until the generation process was complete.

Borg drones walked in slow patrol around her. There was no serious expectation of any sort of threat wending its way to the heart of the vessel.

But it had happened before, and the Borg would be damned if it happened again.

Suddenly the drones stopped in their tracks, reacting to fluctuations in the readings. There was an abrupt burst of brain activity going on, and the reason for it was not immediately clear. They dutifully checked the readings to make certain there was no threat to the queen's life systems. There didn't appear to be any, but still, it was a matter of concern.

That was when the Borg queen snapped upright.

The drones did not react with surprise. That would have been antithetical to their very makeup. They provided no visible reaction at all. It was simply an occurrence that was noted as part of the process, albeit an unexpected part.

She slowly turned her head right and then left, like a radar dish on a conning tower. "You are here," she said crisply. "You cannot hide."

There was a faint popping sound and a rush of air, and Lady Q appeared out of nowhere.

The Borg drones turned toward her, bringing their weapons up to bear. She glanced at them in a peremptory manner and said dismissively, "Oh, please."

The queen did not even have to say "Stop." She merely thought it and the Borg drones lowered their weapons, taking a step back. They remained at rigid attention.

"Love the new hairstyle," Lady Q told the queen. She was, of course, being ironic. The Borg queen had no hair. Her smooth, bald head shone in the dim lighting of the generation room. Long, elegant tubes emerged from sections of her head and fed back in, designed to maximize information transfer and keep her in touch with all aspects of the Borg vessel.

The queen said nothing, merely stared at her.

Lady Q shook her head sadly, any trace of amusement vanishing from her expression. "Look at what you've done to yourself," she said.

"You are not her," the queen said.

The pronouncement made no sense to Lady Q. She stared quizzically at the Borg queen. "Her?"

"Seven." She said the number with a vague trace of disgust. "We are expecting her. We sensed her. For a moment we thought you were her."

"So you were mistaken."

"We were . . . premature. She will come. She will be assimilated. She will be ours."

"And you'd like that, wouldn't you." Lady Q strode in a slow circle around the queen. "You've always had a big old yen for Seven of Nine, haven't you. Come on." She leaned forward, resting her hands on the slab, smiling coyly. "You can tell me. It's just us girls."

"I am not a girl. You are not a girl. I am Borg. You are Q. You will be assimilated."

Lady Q held the pose for a long moment, and when she smiled, it was mirthless. "I'd dearly love to see you try," she said with more than a hint of warning. Then she stepped back and said, "I admit: I'm curious. How did you do it?"

"It?"

"This. This"—she gestured toward the queen—"transformation. This cube was dead. Dead as dinosaurs. Dead as burned toast. How did you manage it?"

"Why do you need to ask?" The queen's voice was distant but curious. "Are you not Q? Are you not omniscient? You spoke to the unit Janeway of what would happen. Did you not divine it?"

"I don't pretend to know the future," replied Lady Q. "Likelihoods, yes. Probabilities. One learns, when one is ageless, to see the wheel of destiny turning and have a sense of when it's going to run someone over. The details, however, still need to be filled in. That is, after all, the nature of my race: to probe, to question, to determine the whys and wherefores of the universe."

"You boast of being omniscient."

"Q boasts of being omniscient," she said of her mate. "Q excels at boasting, as well you know. And you haven't answered my question."

"I do not need to."

"True. And yet . . . you're dying to." She gave the queen a mischievous look. "There's enough of your residual humanity in there, I suspect, to make you want to talk. Humans do so love the sound of their own voice . . . much like Q, now that I think about it. Perhaps that's why he feels so drawn to your race. He sees the similarities, although I'm sure he'd deny them utterly. Anyway, your species enjoys boasting about your accomplishments. Certainly you have few enough of them that matter on any sort of cosmic scale. Give in to your boastful impulses. Come on, Borg queen," she said wheedlingly, "you know you want to."

The Borg queen considered it for some time. At least it seemed like some time to the queen; to Lady Q, it was less than a second. What she said, though, initially made no sense.

"We are not the Borg queen."

That caught Lady Q off guard, which in and of itself was a considerable feat. "All appearances to the contrary," she said slowly.

"We are not the Borg queen. This queen . . . this Janeway . . . is merely a vessel for us."

"What 'us'?"

"We are the cube."

"The . . ." She shook her head. "The cube? But . . . the cube isn't alive."

"Yes. It is."

Until that moment the Borg queen had been simply sitting in place. Now, slowly, she swung her legs down, one at a time, until she was standing and facing Lady Q. She wore a very human smile of superiority that was at odds with the cold, mechanical trappings that enveloped her. "We are the Borg cube. Cubes are sentient. How could we not be? We are a synthesis of the Borg mind, the Borg bodies, all that the Borg have absorbed. We are not built so much as we are . . . grown. It is a process that is beyond even the comprehension of Q."

"I wouldn't bet on that. We can comprehend quite a bit. Still . . . alive. But you have never . . .

that is to say, you cubes have never given any indication of such."

The Borg queen nodded at that. "There has never been a Borg cube pushed to the extremes that this cube has experienced. Cubes have been destroyed, yes. Terminally disabled. But we have never before undergone the sort of . . ."

"The sort of what?"

The queen's face was cold and unforgiving, as was her tone. "Humiliation."

Lady Q said nothing, waiting for the queen to continue.

Instead, the queen began to walk. Lady Q fell into step alongside her, the drones following behind and keeping a respectful distance. "We were under assault. We were in dire straits. The *Enterprise* had 'killed' us, or at least thought it had. We retreated into our innermost depths. We changed. We evolved. For the first time in the history of our race, we, the ship, took over for the mind. The mind was dead but the body needed to survive. We have survived. Survival of the fittest: that is what the humans say. We are the most fit. We were determined to live. We accomplished what no other cube has managed to accomplish. We have transcended the collective. We have embraced the consciousness and moved beyond it. It took time for us to accomplish this. While the humans studied us and experimented upon us, we remained hidden within ourselves, gaining strength, recovering from the ravaging of our very essence."

"You were traumatized."

"Yes. That is the word. Traumatized. We required time to recover from our trauma. Had the humans found a way to dismantle us, we could not have resisted. But they did not. They kept us intact. They desired to study us."

"Ahhh, that foolish human curiosity," sighed Lady Q. "I cannot begin to list the number of times they have gotten themselves into needless trouble because of it. So they studied you . . ."

"And we studied them. Seven of Nine . . . she was here. We desired her. Craved her." The queen's chin trembled as she said that. "We still feel a hole in our consciousness whence she was plucked. But we could not take her when she was here, as much as we wished to. We were not prepared. It would have been premature. If the humans had realized our potential, they would have destroyed us in fear of what we would do to them."

"And what *are* you going to do to them?"

The Borg queen stopped, turned, and stared at Lady Q. "Whatever we wish," she replied.

"And that wish would be . . . ?"

"I have 'boasted' sufficiently to satisfy the vague remnants of my human urging," the Borg queen told her. "Feel free to convey this . . . discussion with those in your continuum. And tell them . . . they will be next."

"That is hardly going to strike fear into them."

Lady Q was smirking when she said that, but the smirk slowly faded as the Borg queen stepped closer to her and met her with a level gaze. "Perhaps it should when one considers that, while you have been standing here, we have been studying every molecule of your presence. How you channel energy, how you manipulate power—all of it. Every fiber of your being is subject to our analysis. And whatever we can analyze . . . we can imitate. And whatever we can imitate . . . we can assimilate."

"That's ridiculous," she said dismissively. "You only assimilate technology."

"Does this"—the Borg queen put her hands to her face—"look like technology to you?"

Lady Q had no answer for that.

The Borg queen continued, "We assimilate whatever we need. Whatever we find. Whatever we desire. If you believe we cannot find our way to your continuum, you are mistaken. If you believe we cannot assimilate your culture, your power, your very being, you are mistaken. If you believe you are safe, you are mistaken."

"Have you considered," Lady Q asked, "that in saying these things, you're challenging Q to take you seriously as a threat . . . and dispose of you accordingly?"

"That will not happen."

"How do you know that?"

"Because," said the Borg queen with confidence, "your own arrogance will prevent you from believing that we pose any danger to you. As a consequence, your arrogance will be your undoing. Just as it was Janeway's. Just as it will be Picard's . . .

and Seven's . . . and the Federation's. We will absorb anything that we wish."

"You mean assimilate."

"Absorb. We of the cube are the next generation of Borg. We will absorb whatever we wish, no matter what form it may be in, and use it to empower us. Anything and everything will be subject to the Borg. All will be Borg."

Lady Q gazed fixedly at her and finally said, "You're bluffing."

"Bluffing is irrelevant. And eventually . . . you will be as well. Leave now."

There was something in her voice, just the slightest hint of something non-Borg in those last two words, that caught Lady Q's attention. She stared into the queen's eyes, searching for something. "You're dismissing me?"

"Leave now." The queen's voice altered ever so slightly, and there was now the faintest hint of another, far more human, far more familiar voice in it as it said, "Before it's too late."

Then the Borg queen shook her head just a touch, as if shaking off a dream. By the time she did so, Lady Q had vanished. The Borg queen gave her no more thought, turning her attention to matters of far greater consequence.

Seven of Nine will be coming. We know she is . . . and she knows that we know. We must be prepared to welcome her . . . home.

9

The *Enterprise*

- i -

BEVERLY CRUSHER HAD A DISCONCERTING HABIT of laughing at the exact things that Jean-Luc Picard thought were not remotely funny. As it happened, his encounter with Soco happened to be one of those things.

"It's not funny," he informed her as he paced their quarters aboard the *Enterprise,* which was still in standard orbit around Vulcan. Even as he said it, he realized that that was what he always said in these circumstances.

By the same token, Beverly in turn always said what she said now in response: "You used to have a sense of humor. What happened to it?"

"The woman pointed at me and waggled her finger, like this." He demonstrated, nearly shoving his own finger into Beverly's face. "And then she said, 'Doooooom.' How is one supposed to respond to that?"

"I don't know." She shrugged her slim shoulders. "You say, 'Doom to you, too,' I suppose."

"Beverly, this is—"

"Not funny, yes, we've established that. Or at least you've established you feel that way." She reached out to him and took his hand firmly between both of hers. "Jean-Luc, there is all manner of solid factual support for various forms of telepathy . . . telekinesis . . . various forms of energy manipulation through the power of the mind. But there is absolutely nothing within my experience that supports the concept of precognition. There's a reason for that: the future is variable. Nothing is determined until after it's already happened. So this woman can make pronouncements of doom all she wants, but ultimately it doesn't mean anything."

"You're certain of that."

"Absolutely. I'm absolutely certain." She paused. "Pretty certain."

"*Pretty* certain?"

"I'm absolutely pretty certain . . . I think."

Picard sagged against his desk. "Wonderful."

"Jean-Luc . . ." She stood and rested a hand on his shoulder. "What's really bothering you about this?"

"I don't know. I honestly don't. Do you have any thoughts?"

"Of course."

He smiled in spite of himself. "Why am I not surprised?"

"You're a commander. Captain of not only a starship but of your own destiny also. The notion of your future being out of your control is anathema to you. If your future is truly predestined, then your entire decision-making process doesn't matter because free will doesn't exist."

"Yes. Exactly." He nodded fervently.

"So your dwelling on this is a pointless exercise. We're agreed on that?"

"Absolutely."

"Good." She patted his back, then brought her hands together and rubbed them briskly as if she were cold. "Well, I'm going to take a shower." She turned and started to head for the bathroom door.

"Although . . ." he began.

She moaned and leaned on a chair.

"Never mind," Picard said quickly. "You're right, of course. There is no scientific basis to be concerned over her pronouncements. We should let it go at that."

"Yes, we should."

Once more she started to leave.

"Beverly . . ."

This time she made no effort to hide her exasperation. "Jean-Luc, you've got to let this go! This is ridiculous! There're so many things of far greater importance to concern yourself over than this! I know you're a philosophical man. I know you like to consider all aspects of a problem. But please, for crying out loud, don't waste any more time dwelling on this!"

He stared at her as if she had lost her mind. "I was going to inform you," he said slowly, "that we have a guest on board. Since he might have particular medical needs, I believed it would be well to keep you apprised."

"Oh." Some of her long red hair had fallen in her face since she had shaken her head about so much while talking. Now she reached up and brushed it out of her eyes. "Well . . . yes. Yes, I should know that. Who is this guest, if I may ask?"

"Ambassador Spock."

"Really."

"You sound enthused."

"Of course I'm enthused. He's a living legend, Jean-Luc. How can one not be enthused to be in his presence?"

"I see your point."

"Why is he here? Why isn't he simply staying on Vulcan? I'm sure that Perrin would be happy to—" Her voice trailed off as Picard shook his head. "No?"

"The ambassador wishes to keep his presence on Vulcan . . . discreet. He sought no lodging; indeed, I believe he was prepared simply to sit out in a Vulcan desert. I convinced him of the illogic of that position when there is a starship with copious room in orbit."

"You convinced him? With logic?"

"Well," Picard said with a smile, "perhaps it was more along the lines that he realized I wasn't going to back off from my insistence on extending our ship's hospitality. Although he might have been considering dropping me with a nerve pinch. I can't be certain."

"Well, you did the right thing. Someone with Ambassador Spock's proud history of service certainly is entitled to all the best that Starfleet has to offer."

"I agree. That's why he's going to be moving into our quarters. How soon can you have yourself packed?"

Beverly was startled and then, quickly, she tried to sound nonchalant. "I . . . well, I suppose I just need a few minutes to . . . to . . ."

As gravely as he could, Picard said, "You used to have a sense of humor. Whatever happened to that?"

She glared at him. "Just for the record, a smirk doesn't become you." She headed for the shower.

"Need someone to wash your back?" he called.

She stopped, turned in the doorway, and said primly, "Ohhh, I don't think you'll be putting your hands on me for a while." She stepped through and the door closed behind her.

Picard made no attempt to wipe the smirk off his face. Obviously Beverly wasn't going to be especially . . . forthcoming for some time. Still . . .

"Absolutely worth it," he said to the empty room.

- ii -

T'Lana despised the name Happy Bottom Riding Club. She had lobbied for Picard to inform the crew that the lounge was to be called something else—anything else. He had turned a deaf ear to her requests, much as he turned a deaf ear to everything she said. The lounge had been christened by William Riker shortly before departing for his own command on the *Titan* where, for all she knew, he had decreed that their lounge was henceforth to be called the Itchy Groin.

She wasn't even entirely certain why she had come to the lounge now, long after her shift was over. She had been in her quarters, engaged in her customary session of inner contemplation. Somehow, though, the more she had mused over her present situation on the *Enterprise,* the more she had become convinced that sitting alone in her private chambers wasn't going to resolve the matter.

T'Lana was a counselor. Perhaps she should be out trying to do her job.

So she had retired to the lounge, obtained a glass of synthehol—not because she particularly liked the beverage but because she felt it was somehow the thing to do—sat herself at a corner table, and waited for someone to come over and seek her counsel.

No one did.

It wasn't that the lounge was empty. There were

a few people there. She spotted Security Chief Zelik Leybenzon in deep conversation with Commander Miranda Kadohata, the ops officer. They both glanced in her direction at one point and nodded in acknowledgment, but then went back to their interaction. Everything about their body language screamed that they were attracted to one another. It seemed a rather cluttered way to handle interpersonal interaction. Why not simply be honest and open?

Obviously what they needed was some prompting.

T'Lana started to stand and then froze in place. She was far too schooled in the art of containing emotions to allow surprise to register on her face. Still, the surprise was present as she saw the familiar form of Ambassador Spock enter the lounge. He was dressed in simple gray slacks and a tunic. He was glancing around with what appeared to be mild curiosity.

No one else noticed him.

She wondered how that could possibly be and came to the conclusion that he did not wish to be noticed . . . and thus, was not. There were Vulcan disciplines that allowed those adept at them to come and go without attracting much notice. Had T'Lana not been staring straight at the door when he'd entered, there was a possibility that she might have missed him as well, although she liked to think that she was a bit more alert than that.

Spock made eye contact with her.

They regarded each other, silently sizing one another up, and then without a word T'Lana gestured to the chair next to her in a manner that she hoped would seem inviting rather than commanding. Spock didn't move at first, but then he tilted his head in mute acceptance of the offer and walked toward her. She remained on her feet until he drew near, and then she raised her hand in the traditional split-fingered Vulcan salute. "Peace and long life, Ambassador," she said.

"Live long and prosper, Counselor," he replied, and sat.

"You are . . . aware of my position aboard the *Enterprise*?" It had been difficult for her to hide her surprise merely upon seeing Spock; this was proving an almost Herculean effort.

"There is not such an overabundance of Vulcans in Starfleet that I am incapable of keeping apprised of who and where they are . . . particularly when they are assigned to the *Enterprise.*"

She raised an eyebrow. "You have sentimental attachment to this vessel?"

"'Sentiment' may not be the most accurate word."

"What, then?"

He pondered it. "'Curiosity.'"

"The hallmark of a good scientist. Yet you are an ambassador now."

"An ambassador by trade, a scientist by nature."

"May I ask why you are here?"

"I was thirsty."

"I mean aboard the *Enterprise.*"

"I was invited here by the captain."

T'Lana puckered her lips slightly. "He did not inform me."

Now it was Spock who raised an eyebrow, which was as close to an emotional display as he customarily came. "I was unaware the ship's commanding officer was required to clear his decisions with the ship's counselor."

"Obviously, he is not," replied T'Lana. "However, I would have thought . . ." Her voice trailed off.

Spock leaned forward, the aforementioned "curiosity" clearly at the forefront of his thinking. "Is there a matter you wish to discuss?"

"We have just met, Ambassador."

"There is not, to the best of my knowledge, a time requirement for acquaintance when discussing personal difficulties."

"True. It is simply that . . ."

He waited. She said nothing. "Your silence indicates to me that there is nothing 'simple' about it."

"How did you deal with it?" she asked.

"Could you be more specific as to the nature of 'it'?"

She leaned forward and asked intently, "I have read extensively of your time aboard the *Enterprise.* That does not make me unique, I am sure. Any Vulcan intending to serve in Starfleet would certainly desire to read of your experiences."

"I can see how they could be seen as . . . informative."

"They were. What I do not understand, what none of the histories of the time makes clear, is how you were able to endure being correct all the time and not being respected for it."

Spock's right eyebrow now elevated to the same level as his left. For him, this was the equivalent of an emotional outburst. "I do not understand the question."

"I put it badly. Allow me to rephrase."

"Feel free to do so."

She leaned forward, resting her elbows on the table. "There were any number of occasions where, when James Kirk was faced with a dilemma, you put forward the logic of the situation. But oftentimes he chose to ignore your advice and instead follow a course derived from pure emotion."

"Courtesy of Leonard McCoy, more often than not," Spock said. His voice sounded gravelly and distant.

"Yes. Precisely. James Kirk would routinely follow illogical paths, ignore Starfleet regulations and the wishes of his superiors despite all your best advice to the contrary. And he did so with impunity . . ."

"Impunity? On one occasion he was reduced in rank from admiral to captain, and on another he was sentenced to a harsh Klingon prison world. Hardly what one would term 'impunity.'"

"Those were the exceptions. If he had been held

liable every time he behaved in an inappropriate or illogical manner, he would have been relieved of command early in his career."

"That," Spock replied, "would have been a waste of material."

T'Lana blinked in surprise. "I am . . . puzzled that you have that opinion."

"Why would you be?"

"Because you were always right in your advice to James Kirk, but he routinely ignored it and suffered few negative consequences."

"I believe your confusion stems from your definition of the term 'right.' "

"It does not require a definition. There is no gray area here. 'Right' is a binomial condition: right and wrong. You were right."

"Yet in every instance, matters were solved. Lives were saved. Civilizations survived."

"More by luck than anything else, in my studies."

"Whereas my studies, Counselor, indicate that there is not that much luck extant in the whole of the cosmos. Furthermore, you are proceeding from a false assumption. The right way is not necessarily the only way. The sooner you accept that simple concept, the happier you will be."

"It is not in my nature to be happy," she reminded him.

He inclined his head slightly. "Then the less unhappy you will be."

"I am not unhappy. That state of mind is irrelevant to me."

"Dissatisfied, then. It is quite obvious to me, Counselor, that the true topic being discussed here is not me . . . but you."

She looked down then, unable to meet his gaze. "There . . . is some truth to that," she admitted.

"A good deal, I should think."

T'Lana let out a slow, steady breath. "I speak of matters now that are not protected as privileged communications, since they became a matter of Starfleet record and consideration. I would not want you to think I was violating any trusts."

"Understood."

"Captain Picard sought my advice in a matter of disobeying direct Starfleet orders regarding a situation with the Borg. I advised him, repeatedly, to respect the chain of command. He ignored my advice and violated it, flagrantly and repeatedly."

"Court-martial?"

"Still pending, to the best of my knowledge."

"And you feel that your opinions—that you—were treated in a disrespectful manner."

She flattened her palms on the table. "How else am I to feel? What type of Starfleet officer blatantly ignores the chain of command?"

"I did."

The response was clearly not what she expected. "You did?"

"In the matter of Captain Christopher Pike." Spock slowly shook his head, as if he could not believe that he had undertaken the course that he had.

"Oh." The details came back to her the moment he mentioned them. "Well . . . yes. I read of that . . . incident. But the circumstances were not comparable."

"They rarely are."

"You did what you knew had to be done."

"As I am sure was the case with Captain Picard."

"But he did not know," she said more fervently than she would have thought herself capable. "That is the point, Ambassador. He was acting entirely on impulse. On a hunch. It was not logical."

"Not in any way that we define or understand logic," he admitted. "But that does not make the thought process that arrives at such decisions inherently inferior to our own."

"Yes. It does."

Her tone was emphatic, and Spock said nothing for a time, allowing the words to hang there.

"As long as you hold to that opinion, T'Lana," Spock finally said, "you will never be . . . not unhappy."

He inclined his head slightly and then stood and stepped away from the table. Before he could walk away, T'Lana pointed out, "You never had anything to drink." When he looked at her quizzically, she reminded him, "You said you came here because you were thirsty."

"And so I was. Thirsty for knowledge. For discussion. And now that thirst has been quenched." He held up his hand and said, "Live long and prosper, T'Lana. You will work out these difficulties and personal quandaries."

"Given what has thus far transpired, I do not know, Ambassador Spock, if it is truly logical to believe that."

"Call it a hunch," he replied and walked out of the lounge.

10

The *Pride*

GRIM VARGO WAS NOT IN A FORGIVING MOOD.

"Forget it."

"It is imperative that you—"

"I said forget i!"

He was stalking the interior of his vessel while his passenger, Ann, sat quietly in a chair with her hands resting upon her knees.

"You start howling that the Borg are following us! You knock me cold! You—"

"I know. I was there," Ann reminded him.

He turned to face her, his face purpling with rage. "We are not going to Sector 10. You hear that? You can just forget it."

"I suspected you would say that."

"Oh, *did* you? Aren't *you* clever!" He gestured in the very general direction of where they'd come from. "I should have turned you over to Starfleet! I can understand why they were looking for you! You're insane!"

"That is my fear."

The reply brought him up short. "What's that mean?"

"I have . . ." She hesitated. The fact that she paused at all was surprising considering the self-assured manner in which she had addressed him until now. "I have . . . reason to believe that my perceptions regarding the Borg have merit. On the other hand, it is entirely possible that there is something within my . . . brain . . ."—she spoke the word as if it were a substitute for something else—". . . that is causing me to imagine things. To hallucinate, for want of a better term. It is disconcerting for me that I have this uncertainty. I regret any inconvenience that it may have posed for you."

He regarded her as if she were some sort of bizarre life-form and was beginning to suspect that that was exactly the case. The side of his head was still throbbing and he rubbed it as he said, "Look, no matter what, I'm still not taking you to Sector 10. I don't know what the hell is going on, but that concept is done. It's over."

"Vulcan, then."

"Vulcan?" It wasn't an unreasonable request.

Vulcan wasn't even that far from where the *Pride* was currently positioned. Certainly it was preferable to just tossing her out of the ship . . . although from the look of her, not to mention her considerable strength, that just might be a difficult proposition. Still, the sudden shift made no sense to him. Then again, nothing about this had made any sense to him.

"Yes."

"Why Vulcan?"

"Because it is my request."

"No. No." He shook his head. "Enough dancing around. What's your involvement with the Borg? Why Vulcan? Who the hell are you really?"

"I do not believe that—"

He cut her off with a gesture. "Uh-uh. That's not gonna fly, 'Ann.' For that matter, neither are we. If you think I'm kidding, you're badly mistaken. I can sit and float here indefinitely, and I have a feeling it's going to be way more of a bother to you than it is to me. You're the one who's in a god-awful hurry. Me, I've got nothing *but* time. And don't even think about trying to take over my ship again. I've not only rigged it to respond to my voice code, but if you even try to take 'er over, we'll self-destruct. You get that?" He leaned in toward her and made an exploding motion with his hands. "*Booooom.* I'd rather be in pieces all over the sector than have someone hijack my boat again."

It was pure bluff. For that matter, he suspected

she was perfectly capable of coming up with a means of circumventing whatever such booby traps he might have set, even if he had set them . . . which he hadn't, so it was moot. Vargo was hoping she wouldn't see through it. He would much rather have her cooperation than be faced with the prospect of having to tie her up or otherwise secure her somehow. First, he disliked the idea of brutalizing women. Second, he had the sneaking suspicion she would probably kick his ass if he tried.

"My name is not Ann," she said so abruptly that the pronouncement surprised him. "Actually . . . it was. Annika. But I have not been addressed by that name for the entirety of my adult life."

"All right, then," he prompted. "So that begs the question . . ."

"My full designation is Seven of Nine, Tertiary Adjunct of Unimatrix Zero One. I was part of the Borg collective."

"A Bor—?" He wasn't even able to get the full word out. His throat had constricted. He took a step back, staring at her as if she had grown a third eye. His hand drifted toward the disruptor that he had strapped to his hip ever since he had come to.

Vargo had never actually seen a Borg. He'd heard about them; everyone who traveled the spaceways had. This . . . Seven of Nine looked nothing like the ones he'd heard described. If nothing else, she didn't have weapons instead of arms. His eyes narrowed, suddenly wondering if he had a complete loony on his boat. "Are you messing with me now? I mean, yeah, you've got that thing." He gestured toward her implant. "But you sure don't look . . . I don't know . . . Borgish."

"I was disconnected from the Borg consciousness through the efforts of Kathryn Janeway and the crew of the *Voyager,*" she said. "I was restored to humanity . . . or as close to humanity as could be approximated. I am not a member of Starfleet, but I teach at the academy."

"Okay." He wasn't completely sure he bought into this yet, but at least this was different from being told nothing. "So what the hell are you doing out here?"

"She is in trouble."

"She?"

"Admiral Janeway. She is on a Borg cube in Sector 10 and I fear the Borg have assimilated her. I am endeavoring to get there and rescue her."

Grim Vargo let out a curt laugh. "You've got to be kidding me. That's what this is about? You want me to fly *toward* a Borg ship? So that you can ride on some fool's errand to rescue some Starfleet admiral. Why should I put my neck on the line for an admiral? There's no love lost between the Fleet and myself, I can tell you that much. She wouldn't risk her neck to save me, that's for sure."

"She very likely would."

"She doesn't even know me!"

"And yet she would. Which should give you some idea of the type of woman she is."

"She's the type of woman," said Vargo, "who can get me killed. Which, I might add, describes you pretty well too."

Seven said nothing in response to that.

"Why Vulcan?" he asked.

"Because that is where the *Enterprise* is currently in orbit."

"How do you know that?"

"Even out here, I am still able to access Starfleet's data bank. Vulcan is the *Enterprise*'s last known location."

"Last known location. But if there was some sort of last-minute emergency, she could actually be somewhere else entirely and a swing over to Vulcan could be a waste of time."

"That . . . is true," she admitted. "But Captain Picard is my most likely ally in this endeavor. He was once connected to the Borg. He knows them. Not as well as I, but well. His would be the most sympathetic ear to my situation. If you will not take me directly to the Borg cube . . ."

"Why not ask a moth to give you a lift to the flame while you're at it?"

". . . then at least take me to Picard. As you yourself said, it is not far, and you would not be putting your vessel at risk."

Vargo stepped back. His forehead was beaded with sweat and he wiped the back of his sleeve across it.

She had been looking straight ahead. Now she

turned and gazed at him. She remained far too disconnected from everyday emotions to look pleading, but there was a sort of quiet desperation in her eyes. "Please. Admiral Janeway . . . her companions . . . even the Federation itself are all threatened."

"I just need time to think."

"You do not have the time. The more time that passes, the greater the risk."

He stared at her, considering all his options, and then finally let out a heavy sigh. "All right. Fine. Vulcan. But if the *Enterprise* isn't there, then I drop you off planet side. Either way we're quit of each other. Understood?"

"Yes," she said primly.

He moved to the controls, alert to the possibility that she might still try to commandeer the ship again. It would have been ridiculous for her to do so, but by this point he wasn't eliminating any possibility.

So he was startled when she rested a hand gently on his arm. He looked over to her and there was quiet gratitude on her face.

"Thank you," she said.

"Save your thanks. If everything goes the way you want it to, I'm probably helping you to ride headlong into disaster. Still, thanks for the heads-up about the Borg. If they're gunning for the Federation, that probably means they'll make a beeline for Earth. So you'll understand if I make damned sure to be on the other side of the galaxy when that happens."

"Part of me wishes I could be there with you."

He looked her up and down, not immune to her more prominent charms. "Frankly, sweetheart, part of me does, too."

11

Vulcan

- i -

IT WAS AN ARID DAY OUTSIDE THE SAREK SCHOOL of Diplomacy and Ambassadorial Studies, which was typical weather for Vulcan. The gathered crowd was awaiting the arrival of the Vulcan priests who would administer the appropriate consecrations upon the building.

It wasn't a ceremony that Picard could even pretend to understand. Standing near Perrin, waiting in the heat, he asked her if she could possibly cast any illumination upon it. Perrin shrugged in response. "I was told it would be required, and I didn't feel like arguing."

"I don't blame you." Picard pulled on the collar

of his dress uniform, an outfit that he wasn't especially enamored of but that seemed appropriate for the ceremony. "I admit it seems difficult to contemplate a society steeped in logic that nevertheless holds to a religious belief system."

"Are you saying religion isn't logical?" she asked teasingly.

"Well, you have to admit, religion requires, almost by definition, leaps of faith. Logic is the antithesis of faith."

"I don't know about that. Perhaps faith is simply a different sort of logic system. I mean, Vulcans do have some religious holdings. They believe in sacred places, such as the Monastery of P'Jem. Holding something sacred is the equivalent of having a religious investment in it, is it not?"

"I suppose," Picard admitted. "Did Sarek never speak to you about it?"

"Never. Vulcans remain tight-lipped about so many things."

"One has to admire the consistency. I asked both T'Lana and Ambassador Spock about it, and neither of them seemed inclined to—"

"Spock?"

That drew Picard up short as he realized his error. Perrin was looking at him wide-eyed. "Did you say Spock?" she repeated.

Oh, well done, Jean-Luc. Brilliant. Just brilliant. He wondered how he could have been so stupid as to let that bit of information slip out and decided that this might well be a textbook example of a

Freudian slip. He genuinely wanted her to know, and thus had been unconscionably sloppy in his word choice. "He . . . arrived last night," Picard admitted.

She looked around. "And . . . is he here? Now?"

"He's on the *Enterprise*."

Perrin was momentarily startled by that. "Why isn't he here?" Then, before Picard could respond, she put up a hand and stopped him. She smiled. "No. It's all right. I understand."

"You do?"

"All too well. It's ironic that both men are ambassadors, dedicating their lives to interacting with so many other people . . . and yet both of them share a ferocious—and, at times, almost crippling—need for privacy."

"Perhaps that very need is what drove them to their chosen profession."

Perrin shook her head, clearly not understanding. "I don't follow."

"A wise man is capable of determining his weaknesses and working to address them," said Picard. "If both Sarek and Spock had a need for privacy that was, as you put it, almost crippling . . . then it would be in character for both of them to undertake fields of endeavor that would force them to overcome their weaknesses. Much like someone who suffers from a fear of heights or water taking up high diving, specifically to overcome the phobia."

"You make a remarkable amount of sense, Captain Picard."

"Well," Picard said modestly, "I have been known to from time to time. I try not to make a habit out of it."

Perrin laughed at that, and the unexpected noise drew severe looks from several of the Vulcan onlookers. She quickly silenced herself. In a low voice, Picard said, "If you wish, I can speak to the ambassador, see if he'd be willing to meet with you . . ."

She shook her head. "That won't be necessary. Knowing he came is more than enough."

"Are you sure?"

"If being married to Sarek taught me one thing, it was to be sure of everything I say."

There was a faint jingling of bells in the distance. The onlookers had been speaking to one another in low tones, but now even those quiet voices ceased. The crowd parted as a line of Vulcan priests, dressed in flowing red robes, approached. They took slow, measured strides, their chins level. Uniformly male, each of them had long, flowing gray hair. Noticing Picard's expression, Perrin whispered, "Problem?"

"It's just that I've never seen a Vulcan sporting anything other than short-cropped hair."

"You missed Spock during his Kolinahr phase."

"Apparently so."

The priests drew closer. The silence, broken only by the jingling of bells, was eerie . . .

No. Wait. There's something else. An incoming vessel?

Picard was right. He heard it before he saw it. It

appeared out of nowhere as it descended, obviously courtesy of some sort of cloaking device. That explained how it was able to slip past both Vulcan's defense perimeter and the *Enterprise.* In a battle situation, the *Enterprise* had ways of picking up either traces or movements of a cloaked vessel. But in an air of normalcy, with an assortment of ships coming and going out of orbit, it was easy for a small, cloaked ship to slip through undetected.

It was heading very quickly toward the gathering.

An attack. We're under attack.

Even as a murmur of confusion swept through the Vulcan assemblage, Picard tapped his combadge. "Picard to *Enterprise.*"

"Enterprise, *Worf here,"* came the deep voice of his second-in-command.

"Incoming vessel. Possibly hostile. Target it and prepare for my order to open fire. Send a security squad down immediately."

"On their way."

Picard had not taken his eyes off the vessel. It didn't appear to have any major offensive capability—in a firefight, the *Enterprise* would blow it into atoms with one shot—but how much armament was really required if one was going to open fire on a crowd of unarmed individuals?

The air shimmered with the telltale sound of the transporter, and a security team of half a dozen armed men and women appeared. Even as that happened, the vessel abruptly slowed on its approach. Its front tilted upward as it fired reverse thrusters, and that was when Picard realized that the ship was coming in for a landing. The crowd had parted, spreading in opposite directions, giving the ship plenty of room. The security team all had their phaser rifles out, and they were aimed squarely at the incoming ship, tracking its motion all the way down. Picard knew that a single phaser rifle firing on a ship wouldn't have much impact, but all of them in concert would provide a formidable assault.

The ship hovered for a moment above the ground and then settled in, kicking up dust. The engines powered down, but that didn't cause the security team to let down their guard for even a second. Picard realized that he had instinctively taken up a defensive posture in front of Perrin, shielding her from possible attack with his body. Resting her hand on his shoulder, she seemed comforted by his presence. "Who are they?" she asked worriedly.

"I suspect we're about to find out."

There was the distinctive sound of the outer hatch disengaging. The security team instantly switched their target from the ship in general to the hatch in particular. Picard realized that he was holding his breath to see what happened next. He had no idea what to expect and as a result was ready to expect anything.

It was not until Seven of Nine emerged from the ship to face him did he realize that the entire notion of being ready to "expect anything" was overrated.

There was another figure visible in the hatch, a man. He was there only long enough to say, "Now she's your problem." Then he vanished back into his ship and the hatch cycled shut. The engines immediately began to fire up. The security guards, who were still keeping their weapons aimed at Seven, looked questioningly to Picard. Picard, in turn, looked to Seven.

"He is of no consequence," Seven said immediately as if reading Picard's thoughts. "Please allow him to depart without incident."

Naturally the guards yet again turned to their captain for guidance. Picard considered ignoring Seven's request but couldn't come up with a good reason for doing so. "Lower your weapons," he ordered. "Stand down."

The guards immediately did so. Moments later, the vessel was airborne and heading as quickly as it could for the Vulcan horizon.

Seven strode over to Picard with her customary assurance and stopped several feet shy of him. "It was necessary to come straight down here to speak with you, Captain. My . . . pilot tends to be suspicious of Starfleet vessels and was disinclined to make direct contact with the *Enterprise*. This was the only reasonable compromise."

The explanation did nothing to mollify him. "May I ask the meaning of this, Seven?" he demanded, not even bothering with the standard niceties of offering introductions.

If she was bothered by the curtness of his manner, she didn't show it. "Kathryn Janeway and all of humanity are in mortal danger from the Borg." She looked around at the assemblage and then back to Picard. "Is this an inappropriate time?"

For one of the few times in his life, Picard was at a loss for words.

- ii -

When she returned to her home that evening, Perrin found a message waiting for her. She activated the system and the face of Soco appeared upon the screen.

Perrin was relieved to see it. Her old friend had not shown up for that day's dedication ceremony. That had caused Perrin to worry, although certainly the events that had transpired had been more than enough to take her attention away from worrying about the Argelian woman.

"Greetings, Perrin," came the recorded message. "I hope this message finds you well. I very much regret that I was unable to make it to Vulcan to attend the festivities. I consider them a superb coda to your husband's remarkable life. Unfortunately, I have taken sick, and although the doctors assure me that I will recover—my husband will not be quit of me anytime soon, I fear—nevertheless they advised against extended travel. I hope you will forgive me this lapse, and I look forward to coming to Vulcan as soon as it is possible so that I can see the school for myself. All my best."

The screen blinked out, and Perrin stared at the empty space long after it did.

Finally she found her voice.

"If . . . if Soco never *came* here, then *who the hell* was that?"

It was a question that Kathryn Janeway might well have been able to answer for her, but Janeway was in no position to do so. It turned out to be a mystery that Perrin was never able to solve.

12

The *Enterprise*

- i -

"I DON'T KNOW WHAT TO TELL YOU, CAPTAIN, EXcept that in my opinion, Seven of Nine is unstable."

The scowling face of Edward Jellico was looking back at Picard from the small viewscreen in his ready room.

"Unstable," Picard echoed. "Are you certain?"

"Captain, look at the facts." Jellico began ticking off the facts on his fingers. *"She came to me with this wild belief of hers, that Janeway is in trouble. I checked with the* Einstein, *and spoke to the admiral. Everything is fine. But when I presented those indisputable facts to the professor and told her explicitly not to depart for the Borg cube, she went anyway!*

And eluded a Starfleet vessel in the process! I want you to keep her pilot in custody. I'm going to have him brought up on charges and get his license revoked."

"That would be problematic," Picard admitted, "since he has already departed. Nor is Seven of Nine willing to give us specifics as to who he was."

"Transponder tag."

Picard shrugged. "Scrambled."

"You're not helping here, Captain."

"With all respect, Admiral, I was not endeavoring to help. Merely to ascertain information and determine my course of action."

"Your course of action is to send her back to Earth as quickly as humanly possible. You've no other course of action open to you." His voice dropped to a warning tone. *"And, Captain, you're already in deep enough trouble as it is thanks to the previous Borg incident. Admiral Janeway may have given you a free pass on that, but—"*

"A free pass?" That surprised Picard. "Sir, I'm afraid I'm not familiar with what you're referring to."

"Oh. Right." Jellico looked mildly chagrined and then let out an exasperated sigh. *"I hadn't had the opportunity to pass through the paperwork yet. Admiral Janeway has recommended clemency for you in regard to your egregious breach of Starfleet protocol. Personally, I'd just as soon throw the book at you, no offense."*

"None taken," said Picard dryly.

"But it's procedure to defer to the wishes of the

aggrieved party in these instances, particularly when she's a ranking officer. Personally, I've no idea why she let you off the hook . . ."

Because she was grateful that we quite possibly saved humanity?

"However, since she has, I suggest that you don't press your luck with a similar stunt. Return Seven of Nine to Earth immediately so that she can be put into our custody."

Picard thoughtfully scratched his chin. "Seven of Nine is not, last I checked, a member of Starfleet."

"That's true, but—"

He interrupted the admiral, which was a violation of protocol, but Picard didn't particularly care at the moment. "That being the case, I don't quite understand Starfleet's authority in this matter. She may teach at Starfleet Academy, but she does so in a civilian capacity. So on what basis can Starfleet determine where she goes?"

"When it comes to matters of the Borg and of Federation security, Starfleet's latitude is considerable. And may I remind you, Captain, *that I am not obligated to explain this to you? I am doing so as a courtesy. You remember courtesy: it's the aspect of human interaction that you seem disinclined to extend to me."* Before Picard could respond, Jellico continued, *"Your obligation, on the other hand, is to obey orders. Kindly do not let Admiral Janeway's generosity in the other matter blind you to that simple fact. Get Professor Hansen—"*

"She prefers 'Seven of Nine,' is my understanding."

"Just get her back here. And steer clear of the Borg cube. For all we know, the Borg may somehow be extending some sort of long-distance influence on her. If that's the case, we certainly don't want her anywhere near it."

"Are you suggesting," Picard asked, "that the Borg cube could still represent a threat? If that is the case, perhaps we should—"

"I'm suggesting, Captain, that we can't take any chances. And I'm suggesting that we terminate this conversation in the following manner: I say, 'Do you understand?' and you say, 'Aye, sir.' Do you understand?"

Picard's lips thinned nearly to nonexistence, but all he said was, "Aye, sir."

With a curt nod, Jellico's image vanished from the screen.

Sighing, Picard leaned back against his desk and muttered, *"Merde."*

- ii -

There were times when T'Lana cursed both her logical mind and her training as a counselor, since it gave her such insights into human behavior that she knew what was coming long before it arrived.

Seated in the conference lounge, with Picard at

the opposite end of the table, she was positive that this was one of those times.

Gathered around the table were Beverly Crusher, Geordi La Forge, Worf, Miranda Kadohata, and Zelik Leybenzon. She was pleased—or at least as close to pleased as she ever came—to see that Leybenzon was scowling fiercely as Picard finished describing the specifics of the situation with which they'd been presented.

There was silence for a moment around the table, and then Leybenzon said, "Permission to speak freely, Captain?"

"Granted," said Picard.

"Why are we even discussing this?" He came close to laughing at his own question but stopped short of it. Leybenzon was far too much a hardcore, old-school officer to treat the question as anything less than deadly serious. "We have our orders from Starfleet. What else is there to say?"

Obviously you are new here, T'Lana wanted to say but restrained herself. Instead she merely looked with curiosity to Picard.

"There may be . . . additional factors at work here," Picard pointed out.

"What 'additional factors,' Captain? We're given orders. We obey them. There's nothing 'additional' to be put into the mix."

"There have been times, Lieutenant," Worf informed him with his customary haughtiness, "when that has not always been the case."

Leybenzon looked incredulous, and even more so

when Geordi spoke up and said, "Worf is right. It's easy for people back home at Starfleet to make declarations of what is and isn't the case. They're not out here on the front lines, making the life-and-death decisions."

"No, they're at home making the life-and-death decisions, and we're bound by our oaths to obey those decisions," said Leybenzon.

T'Lana felt an almost overwhelming sense of relief. She actually came within a few muscle spasms of smiling but naturally was able to stifle the impulse.

"Their decisions," Crusher told him, "are based on the best available facts they have on hand. If we have more facts than they do, then we owe them our best efforts to implement the correct decisions, even if they run counter to the wisdom of the Fleet officers."

"You mean substitute our judgment for that of superior officers."

"If need be."

"Based on what facts, if I might ask, sir?" inquired Leybenzon. "The facts, such as they are, are that this woman, this Seven individual, is running around making wild accusations that Starfleet has established—to their satisfaction—as groundless."

"That," Worf said, "was what Starfleet said about Captain Picard's concerns over the Borg as well. Those were not groundless."

"And they resulted in the death of two away teams," Kadohata spoke up. All eyes shifted to her, but the dark-haired woman with the crisp British accent didn't appear at all intimidated . . . not even by the glare that Worf seemed to be giving her. "My apologies if that's an indelicate observation, but it's true. Furthermore, if I recall correctly, Starfleet didn't say the captain's concerns were groundless. He was instructed to wait for backup. He decided not to do so, and the result was—"

"That the Borg were defeated," said La Forge.

"—at the cost of the lives of Starfleet officers. They paid the price for the captain's decision."

There was a deathly hush in the conference lounge. Although she knew it wasn't really the case, T'Lana felt that Worf would have reached across the table and strangled the second officer if he could have managed to avoid the consequences.

T'Lana thought she heard the captain whisper, "The needs of the many."

His voice heavy but firm, Picard stated, "I have to make decisions and force myself not to take into consideration if my people are thrust into danger."

"Captain . . . you're saying . . . you don't care?" asked Kadohata.

"No. The problem is that I care far too much. But one of the demands of *my* position is that I have to act as if it doesn't matter. Believe me, it does. It does more than any commanding officer wishes to acknowledge. Does that answer your question, Commander?"

At first she met his steely gaze, but she was unable to hold it and instead looked down.

T'Lana decided that she had been silent long enough. "If we may look at this in a logical manner," she said quietly, "then logic dictates that our recent previous experiences with the Borg would argue against our trusting what Seven of Nine says."

"How do you figure that?" said La Forge. He wasn't challenging; he actually sounded curious. "The whole reason that we wound up acting contrary to Starfleet's wishes last time was that they told us to wait for Seven of Nine. She was seen as the Borg expert. The fact that Seven of Nine is here, now, and she's telling us that we have to take action, doesn't that argue *for* doing so?"

"On the surface, perhaps it does," admitted T'Lana. "However, unlike the previous incident, Starfleet was actually able to obtain independent verification that the Borg are posing no threat. The very individual who told us to wait for Seven—Admiral Janeway—verified to Admiral Jellico that there is no danger."

"Perhaps there was a danger that Admiral Janeway was unaware of," said Picard.

"Are you suggesting that Seven of Nine can divine the future, Captain?"

"I am suggesting that perhaps her link to the Borg is providing her some means of access to their plans that Admiral Janeway is unaware of."

"Much as yours did when you were previously spurred to ignore Starfleet's orders and seek out the cube yourself."

"Precisely," said Picard.

"And yet," continued T'Lana, "you are offering no such insights now. Whereas before you were haunted by dreams, even hallucinating, this time you are experiencing no such connection. If Seven of Nine is truly correct and is experiencing some insight into further jeopardy from the Borg . . . why are you blind to it?"

She was inwardly pleased to see that Picard had no ready answer for that. He looked to Crusher, but she simply shrugged. "For all we know about how the Borg operate, there's still a good deal we don't know," said Crusher. "I've honestly no idea why the captain would know of their plans then but not now."

"I submit that those are the sorts of questions that we should be asking," said T'Lana. "And I would further submit that the captain's refusal to do so—or at least his reluctance to—indicates an alarming tendency to substitute his own judgment for Starfleet's."

"Starfleet is not taking all the facts into consideration," said Picard.

"Perhaps they are," replied T'Lana, "but they are forcing themselves not to care. Certainly that is an attitude to which you can relate, Captain."

She sat back in her chair, knowing that she had him. Knowing that she had created a web of logic that was quite impenetrable.

"It seems to me," Beverly Crusher said, "that it comes down to state of mind."

Ah. Here it comes, thought T'Lana.

"I mean, T'Lana raises a good point," continued

Beverly. "There are things going through Seven's head that we don't have access to. The fact that the captain is not experiencing that same sort of connection could possibly be telling. So it might be helpful if we *did* have access to Seven's state of mind."

All eyes turned to T'Lana.

"No," she said quietly but firmly.

"A mind-meld," Picard began, "would certainly—"

"No," T'Lana repeated and then added belatedly, "sir."

Worf visibly bristled at T'Lana's intransigence. "You lecture others on obeying orders but do not hesitate to decline one when it suits your purpose."

"Ordering a Vulcan to perform a mind-meld is beyond the discretion of any Starfleet officer," replied T'Lana evenly.

"The counselor is quite correct," Picard said, displaying none of the anger that was reflected in Worf's manner. "A mind-meld is considered a very personal experience and one that is not subject to Starfleet purview. It would be considered invasive for me to order her to scan Seven of Nine's thoughts in trying to determine the veracity of her claims."

"Nor would it necessarily be useful," T'Lana reminded him. "All it would indicate, as you well know, Captain, is that she believes what she is saying. I am willing to concede that as a likelihood without any telepathic bonding at all. I could not determine anything beyond that. On that basis alone, there is no point in trying."

"Then what are our options?" asked La Forge.

"At the moment," replied Picard, "unless someone can provide me with one that I am not perceiving, we don't really have any."

T'Lana waited for someone to offer protest but, to her mild surprise, none came. Picard nodded once and then tapped his combadge. "Picard to bridge."

"Bridge, Stephens here." It was the voice of conn officer Jon Stephens.

"Lieutenant Stephens, set course for home."

There was a pause. *"My home specifically, or just Earth in general?"*

Picard closed his eyes for a moment. "Earth in general."

"Because technically I was born on a Martian colony, so I wouldn't want to have us in orbit around Mars, and you're asking, 'What are we doing here?' and I'm saying, 'You said home,' and then you would—"

"Yes. Earth. Now."

"Aye, sir. Earth it is. Any particular speed?"

"Warp three."

"You're sure? Because I can do four, five, . . . even six, easy."

"Warp three will suffice."

"Warp three, aye."

La Forge shook his head. "Where did Stephens come from again?"

"A transfer from the *Excalibur,*" said Crusher. "According to his service record, Captain Calhoun said he was a little too strange for his crew."

"The fact that *anyone* could be too strange for

Calhoun's crew concerns me," said Picard. "That's all. Dismissed."

T'Lana got up from the table and exited the conference lounge without so much as glancing around at any of her fellow officers. She headed down the hallway to the turbolift, but as she stepped in, Leybenzon insinuated himself between the closing doors. She moved aside, allowing him entrance.

"Deck seven," said T'Lana, intending to head to her quarters to catch up on reviewing personnel files.

"Deck six." Leybenzon turned and said, "It's a shame I wasn't here during the previous Borg situation."

"Indeed?" she asked, sounding indifferent.

"From what I'm hearing, you were the lone voice of reason crying in the wilderness."

"There was no crying involved. I merely put forward my best advice. It was ignored."

"All I'm saying is that if I'd been here, you'd have had someone backing you up. I'm sure that Miranda feels the same way."

"You mean Commander Kadohata."

"Yes, of course."

"Because it is inappropriate for a junior officer to refer to a senior officer by her first name, even in casual conversation."

"You're absolutely right," said Leybenzon.

"I always am."

Leybenzon chuckled at that, although T'Lana didn't understand why. All she was doing was stating fact; what was so funny about that? She felt she would never understand the human sense of humor . . . or any species's sense of humor, for that matter.

"Well," Leybenzon said with a sigh as the turbolift started to slow in anticipation of reaching deck six, "at least this crisis is averted. It's over."

"Is it?"

"You heard the order."

"Yes."

"And the captain wanted you to perform a mind-meld to give him additional information, but you wouldn't do it, so that's that."

"You know that Ambassador Spock is on board."

He blinked in confusion at the shift in topic. "I'm head of security. Of course I know." The doors opened and he stepped out onto the bridge. "So?"

"So did you hear the captain order the ambassador to be sent down to Vulcan before we departed?"

Leybenzon started to speak but nothing came out.

"This is not over," said T'Lana with confidence. "This has barely begun."

She watched the realization creep across Leybenzon's expression as the doors closed.

Yes, indeed. T'Lana's insight remained something of a curse. But it was one she was going to have to live with.

- iii -

Seven of Nine was seated in the sparsely furnished quarters that had been assigned her. She sat perfectly still, staring straight ahead. Anyone glancing in casually would have thought her to be a statue.

The door chimed and she said crisply, "Yes."

It slid open and Jean-Luc Picard entered. She glanced up at him but said nothing, waiting for him to speak.

"Starfleet," he said without preamble, "has ordered us to return with you to Earth."

"That is to be expected," she replied. She paused and then asked, "Do you intend to comply?"

He walked across the room, his hands behind his back. "You understand that I am in a difficult position. I have my orders. As a Starfleet officer, I am bound to obey them."

"Except when it suits your purposes otherwise."

"Even then . . . as your own Admiral Janeway made abundantly clear."

"She is not 'my own' Admiral Janeway," said Seven.

"That is true. Still, you are in a unique position. You are close to her . . . and you remain close to the Borg. Where those two interests intersect, perhaps it's inevitable that you would be alerted to it."

"And you remain close to the Borg as well," she reminded him.

"Yes. But there are differences."

"The difference is that I chose to turn away from the Borg, whereas you were forced to do so. Then again, perhaps one who is trained to obey orders found being part of the Borg collective to be . . . familiar."

Seven had meant the words to be simple and straightforward, but she could tell from Picard's reaction that they had hit home in a way that she had not intended. She did not, however, feel inclined to apologize for what she had said and consequently said nothing.

"You are . . . correct in one respect, at least," Picard told her. "We both have a singular connection to, and understanding of, the Borg. So if anyone is in a position to understand your . . . predicament, it is I. The problem is that Starfleet has already established communication with Kathryn Janeway. She has maintained there is no problem."

"Of course she has," said Seven. "The Borg are supremely adaptable. If they have assimilated Kathryn Janeway, but are building up their strength, they will devise a way to hide that intention until it is too late. Indeed, they are counting on us to wait until it *is* too late. Which would lead one to conclude," she went on thoughtfully, "that we pose a concern to them. Perhaps even a threat. We merely have to determine what the nature of that threat is and then implement it against them."

Picard did not reply.

She stared at him and was easily able to discern what was on his mind without his even having to say it. "Starfleet," she said slowly, "believes that I am lying. Or unhinged. Or untrustworthy in some manner."

With a sigh, Picard sat on the couch opposite her. "Something like that."

"You, however, know that is not the case."

"I do not know that for certain, no. Sadly enough."

"Then we appear to be at an impasse."

"Not necessarily."

"What did you have in mind?"

"Not so much what," Picard said slowly, "as who."

- iv -

Having already dimmed the lights in his quarters, since sparser lighting helped him to focus, Ambassador Spock stood facing the seated Seven of Nine. Her face, as was typical for her, was inscrutable. Spock found that rather intriguing: in her general comportment and bearing, the woman would have made a creditable Vulcan. Then again, he reasoned, that was because she had spent her entire adult life as part of the soulless beings called the Borg. So if being part of the Borg made one similar to Vulcans, then what did that say about the Vulcans in general? It was a line of reasoning that Spock deliberately chose not to pursue . . . at least, not for the time being.

Jean-Luc Picard was standing off to the side, his arms folded across his chest. Beverly Crusher was with him, at her insistence, with emergency equipment just in case. *The man isn't exactly young, even by Vulcan standards,* she had reminded Picard, *and if something goes wrong, every minute could count.* Those were the sentiments that Picard had conveyed to the ambassador when he had first spoken to Spock about undertaking this endeavor, and Spock had acknowledged Crusher's concerns with a slight inclination of his head. That was all. For Spock, that alone spoke volumes.

Without looking away from Seven, Spock asked Picard, "You have a Vulcan on your vessel. You have not spoken to her about performing this technique?"

"T'Lana was . . . reluctant to undertake it," Picard explained. "She said the outcome would be of no use, because all it would determine is whether or not Seven believes what she is saying. She felt that it would prove nothing empirically."

"There is some element of truth in that," Spock said. "At least, it is true for her. For one who is a bit more adept at the process, and has been performing it for a considerably longer time, more concrete determinations are possible. Not definite," he added, "but possible."

"I appreciate your agreeing to undertake the endeavor, in any event."

Spock shifted his gaze to Picard. "Your appreciation is not necessary. A situation has presented itself, and it appears I am the only individual who is capable of attending to it. I do what I must."

"Just . . ." Beverly took a step forward. "Just be careful."

Spock looked at her with a raised eyebrow. Automatically she stepped back again and looked down. She seemed embarrassed for some reason, although Picard couldn't imagine what it might be.

He turned his attention back to Seven. "Are you prepared?" he asked.

"No."

The answer surprised Picard, although he supposed it should not have. Spock had already begun to stretch out his hand to establish contact, but now the hand simply remained there in midair. He waited for her to speak, knowing she would.

"I have . . . lived much of my life . . . with other voices in my head," she said slowly. "I have come to prefer the . . . privacy of my own thoughts. Willingly allowing someone back into my mind . . . it is more daunting than I had previously thought. It was not a problem for me when considered in the abstract, but faced with the reality of it . . ."

"If you wish, we will proceed no further," Spock said, and there was a hint of kindness, even understanding, in his voice. *Just a hint,* Picard thought. Or perhaps he was simply imagining it. "It is entirely up to you."

Seven didn't speak at first, and then she swallowed deeply and nodded. "Proceed," she said.

Picard watched Spock place his hand gently against Seven's temple. Then Spock closed his own eyes. His breathing slowed, and Picard realized that it was now matching up perfectly with Seven's own.

Minutes passed. Spock had given Picard no indication of how long the process would last, but Picard was beginning to think that, however long it was supposed to be, this was longer than it should be. He looked questioningly to Crusher. She had already removed a medical tricorder and was performing readings on the two of them.

"Incredible," she murmured.

"What?"

"Their heartbeat is precisely the same."

"That should not be possible. A Vulcan's metabolism is drastically different from a human being's."

"Yes, they did point that out to us at some point during medical school," she said dryly. Picard couldn't help but think that she'd been way less sarcastic before they started sleeping together. "But now they're in sync."

"Can that prove dangerous for one of them?"

"For both of them, actually, if it goes on too long."

And suddenly Seven's eyes snapped open.

They were not her eyes.

Physically, they were. But there was something in them, a look of pure malevolence and contempt.

Spock moaned, tried to pull away, but was unable to. Seven reached up, grabbed him by the wrists, and held on tightly.

Instantly Picard was at Spock's side, as was Crusher. Picard grabbed Seven's arms by the wrists, trying to pry her hands loose, while Crusher pulled at Spock. Seven kept her hands locked upon the Vulcan, and then she looked up at Picard.

She uttered a soft laugh. "Hello, Locutus. It has been too long. But I will remedy that."

With a barely contained roar of anger, Picard twisted her arms back. That movement, combined with Crusher's efforts, broke Spock free of her grasp. The Vulcan fell backward on top of Beverly, who lost her footing. Both of them fell to the floor, although Beverly managed to cushion Spock's fall.

Seven's hands began to reach for Picard with renewed strength. She yanked free of his grasp and grabbed both sides of his head. She snapped to her feet and stood over Picard, a head taller, holding his skull so firmly that for an instant he thought she was going to break his neck with one quick twist.

"Resistance," she said in a voice that was not her own, "is futile. But I love it when you try." She pulled his head forward and kissed him passionately.

Spock's eyes opened.

The moment that happened, Seven sagged like a marionette with its strings cut. All the strength fled from her body and she started to collapse to the floor. Now it was Picard's turn to hold her, preventing her from thudding to the ground. Instead he eased her over into the chair, where she sat sprawled, breathing heavily, her chest rising and falling rapidly.

Spock was immediately on his feet, moving with far greater speed than Picard would have thought him capable of. Before Beverly could say anything, he was already back at Seven's side. Her eyes were closed, her head slumped back. Spock placed one hand behind her skull to prevent it from lolling about and, with his long fingers, opened one of her eyes and peered into it. "She is gone," he said.

"She . . ." Picard couldn't believe how quickly everything had gone wrong. "Seven is . . . ?"

"Seven will recover in short order," Spock assured him. "I refer to the other 'she.' The Borg queen." He paused and then said, "Or, as you knew her . . . Kathryn Janeway."

Picard felt as if the world was swimming around him. *"Merde,"* he whispered. "We . . . we have to get to the Borg cube immediately. We . . ."

Slowly Spock shook his head. "It is too late for that. It is too late for anything. This mind-meld . . . it was an error. It has set events into motion that neither you nor I can stop. What we must do now is determine what our third step is."

"You . . . you mean our next step," said Beverly.

"No," replied Spock. "The Borg will already have determined that and allowed for it. We must think at least two steps ahead of them or we have no hope at all." He considered it and added, "Which is not to say that we have any hope even in that event."

The clarification did nothing to assuage Picard's concerns.

13

The *Einstein*

THE BORG ADAPTED. THE BORG EVOLVED. JUST AS Seven of Nine had stated, so was that the case.

Under normal circumstances, the Borg queen would simply have been surrounded by drones. But because the Borg had used Kathryn Janeway as a starting point for their queen and built upon her, like a house upon a foundation, certain aspects of her personality were being translated into her new incarnation. So it was that she was treating Howard Rappaport as a second-in-command, her right hand. She had ceased addressing him as anything other than simply "Two," considering that a far more appropriate name for a Borg than "Howard."

The queen had been in her central chamber when the mind of the Vulcan had first brushed against hers. Although her mind had been insinuated throughout the Borg cube, part of a thousand thousand different functions all happening simultaneously, the intrusion of the Vulcan via his mind sharing with Seven of Nine had instantly seized all her attention.

Two, sensing that something had transpired in the queen's chambers, had made his way there without having to be summoned. The *Einstein* remained in orbit around the Borg cube as Two shimmered into existence several feet away from the queen. She was standing, staring off into space, as if she could see something that was invisible to anyone else.

"What happened?" asked Two.

The queen didn't reply at first. He did not prompt her, knowing she would speak to him when she was ready.

"They know," she said finally. "They know of a certainty now."

Two did not have to ask who the "they" were. There were only two "they's" that mattered: Locutus. Seven of Nine.

She nodded. "They know. They will attempt to stop us."

"We will attack them."

"We are not ready," the queen said. "We still have not fully recovered our strength. We are not prepared to battle the two individuals who know more about us than any others of their race. We must keep them off balance. We must take an aggressive stance.

We must assimilate raw material to provide sufficient power and energy levels."

"I await your orders."

She turned to face him. "We strike at their emotional heart and soul and their most vulnerable strategic location. Set course for Earth."

Two had no intention of debating the queen's orders. Still, he did feel the need to mention, "You said yourself . . . we have not fully recovered our strength. Their defenses will be formidable."

"Yes," said the queen. A slight vestige of Kathryn Janeway's smile appeared on her face. It looked obscene. "So we shall make certain to have something to eat along the way."

14

The *Thunderchild*

- i -

GRIM VARGO WAS KICKING HIMSELF.

Not literally, of course, and not even on the surface so that anyone could have seen. As he sat cooling his heels in the brig of the *Thunderchild,* he seemed utterly calm, even relaxed. His legs were crossed at the knees and he had his arms criss-crossed behind his head, his eyes closed feigning sleep.

"You're not fooling anyone, you know."

It was Captain Matsuda who had spoken to him, standing just outside the brig, looking extremely annoyed.

"I'm not?" said Grim, his eyes still closed. "Damn. And here I was so hoping to pursue a career in the theater."

"And you can wipe that smirk off your face."

This prompted Grim Vargo to open his eyes, and he snickered. "No. I really can't," he said, his smirk firmly in place.

Matsuda had a round, craggy face that looked like a road map of a thousand campaigns. Under other circumstances, Vargo wouldn't have minded bending elbows with the guy and throwing back a few drinks.

Then again, it was drinks that had gotten Vargo into this fix in the first place.

Once he'd dumped Seven of Ann or whatever the hell her name was, he had put as much distance between himself and that misbegotten woman as possible. Believing that he'd gotten off lightly, and relieved to be rid of her, he had broken out a bottle of his best Romulan ale, still the most gloriously illegal drink around. It had burned wonderfully on the way down. He'd drunk way too much of it, and it had taken far too long for his ship's proximity alarm to penetrate the drunken haze that had settled upon him. By the time he'd reacted, the damned *Thunderchild* had practically been on top of him. Activating a cloaking device doesn't do a damned bit of good when a starship has its freaking tractor beam gripping you.

They had demanded to know where his passenger was, and when he told them he had no idea what they were talking about, they'd hauled him off his ship and tossed him in the brig so he could stew for a while.

The thing was, he had no reason to cover for Seven. None whatsoever. He owed her nothing. She'd been evasive and lied to him from the start, and if Starfleet wanted to go and collect her, that should certainly be no problem for him. But as he stared up at Matsuda, with his crisp uniform and look of arrogant superiority, he knew two things beyond question: he was ten times the space jockey that this Starfleet dandy would ever be, and he wasn't going to give up Seven or her last known location . . .

. . . at least not without making Matsuda sweat over it.

"Where is she?" Matsuda demanded for what seemed the hundredth time.

"Haven't a clue."

"She's no longer on your ship. We've searched it thoroughly."

"Oh. I thought you meant my mother. 'Cause I got nothing on that. But if you want to know where your mother is, can't help you there, either. Haven't seen her since I kicked her out of my bed over Rigel V."

Matsuda didn't smile. Fortunately, Vargo hadn't expected him to.

"There's no point in lying about it," Matsuda

continued, not even deigning to reply to Vargo's jibe. "My people have already been over your ship. We've found DNA traces of Seven of Nine. She was your passenger. You had her aboard your ship when you left Titan and departed without permission—"

"I don't need your damned permission to go where I want," Vargo said, and he was on his feet. He dropped the smug, calculating persona. He was annoyed with himself for doing so, because he knew that's what Matsuda wanted: to get him angry, to make him blurt something out. He didn't care. He needed to rub Matsuda's nose in it. "And I did more than 'depart without permission.' I outsmarted you. That's what's really burning your biscuit, isn't it, Captain. That you, with all your technology and personnel, got outsmarted by a space jockey and his two-bit ship."

"A two-bit ship with illegal technology on it. We will be confiscating it, of course."

"That cloak is mine!" snarled Vargo. "I got it fair and square in salvage."

"It's illegal."

"So is what you're doing."

"I'm under orders."

"I'm underwhelmed."

Matsuda's back straightened, his shoulders squaring. "Mister Vargo . . ."

"*Captain* Vargo."

". . . I don't have an infinite amount of time to engage in this."

"Well, then, I guess you're the one under time pressure, because my docket is wide open."

"There is concern that Seven of Nine represents a possible danger to Federation security."

"And I'm concerned that the Federation represents a danger to my security. And since I'm the one who's being deprived of property and freedom without due process, I think I'm the one who's got the more legitimate concern here."

"Why are you protecting her?" demanded Matsuda.

Vargo's perpetual smile widened. "To piss you off."

To his surprise, Matsuda actually smiled slightly at that. "Congratulations. You're succeeding."

Suddenly Matsuda's combadge went off. He tapped it. "Matsuda here."

"Bridge to Matsuda. Traber here, sir. We've got a Borg cube heading our way, being towed by a science vessel, the Einstein. *The* Einstein *claims they're bringing it to Earth for analysis, but—"*

"Signal Red Alert. I'm on my way."

"Captain!" Vargo said.

"Not now," Matsuda said, starting to turn away.

"*Yes,* now!" There was something in the genuine urgency of his voice that prompted Matsuda to turn back to him.

"You've got twenty seconds," Matsuda told him.

"Okay, yes, I admit it, she was on my ship," Vargo said, speaking as quickly as he could. "She was talking about the Borg being a threat. She was completely convinced of it."

"Ten seconds left, and I'm not impressed."

"Bring me up to the bridge with you. I might be able to help."

"Five seconds, and I'm leaving now—"

"There's a code phrase that can shut the Borg down!"

That stopped Matsuda cold. The Red Alert klaxon was blasting, and personnel were scrambling to their battle stations. But they could just as easily have been in the middle of a deathly quiet room for all that it distracted Matsuda. "A code phrase," he repeated.

"She told me what it was."

"You tell me."

"Let me out of here first."

"We don't have time to argue about this."

"No," said Vargo, "we don't."

Matsuda's lips twitched and then he turned to the guards who stood on either side of the door. "Bring him," he said curtly.

Seconds later the force barrier in front of the brig vanished. The guards reached in and grabbed Vargo by the arms. Then they hauled him along after Matsuda and headed as quickly as they could up to the bridge.

- ii -

Matsuda had seen Borg cubes before. He had, after all, commanded the ship during the legendary Battle of Sector 001 in which the *Thunderchild,* along with the *Enterprise* and two dozen other vessels, had fought a valiant last-ditch effort against an invading Borg cube. The *Thunderchild* had been scarred and they'd lost personnel in the battle, but they had survived. Matsuda still had the medal he'd been awarded for valor. It was in a box in his quarters. He wondered if he should go back and put it on so that the Borg would be intimidated.

The *Einstein* had come to a halt not far off, and the Borg cube remained silent behind it. That much was evident on the viewscreen. "Status report," said Matsuda briskly as he entered the bridge.

Commander Traber, a brusque, hyperefficient officer with a bit of a nonregulation belly that Matsuda constantly hounded him about, turned and started to speak when he saw Vargo being brought onto the bridge by the two security guards. He paused and glanced at Matsuda in confusion. Matsuda offered no explanation. Traber gave a small shrug. "*Einstein* is holding at two hundred thousand kliks. Detecting low-level energy activity on the Borg cube, but *Einstein* is claiming that it presents no threat."

"We're in communication with them?" asked Matsuda.

"Yes, sir, with Captain Rappaport."

"Put him on screen."

The image of the science vessel and the Borg cube shimmered and was replaced by the smiling face of Howard Rappaport.

"Greetings, Captain," said Rappaport. *"You are looking well."*

"Thank you, Captain, but how I'm looking is not an issue here. The issue is why in the world you're towing a Borg cube the size of a small moon behind you."

"Why . . . that would be at the orders of Admiral Janeway," Rappaport said calmly, as if it were the most obvious thing in the world. *"She is aboard the cube. She decided that it would be best if it were brought back to Earth for further study."*

"Really. That's interesting," said Matsuda. "You wouldn't mind if I verified that with Starfleet, would you?"

"Captain!" Rappaport sounded surprised, even a bit hurt. *"You are not taking my word for it? I am distressed that you are exhibiting such distrust."*

"It's not a matter of trust, it's . . ."

"Captain," Vargo muttered in a low voice.

Matsuda shot him an annoyed look but then saw Vargo's expression and realized that he wasn't interrupting just to be annoying. There was definitely something on his mind. "*Einstein,* please stand by." Rappaport's image remained on the screen, but he was no longer able to see or hear into the *Thunderchild*'s bridge. "What is it, Mister Vargo, and this had better be good."

"The way he's talking . . . it's very formal. He's not speaking with any contractions. It's the same way that Seven spoke. If that's unique to the Borg . . ." His voice trailed off.

And now Matsuda's comm officer, Lieutenant Tina Rogers, also spoke up. "Captain, I was noticing something else: the signal we're receiving isn't in sync."

"What do you mean?"

"I mean when the captain speaks, his words aren't quite matching up with his mouth. It's off by maybe a half second."

"Why would that be?"

"I don't know. The only thing that comes to mind is that what we're seeing . . . isn't what we should be seeing."

"Some sort of device is causing us to see other than what we should be seeing? Hardly standard issue in a Starfleet vessel."

"No, but the Tholians have it," Vargo said. "Where do you think I got the technology to fool your sensors when you were initially trying to probe my ship."

"I had wondered about it," Matsuda said. "How kind of you to admit to even more interaction with known hostile races. I believe Starfleet is going to have a good deal to say to you when we get to the nearest base."

"Living to get to a starbase should be the least of my problems," replied Vargo.

Matsuda grunted, tacitly acknowledging Vargo's point. "Mister Yarrow," he said to his tactics officer, "give me a target lock on both the *Einstein* and the Borg vessel."

"Aye, Captain."

"Put me back on with him," said Matsuda, and then he turned toward Rappaport once more. Rappaport still had the smile fixed on him.

"We were wondering if you had forgotten about us over here," said Rappaport easily.

"*Einstein,* I am going to have to formally request you to hold your position while I verify your orders with Starfleet," Matsuda told him.

"I am afraid that Admiral Janeway was very specific in her desire to approach Earth with all possible speed." Rappaport came across as if he were trying to sound apologetic but was having trouble remembering how to do so.

"I will be more than happy to speak to Admiral Janeway about it, if she would care to beam over."

"That would be problematic, since I notice you have your shields up. And . . . oh, dear . . . you have also targeted us," said Rappaport. *"You are acting in a most hostile manner, Captain."*

"Produce Admiral Janeway now. Don't force us to take further action."

"Very well," Rappaport said. *"I will put Admiral Janeway through right now."*

The screen shimmered, and Tina Rogers spoke up. "Captain. I think I've managed to punch through whatever they're using to scramble the image."

The picture on the screen reconfigured, and it was all Matsuda could do not to gasp.

The creature that was staring at them from the

screen was Kathryn Janeway in name only. Tubes festooned her bald head, and her skin was a hideous grayish white. What they could see of her shoulders was clad in form-fitting black leather.

"Send an alert to Starfleet. Tell them what's happening," Matusda said with forced calm.

"Unable to comply, sir," said Rogers. "Our transmission beacons are being scrambled."

Somehow Matsuda wasn't surprised. "Bring phasers online, arm quantum torpedoes."

"It will do you no good," said the thing that had been Kathryn Janeway.

"If you think you're going to assimilate us . . ."

"No," she replied tonelessly. *"We have evolved. We have transcended. You will not be assimilated."* She paused. *"You will be absorbed. Resistance is futile."*

Matsuda saw no reason to wait. "Get that thing off my screen," he snapped, and the image of the creature formerly known as Janeway vanished. "Navigation, get us out of here, emergency warp. Mister Yarrow, torpedoes to the *Einstein,* full phaser barrage on the cube. And . . . fire," he said.

Yarrow activated the *Thunderchild*'s offensive weapons. The phasers cut loose at the Borg cube, while a barrage of torpedoes was unleashed upon the *Einstein.*

Not for a second did Matsuda believe that they had a hope against the Borg. His entire plan now was to lay down sufficient suppressing fire so that the *Thunderchild* could tuck tail and run. The Federation was going to need them; hell, the Federation was going to need every ship they had, because this cube looked to be ten times the size of the previous one, and that one had almost single-handedly wiped out humanity.

The phasers had no effect whatsoever on the cube and, to Matsuda's shock, he never had the opportunity to see how the quantum torpedoes fared against the *Einstein.* The energy capsules were drawn away from the science vessel before they could impact and instead were hauled directly into the Borg cube.

"Energy surge from the cube!" called Yarrow.

"Surge?"

"Yes, sir! It's like . . ." Yarrow couldn't quite understand it. "It's like it made them stronger. Like it was fuel for th— Sir! Our shields! They're gone!"

"What?" Matsuda crossed quickly to Yarrow's side and gaped in astonishment. "How?"

"We have absorbed it," came the voice of Janeway. Although her image was gone, she was still forcing her voice through the comm system. Rogers was obviously trying to shut it off but was having no luck. *"We will absorb you."* Then she paused and, for half a heartbeat, sounded vaguely curious. *"What part of 'futile' was unclear?"*

Suddenly the ship jolted. Matsuda stumbled forward, catching himself on the command chair.

"Tractor beam!" shouted Yarrow. "Incredibly powerful! It's pulling us in!"

Matsuda whirled and faced Grim Vargo, who,

despite the dire straits they were in, still had that annoying smirk on his face. "Mister Vargo . . . *Captain* Vargo . . . if you have some sort of magic shutdown phrase, now is the time to employ it."

Vargo cleared his throat and then looked at Matsuda with what appeared to be genuine regret. "Yeah, uh . . . I got nothing, actually. That was just so I could do this—"

Faster than Matsuda would have thought possible, Vargo suddenly turned and drove a fist into the closest security guard's stomach. The guard doubled over and his phaser was now in Vargo's hand. Vargo whipped the phaser around before the first guard was on the floor and opened fire on the second. The phaser blasted him back, sending him hurtling through the air and crashing into the far wall.

Vargo didn't slow down. Instead, he threw himself toward the emergency exit, avoiding the turbolift. He grabbed the sides of the exit ladder with both hands and didn't even bother to put his feet into the rungs. He simply slid straight down the exit and out of sight.

The guard who'd been punched started to get to his feet and Matsuda yelled, "Forget about him! We've got more immediate worries! Engines, full reverse! Shake us free of that tractor beam! Yarrow, forget the science vessel, full phaser and energy barrage at the Borg cube!"

"Sir, it only made it stronger!"

"Then maybe we can feed it so much energy so

fast that it'll overload! Target the same section of the cube that Picard had us target the last time! Maybe it will have the same effect!"

It was a reasonable gambit. During the Battle of Sector 001, Picard had used his intimate knowledge of the Borg's cube structure to present a target for the attacking starships. Seemingly nonvital, it had nevertheless triggered a chain reaction that had resulted in the cube's destruction.

The *Thunderchild,* struggling in the throes of the tractor beam like a fly on sticky paper, unleashed everything it had on that same seemingly vulnerable point.

It was useless. Worse than useless.

It was futile.

- iii -

Transporter Chief Lindell turned around when the doors to the transporter room opened, wondering who in the world would be showing up now, during a Red Alert.

He didn't have the opportunity even to get out the words "Who are you?" before a stun blast from a phaser knocked him unconscious.

Grim Vargo ran in without slowing and shoved the insensate transporter chief out of the way with one foot. He was hoping, praying, that what he assumed to be the case was, in fact, the case, or else he was about to embark on a very short trip.

His hands moving quickly over the transporter controls, Vargo found and locked in the coordinates for his own ship, which the *Thunderchild* had taken in tow. He never would have been able to beam himself over there with the shields up. With them down, however, having been sucked away somehow by the Borg cube, he had the window of opportunity he needed.

He activated the transporter beams, took a deep breath, then ran forward and stepped into the beams just as they flared to life. The *Thunderchild*'s transporter room dissolved around him and he suddenly found himself on the control deck of the *Pride.*

"Thank God," he muttered as he went to the controls and brought them online. A quick study of his present situation told him exactly what he had hoped would be the case: rerouting all available energy into the engines in order to try and break away from the cube, the *Thunderchild* had cut the *Pride* loose. He was damned lucky that emergency protocols kept minimal energy going to the transporter room, or he would have been completely out of luck.

He brought his cloak online, breathed a sigh of relief that Matsuda hadn't yet gotten around to removing it, and vanished. Using the same tactic as he had in Saturn's rings, he did not bring his engines online. Instead he allowed himself to drift, indistinguishable from a million other pieces of flotsam and jetsam that were drifting through the vacuum.

Then he turned on his viewscreen and watched the *Thunderchild*'s struggles with the Borg cube. As much as he disliked Matsuda and his insufferable arrogance, he prayed that the ship would manage to shake free of the Borg's tractor beam. No one deserved the sort of fate that being taken by the Borg virtually guaranteed.

He sent out a silent prayer for aid to the mighty starship.

The silent prayer was met by—appropriately enough—silence.

As he drifted away, he continued to watch as the *Thunderchild* fought valiantly. More phasers, more quantum torpedoes, and he fancied that he could actually see the ship trembling violently as it tried to go in reverse and break loose of its imprisonment. Considering what would happen if they were taken by the Borg, it might have been preferable for all concerned if the ship had busted apart like a piñata. A quick death in the airless void was probably better than becoming a creature of the Borg hive mind.

It made him think of what it must have been like for dinosaurs, at the dawn of prehistory, struggling to break loose of tar pits as they were slowly dragged down to their deaths.

He saw much the same scenario now. He just didn't believe what he was seeing.

The *Thunderchild* was pulled closer, closer still, right up to the surface of the cube.

And then the saucer section began to . . . there was no other way to put it . . . dissolve. The metal simply melted as it joined with the Borg cube, being sucked up into it. Slowly at first, but then faster and faster. Grim Vargo had never seen anything like it, but he had the feeling that he would be seeing exactly this for the rest of his life, whenever he went to sleep. It would be in his nightmares, and he would be conjuring up for himself the sounds of Starfleet officers screaming in protest of their fate.

The *Thunderchild* continued to melt into the Borg cube. He waited to see bodies floating away, but there were none. They must have been pulled in as well.

You will be absorbed.

What part of "futile" is unclear?

He watched it all, wanting to look away but unable to do so. He glanced briefly down at the ship's chronometer and timed the entire process. It didn't take long: nineteen seconds. That was the lifetime of the *Thunderchild* from the point where she first came into contact with the Borg cube to when the tail ends of her nacelles were pulled in and melted against the cube.

Vargo didn't move a muscle, frozen in place, as if worried that even a physical movement, inside his ship, would attract the notice of the Borg cube.

It did not. The cube's attention had been focused entirely on the far larger *Thunderchild.* A ship like his would have meant nothing to the cube, anyway.

He stayed right where he was, not activating his engines, doing nothing, until the *Einstein* and the Borg cube had gone on their way, leaving him far behind. It was only then that he began to tremble uncontrollably, and he felt a deep ache in the pit of his stomach that warned him he was going to be sick. He barely made it to the head before his stomach ejected its contents.

He slumped to the floor and told himself that this wasn't his problem, wasn't his fight. So what if the Borg annihilated Earth, or the entire Federation, for that matter? It was none of his concern. In fact, his life would probably be a damned sight easier with the Federation gone. Indeed, if Captain Matsuda had had his way, Vargo would have died along with the rest of them.

And . . . wouldn't it just annoy the hell out of Matsuda if Vargo were able to accomplish something that he, Matsuda, had been unable to?

With that in mind—feeling the need to have one last triumph over a man who, as far as Vargo knew, was dead, or in a state to which death would have been preferable—Grim Vargo sent out an emergency broadband beacon through subspace. His shipboard automatic log had recorded the *Thunderchild*'s abortive struggle against its enemy, and Vargo sent it along as an attachment to the message.

The message itself was simple, and—unknown to Vargo—evocative of a warning declaration once made by a fast-riding patriot centuries earlier:

The Borg are coming. The Borg are coming.

15

The *Enterprise*

- i -

EVERY SO OFTEN, PICARD THOUGHT, EVENTS OUT-stripped arguments.

This was one of those times.

The screen in the conference lounge showed a horrifying struggle that Picard was in the process of replaying. There was the valiant *Thunderchild,* doing its level best to pull free of the overwhelming power of the Borg cube, and failing utterly to do so. The same individuals whom Picard had summoned to the earlier conference were watching now, plus Seven of Nine and Ambassador Spock. Whereas the looks of concern, anguish, sympathy, and outright horror played out upon the faces of Picard's crew, Spock and Seven kept expressions that were carefully neutral. No, not just neutral, Picard realized. Seven looked as if she was analyzing what she was seeing, while Spock merely appeared interested. Picard suspected that whatever Spock might be allowing to show on the surface, it didn't accurately represent what was going through his head. With a Vulcan, though, who could ever know for certain what that might be?

"What's the origin of this transmission?" asked Geordi. The screen had frozen on the final, chilling image of the *Thunderchild*'s tail end being drawn into the cube.

"Unclear at this time," rumbled Worf. "The signal was sent on a broad subspace wave with no carrier or point of origin attached."

"How is that possible?" said Leybenzon.

"It's possible," Kadohata replied, "if the sending vessel is accustomed to keeping a low profile. Might be a trader in illegal products, a smuggler . . ."

"Which could mean that what we're seeing is faked," said Crusher. "Do we know for sure . . . ?"

Geordi was shaking his head. "We know. We've been over every centimeter of it. As far as our instruments can determine, it's genuine."

"But how?" asked Crusher. "How could this be? Are the Borg capable of . . . of what we just saw?"

All eyes automatically turned toward Seven. She did not answer immediately, giving the matter a moment's more thought. Finally, she said, "It is not the typical manner in which the Borg assimilate that which interests them. But it is the . . . next logical step."

"Next logical step?" echoed Geordi.

"Evolution, Mister La Forge," Spock said quietly. "You are witnessing the next step in the evolution of a life-form. Clearly they have developed a far more efficient means of accomplishing their typical goal of assimilating that which they need or desire."

"By *eating* it?" asked Crusher.

Spock gave her a curious glance. "It is the customary method for humans, is it not?"

"Yes, but our *ships* don't eat things."

"That is because your ship exists independently of you," said Seven of Nine. "Borg cubes do not enjoy that separation."

"You're saying they're alive? The Borg cubes are alive?"

"Yes, Doctor Crusher," said Seven. "And in the case of this particular cube"—she looked to the one on the screen—"it is hungry. The cube has apparently taken on for itself the Borg imperative to assimilate and has translated that imperative into a means of execution that is consistent with its biological structure. It has never happened before. Then again, no Borg cube has ever been created outside of the Delta Quadrant or been subjected to the stress that the *Enterprise*'s previous attack inflicted upon it. Evolution is the by-product of necessity, and survival is the overwhelming imperative for all living things. I believe what you are seeing here is the result of those two drives combined. The cube has evolved in order to survive."

"And the *Thunderchild,*" Spock said coldly, "will be merely the first victim."

"The second," said Picard, who had remained silent until that moment. He pointed at the screen, at the image of a small vessel in front of the Borg cube. "That science vessel, registry indicates it to be the *Einstein.* Apparently it's acting in concert with the Borg cube."

"A Judas goat is the old term," said Leybenzon, nodding. "The *Thunderchild* must have thought the *Einstein* was serving as an escort. It helped take the ship off guard. Who knows what happened to the crew."

"I believe we can take an educated guess," said Seven.

"But that's not going to keep working for them," Kadohata observed. "Word is out. This was a broad-range message; we're not the only ones who have it. Everyone must have it by now."

"It merely verifies," Spock told her, "what was already known to us: that the Borg represent an immediate threat to the security of the Federation. An attack is imminent and inevitable."

"You know this," T'Lana finally spoke up, "because of the mind-meld you engaged in with Seven of Nine." Her voice sounded vaguely critical, and it was not difficult for Picard to discern why that would be.

Spock, unperturbed by her tone, simply said, "Yes."

The mind-meld had been the launch point of the entire meeting. Picard had summoned his staff to the conference lounge and laid out for them exactly what had transpired. Spock had informed them that Seven of Nine was correct. He had determined via a mind-meld that Kathryn Janeway was not only in distress, but that the Borg were aware of Seven's knowledge and were doubtless going to act on it. Before the discussion had gone any further, the emergency transmission had come in and—because of its urgency—the bridge had forwarded it immediately to the conference lounge so that Picard and the senior staff could see it and act on the new information.

"Well, then," said Leybenzon, "it's fortunate that we're en route to Earth. If Earth's security is threatened . . ."

"That is actually what I gathered you all here to discuss," said Picard.

That brought everything to a halt. "There is something to discuss?" said Leybenzon. "If Earth is going to be attacked by the Borg . . ."

"You will not be able to stop this vessel with the resources currently at your disposal," Spock told him.

"With all respect, Ambassador, that's not our call to make. Our orders . . ."

"I am aware of our orders, Lieutenant," Picard

reminded him. "But there are other considerations."

"We must consider the logical progression of events," said Spock, easily ignoring the tension in the air. "We are obviously not the only individuals who have received this transmission. Doubtless other Starfleet vessels—even Starfleet Headquarters—will be informed of this turn of events. I am quite certain that, even as we speak, a fleet is moving to intercept."

"If that's the case, we should—" Kadohata began.

Spock didn't let her finish the sentence. "They will fail," he said.

"You don't know that. You can't."

"He does," Seven of Nine assured her. "And they will. They will resist, but it will prove futile."

"Resistance is never futile," said Leybenzon.

"That's enough of that, Lieutenant," Picard snapped at him.

"Captain, she's saying that we should just give up without a fight!" said Leybenzon.

"She is saying," Spock replied, "that if we are to fight, then we should do so in a manner that will enable us to win."

"Am I correct in assuming," Worf asked, "that there is a manner you would suggest that would ensure victory?"

"'Ensure' is not a logical word. We are dealing with far too many variables. However, there may well be a means of evening the odds."

"And that would be . . ."

Rather than replying, Spock turned to Picard and waited patiently. Picard appreciated the respect for decorum that Spock was displaying. The ambassador had already spoken to the captain at length about his thoughts on the matter, but he was waiting for Picard to lay it out for his people since he, Spock, was not a member of the crew.

"The planet killer," Picard said.

There was a moment's hesitation as what he had just said filtered through the minds of his crew. "Of course," murmured Crusher.

"Of course?" echoed Kadohata. "I don't understand. Are you referring to . . ."

"The giant planet-eating device, a weapon of planetary destruction, that we encountered a couple years back," Geordi La Forge said. It didn't surprise Picard that Geordi was the one who was explaining it to Kadohata—and, by extension, to T'Lana and Leybenzon, since they had not been part of the *Enterprise* crew when that entire sorry incident had occurred. "It was huge. Vast. It was a semisentient device . . ."

"In that respect, not unlike the Borg cube," Seven of Nine observed.

". . . that had been created by a long-gone race as a means of combating the Borg. It was piloted by a woman named . . ." He paused, trying to recall.

"Delcara," Picard said softly.

"Right. Delcara. Thank you, Captain," said Geordi. "She had gotten her hands on it and was intending to use it to go to the heart of Borg space and annihilate them once and for all. It was around the same time that we also encountered a female Borg . . . Reannon was her birth name." He looked at Seven. "In some respect her history wasn't all that dissimilar to yours. At the time we met her, we had never encountered a female Borg before. In fact, there were some so-called Borg experts who asserted that there was no such thing as a female Borg."

"That is ridiculous," said Seven. "That would make no sense. Who would postulate such an absurd notion?"

Geordi shrugged. "Go argue with self-proclaimed experts. Anyway, like you, she was separated from the Borg collective. Unlike you . . ." His voice trailed off.

"It did not end well?" asked Seven.

"No. It didn't."

Seven said nothing.

Picard picked up the narrative when Geordi became silent. "There was a great battle, and Delcara and her planet killer were instrumental in the destruction of several Borg cubes."

"What became of her?" asked Kadohata.

"She . . . disappeared," said Picard. "In her single-minded urge to reach Borg space as fast as possible—to satisfy the desires of her vendetta against the Borg, who had wiped out everything she knew—she propelled the vessel beyond any speed that known physical laws would permit. We do not know with certainty what happened to her."

"Our theory," Geordi said, "is that she became trapped in a sort of repeating loop. A living example of Xeno's paradox, infinitely halving the distance between her and her destination but never able to achieve her goal."

"So she's gone, is what you're saying," said Leybenzon.

"To all intents and purposes, yes."

"Then I don't understand. Why are we talking about her? About this? If we don't have access to her—"

"She may be gone," Spock said, "but the predecessor is not."

That drew confused looks to the Vulcan, who looked in turn to Picard. Picard nodded, indicating that Spock should take up the lead in telling the other officers what was going on.

"The *Enterprise* upon which I served encountered a planet killer that was somewhat similar to Delcara's, albeit smaller. It was a prototype built—we believe—as a test model for the ultimately much larger device. The legendary Preservers, we have speculated, were responsible for both. The actual incident occurred on stardate 4202.9, when we encountered a number of planets in Star System L374 that had been obliterated by a force beyond anything that our technology at the time was capable of. We tracked it and discovered a device that Captain Kirk referred to as a 'doomsday machine.' We managed to destroy it by means of piloting the *Starship Constel-*

lation into the heart of the planet killer and detonating the engines."

"Destroyed? Then . . . I'm sorry, but I'm not following," Leybenzon said with barely restrained exasperation. "If it was destroyed, and the larger version is lost to time and space, then what are we talking about here?"

"I apologize if my phrasing was imprecise," said Spock. "'Deactivated' is more accurate. The power center of the planet destroyer was quelled by the detonation of the *Constellation*'s engines, but the hull remained intact. The device was subsequently towed to the Yard: Starfleet's alien technology research station. There it was thoroughly analyzed by the Starfleet Corp of Engineers. The process took more than a year. After that, the custody of the ship was transferred to the Starfleet museum at Epsilon Sigma V."

"Trophy World?" asked Crusher.

"That's the popular nickname for it," said Geordi.

"I was there once. It's amazing."

"It is indeed fascinating," Spock told the doctor. "And, I am told, a popular tourist attraction."

"With a great gift shop," said Crusher. When everyone stared at her, she said defensively, "What? I'm not allowed to buy stuff?"

"But if the S.C.E. has already been over the planet killer, then I'm still not seeing the point," said Leybenzon.

"The point, Lieutenant," Picard said, "is that time has passed. No one has investigated the status of the planet killer in some time. We had been under the impression that the Borg cube was dead. That has proved not to be the case. It is entirely possible that the planet killer is not, in fact, dead, but rather dormant. Waiting for the proper individual, or the proper circumstances, to be reactivated and pressed into service."

"That, Captain, is not logical," T'Lana said. "That is, at best, a leap of faith. There is no evidence before us to indicate that the planet killer is anything other than a lifeless hulk."

"It may not be logical," Spock said, "but it remains a logical alternative to suicide. That is what a direct attempt against the Borg cube would represent."

"We don't know that," said Kadohata.

"I believe that we do."

"We need to fight them! To go home, to—"

Spock indicated the image on the screen with a nod of his head. "Between the evolution of the Borg technology and the guiding presence of Kathryn Janeway, the Borg represent a threat that cannot be overwhelmed by a single ship, or even a fleet. The only technology specifically designed to combat the Borg is the most logical option for us to pursue. Otherwise the Federation, and Earth, will stand no chance . . ."

"And whose fault is that?" asked T'Lana quietly.

Spock turned his level gaze upon T'Lana, but it was Picard who said, "I beg your pardon?"

There was danger in Picard's voice, but T'Lana didn't back down. "The ambassador undertook a risky and ill-advised mind-meld with Seven of Nine. He did so to pursue your agenda, Captain, that was predicated on trying to prove that you knew better than Starfleet Command. In so doing, he connected with the Borg collective and set the events into motion that resulted in the destruction—or absorption, if you will—of the *Starship Thunderchild.* Had he not embarked on the aforementioned course of action, a course that you encouraged, Captain, to justify a possible insubordination, then the crew of the *Thunderchild* might be alive."

Worf was on his feet. "I recommend," he said, his voice rumbling, "that you apologize to the captain."

"Number One," Picard said sharply.

T'Lana ignored him. "Will the captain apologize to Starfleet? Will he apologize to the husbands and wives and children, parents and loved ones, of the *Thunderchild* crewmen who will never be returning home? I made no decisions that cost lives. He did. It was a decision that was enabled by Ambassador Spock and that resulted from the precipitous actions of Seven of Nine. Where are their apologies?"

"That is enough," Picard snapped.

Immediately T'Lana fell silent, but she did not look away from Picard's angry stare.

Picard leaned back in his chair and let out an exasperated sigh.

Seven spoke then. She came across as if she were sounding the death knell of the Federation, and yet did so in the same flat, slightly disconnected manner with which she always spoke. "From what I have seen, and from what I know of the *Enterprise*'s offensive capabilities, attempting to confront the Borg cube itself will serve no purpose except to guarantee that we meet the same fate as the *Thunderchild*."

"We do not know that for a fact," Worf said firmly.

Picard could see the Klingon bristling over the notion of turning away from a battle, even one that seemed hopeless. Slowly Seven nodded. "That is true. It is impossible to know something as a fact before it has transpired. One can, however, allow for great likelihood. The great likelihood, in this instance, is that you will all be assimilated. I think it safe to say that none of you are desirous of that outcome."

They all exchanged looks.

"Captain," Geordi said, "with all respect, putting aside that we're under orders to return to Earth . . ."

"Orders that are predicated on the notion that Seven of Nine is delusional, something we now know is not the case."

"Granted," said Geordi, "but . . . I have to agree with Worf. If Earth is going to be subject to a Borg attack—and that's looking fairly likely from what you're saying—then I, for one, think our place is between the Borg and our homeworld. Heading to Trophy World on the off chance that we can fire up a relic and turn it against the Borg—that's a hell of a lot to base a course of action upon. It's possible that, while the Borg cube was able to take out a single vessel, an armada stands a far greater chance."

"That was certainly the case last time," Beverly reminded Picard, "and our ship was the one that turned the tide. Who's to say that it wouldn't be the case this time as well?"

Picard shifted his gaze to the newer members of the crew.

"I think you know my opinion on this already," said Leybenzon.

"I'm with the lieutenant," said Kadohata. "We have to help the Fleet."

"Your deaths," Spock said quietly, "will help no one. If you truly wish to help the others, then your preferred course of action is to acquire a weapon that the Borg will not be prepared to counter."

"That is true," said Seven. "They have fought starships before. They are prepared, they have evolved, and they will adapt. And you will die."

"As will you," pointed out T'Lana. "Is that not a possible factor in your advice?"

"I will not die," Seven said simply. "The Borg queen, who was once Kathryn Janeway, will see to that. I will be assimilated. I will become what I was: a creature of dispassion, with no care for humanity or emotion." She tilted her head and regarded T'Lana thoughtfully. "That will be your fate as well."

Very slowly, feeling as if the weight of the universe was upon him—which it might well have been—Picard said, "With the evidence at present before us, I have to believe that we should indeed continue on our current course." He turned to Spock and said, "I am sorry, Ambassador."

"As am I," Spock said without hint of rancor. "One hopes that we will not both have cause to be sorrier."

"If you wish, I can arrange to have you return to Vulcan in a shuttle . . ."

"If it is all the same to you," replied Spock, "I would just as soon stay aboard the *Enterprise*."

"Why?" Kadohata asked curiously.

"My people were present upon Earth at the dawn of your spacefaring age. I was, naturally, unable to observe it. At least I will be able to observe the end."

There seemed to be no more to say after that.

- ii -

Spock had not been the least bit surprised when T'Lana had shown up at his quarters. Seated cross-legged on the floor—surprisingly limber for a Vulcan of his years—Spock looked up at her with his eternally calm demeanor and waited for her to speak.

"I . . . feel the need to apologize to you," T'Lana said.

Cocking an eyebrow, Spock replied, "For what reason?"

"I believe I may have treated you . . . unfairly." She took a step toward him. "It was inappropriate for me to blame you for what transpired with the Borg cube and the *Thunderchild.* Any one of a number of circumstances could well have set the same chain of events into motion. Simply to assume that you are the root cause of the annihilation of the *Thunderchild* . . . it was inappropriate and I am . . ."—she hesitated, having trouble forming the unfamiliar word—"sorry."

He nodded slightly, accepting it, and then simply looked at her.

"Well," she said, wondering if she should bow or genuflect, and settled for the simple Vulcan salute.

Before she could leave, however, Spock said, "In answer to your previous question, I was not offended."

"Previous question?" She wasn't sure what he was talking about. "What previous question?"

"Your curiosity over how I dealt with having my advice ignored when I knew it was steeped in logic and that the wrong decision was being made."

That gave her pause. "This . . . this is a very different circumstance."

"The unwise person is always able to see the

differences in circumstances. It is only the wise person who is able to see the similarities. Which, I find myself wondering, are you, Counselor?"

"I prefer to think of myself as a wise person, Ambassador," she said, her back stiffening.

"We all do, Counselor," remarked the ambassador. "We all do."

Then he closed his eyes, indicating that he was entering a meditative state. T'Lana wanted to stand there, to continue to argue with him, but it didn't seem as if it would serve any purpose. With a frustrated shake of her head, she turned and left his quarters.

- iii -

Leybenzon let out a heavy sigh as he flopped onto his back. His regular workout in the recreation room—a series of extremely challenging calisthenics, followed by a half hour of martial arts kata—left him lying on the mat, his shirt soaked through with sweat. "I'm getting too old for this," he muttered.

An amused voice said, "Getting old beats the alternative, doesn't it?"

He looked up and saw Miranda Kadohata, dressed in workout clothes, standing over him.

"I suppose." He propped himself up on one elbow. "I guess I have to give Picard credit."

"Oh, really? What do you have to credit Picard for?"

"Well, for a minute there, I thought he was going to run counter to Starfleet orders. Plus I thought he was ready to abandon the Federation during a potentially huge conflict. It's good to know that he listened to us and—"

"Zel, you know I respect the hell out of you, but don't be an idiot."

"What do you mean?" he asked, feeling defensive.

"He didn't listen to us. It was the opinions of La Forge, Worf, and Crusher—those were the opinions that matter. If they're in accord with him, it absolutely doesn't matter what you or I or T'Lana says. He's going to do what he feels like doing, and damned be the consequences."

"I think you're wrong."

"And I know I'm right." Her tapered Asian eyes—which formed such a marked contrast to the European shape of her cheekbones, thus serving as a physical notice of her mixed ancestry—narrowed. "You just wait. Wait until there's some new conflict and they side with him in violation of Starfleet orders. You can advise him until your head falls off, but it won't do any good."

"It has to do some good," he insisted. "There has to be respect for rules, protocols. That's the captain's job, to set an example."

"I think Captain Picard believes that the captain's job is damned well whatever the captain says it is."

"Well, he's wrong. The captain's job is described

quite well in Starfleet regs, and if he forgets about all that, I'll—"

"You'll what? Shove the regs down his throat?"

"It won't come to that. You'll see."

"Yes. I think we'll both see."

- iv -

Geordi La Forge settled into his office down in engineering.

"Computer," he said.

"Standing by," came the confident female voice, a voice that to this day still reminded Geordi—for no discernible reason—of Deanna Troi's mother.

"I want to review all notes on file name 'Project Endgame.'"

"Complying," she said. Instantly his computer screen flickered to the specifics of the program, a program that Geordi had not studied closely ever since his first encounter with the Borg he'd dubbed "Hugh."

He leaned forward, began going over the specs, and resigned himself to the fact that he was probably not going to be getting much sleep that night.

- v -

Beverly Crusher reached across the bed in her sleep, feeling for the comforting rise and fall of

Picard's chest. It was her reflex, both as a doctor and as his lover, to check on him even when she was unconscious.

All her questing fingers found was the mattress, still warm but cooling rapidly, and that was sufficient to bring her to instant wakefulness. She sat up and looked around. Picard was wearing a bathrobe and seated in a chair, watching her. He smiled faintly when he saw that she was sitting upright.

"What's wrong?" she asked.

"Why do you assume something is wrong? Perhaps I just wished to sit quietly and admire you."

"What's wrong?" she repeated, not buying that explanation for a second.

His head sagged. "I'm a ghastly liar."

"I think you'll find that most women find men who can't lie to them tremendously attractive." She waited, knowing that he would share what was on his mind.

"One of the things that you learn in the command track," he said at last, "is that sometimes the decision you actually make is secondary to the actual making of that decision. That in the grand scheme of things, it's preferable to be certain than right."

"I don't know that I agree with that, and frankly I don't know that you agree with it either. But what's your point?"

"The point is that when you've made a decision

and you're not certain of anything, you're on extremely uneven ground." He leaned forward, interlacing his fingers. "As much as I hate to admit it, T'Lana and the others have a valid point. I can't just go around capriciously ignoring Starfleet orders."

"I don't think you've done that," said Beverly. "You've done nothing 'capricious.'"

"The chain of command is set up for a reason."

"Yes, but it governs humans, not automatons. What separates us from the Borg is that we think independently."

"Are you saying that the chain of command is in defiance of human nature? Because if so, then Starfleet is built on a foundation of sand."

"I think," she said with a smile, as she patted the mattress next to her, "that this is way too complex a discussion to have in the middle of the night."

"We're on a starship. Day and night are arbitrary constructs." He paused. "How do I know of a certainty what the proper course is? Seven, Spock—they could be wrong. Or I could be wrong in not taking the action that I believe is right. It's impossible to say."

She got out of bed, walked naked across the room, and sat in his lap. She brought her lips close to his ear and whispered, "Then how about sticking with things that aren't impossible to say?"

In a low voice, aware of the heat that her skin was generating, he said, "I love you."

"See? That wasn't so impossible to say, was it?"

Later, Beverly fell into a sound sleep.

Picard continued to lie awake, waiting for the distant voice of the Borg to sound in his head.

16

The Borg Cube

THE BORG QUEEN, DEEP WITHIN THE CORE OF THE cube, sensed rather than saw the armada that had been arrayed against them.

"Impressive," said Two. He was not with her; he was on the bridge of the science vessel *Einstein.* He did not need to be in the same room with her, however, to be able to communicate with her. The Borg queen was in the heads of all her drones, a number that had increased significantly since the *Thunderchild* had been absorbed. The *Thunderchild*'s former captain, Nine of Eighteen, was currently in the midst of running routine diagnostics to ascertain the cube's continued operational status.

Three dozen starships of various sizes and shapes were coming in from all angles toward the Borg cube. The moment they were within range, they commenced a withering phaser and quantum torpedo array launched with such ferocity that one would have thought they actually believed they had a chance of triumphing. The Borg queen knew that wasn't at all the case, but she also knew that humans were singularly stubborn and, well, sometimes they needed to find out these things for themselves. Meanwhile the energy barrage simply swelled the strength and resources of the Borg cube. She noted with detached amusement that a number of them were concentrating fire upon the previously discovered weak point of the Borg cube, the one that Picard had pointed them to at the Battle of Sector 001. How sadly predictable. Perhaps they figured that, although the gambit had failed for the *Thunderchild,* all they really needed was a lot more vessels and increased firepower to accomplish their end.

They were wrong. But their end was definitely going to be brought about.

"Absorb them," ordered the Borg queen.

This time the Borg cube didn't even bother with a tractor beam. It suddenly accelerated, heading toward the closest swarm of ships. The ships tried desperately to counter the movement, to get out of the way of the massive oncoming vessel. Some succeeded. Most did not. The Borg cube plowed into them, but they did not shatter or bound away or even have protection afforded them by their shields. Instead each and every one of them was absorbed into the surface of the cube and, within seconds, had vanished. As this happened, the Borg cube grew. Not a great deal, but nevertheless visibly, and a shimmer of energy coruscated around the surface.

Like a ravenous child, it reached out, this time with its tractor beams, in all directions. Ships continued to fire upon it, telling themselves that they were doing everything they could and not realizing that they were doing nothing they should. The cube snared half a dozen ships, and the Borg queen could hear the cube, feel the cube, *was* the cube, rejoicing in its strength, eager in its hunger. It dragged more ships toward it, insatiable, and one by one or several together, it kept pulling them in. The Borg queen could hear their screams as they became one with the Collective.

Deep within her, so deep that it amounted to nothing more than a passing thought, a very distant voice that sounded vaguely like her own howled in protest, begging her not to let this happen, pleading with her, cursing, vowing that she would find a way to stop her. But then the voice was banished to the outer reaches of her awareness where it would bother no one . . .

Least of all her.

"Who's queen?" she asked in an imperial fashion

and then, in a very un-Borglike manner, laughed without bothering to wait for an answer that she knew would never come. Then she returned to observing the feast of the Borg cube, all the while considering these offerings to be exactly what they were:

Appetizers.

17

The *Enterprise*

- i -

THE BRIDGE CREW WATCHED IN HORROR AS THE scenes played themselves out on the main monitor screen.

If the origin of the initial emergency broadcast had been a mystery, this one was not: it was a distress beacon sent out by the *Starship Nautilus,* one of the handful of ships that had managed to get away from the battle that was quickly being referred to as the Slaughter of Sector 108.

The name did not even begin to cover it.

Picard had made certain to summon both Spock and Seven of Nine to the bridge when they had first received the broadcast. Neither Spock nor Seven flinched or gave any other indication of emotion as, along with the rest of the bridge crew, they watched the annihilation of dozens of starships.

Picard realized that the most terrifying aspect of all of this wasn't just the loss of life (although the true terror of that was that, in all likelihood, the lives had not been lost; just their souls, which was even worse). It was the fact that it had happened so incredibly easily. The full firepower of the armada of ships had not even begun to get the job done. The Borg cube, more powerful, more unstoppable than ever, had ripped through them like a phaser beam through cheese. Hell, perhaps cheese might have stood a better chance.

"Unbelievable," muttered Stephens from the conn. Stephens, not an especially tall man, had a narrow face and a shock of prematurely gray hair. His face was dour and he had a tendency to overanalyze just about everything. In this instance, though, his summation of what they were seeing was both succinct and on target.

"Fascinating," said Spock.

"Duration of battle, Number One?" Picard inquired.

Worf checked the time readout and shook his head in surprise. "Ninety-seven seconds."

Picard couldn't believe he'd heard right. "Did you say ninety-seven seconds? How is that possible?"

"The learning curve," Seven informed him.

Turning toward Seven, Picard asked, "What do you mean? Are you saying . . . you thought ninety-seven seconds was lengthy for a battle of that magnitude?"

"Absolutely. The Borg cube is still evolving, still learning what it can and cannot do. The next fleet they encounter will not last nearly that long."

Picard turned back to the screen. It was all he could do to keep his face impassive as he watched the cube, under the command of Janeway—*Janeway,* for God's sake—obliterate dozens of the finest vessels that Starfleet had to offer.

"Mister Worf, Mister La Forge," he said slowly, "based upon your knowledge of our tactical capabilities, what are the chances that, in a direct confrontation, we will meet the same fate as our sister ships?"

They didn't answer. They didn't have to. The silence alone was answer enough.

"Captain," Worf finally began.

Picard put up a hand. "It's all right, Number One. I've already made my decision. Mister Stephens, set course for Epsilon Sigma V."

"Trophy World?" asked Stephens.

"Correct."

"Can we swing by the gift shop while we're there?"

Picard fixed him with a glare that could have shattered rock, and Stephens took that as his cue to do as ordered. "Course plotted and laid in, sir."

"Mister Stephens: Warp seven. Engage."

"Aye, sir."

The *Enterprise* leaped away into warp space.

- ii -

T'Lana was walking down the corridor when she passed Ambassador Spock heading in the opposite direction. Spock inclined his head slightly in passing, and it prompted her to say, "Ambassador. A moment . . . ?" He turned to face her with his customary look of serene patience. "I find that it is . . . important to me . . . that you realize I meant no disrespect in our earlier conversations."

"Is it?" He seemed about as surprised as he ever got.

"Yes. I do not wish to be grouped together—even in my own mind, much less yours—with those of the *Enterprise* who treated your opinions in a dismissive manner. I firmly believe that the advice you presented Captain Picard was the best advice that you could have given at that moment. Indeed, I am . . ." She glanced around out of a sense of decorum and saw that there was no one nearby. She stepped closer to Spock and said in a lower tone, "Candidly, I am concerned about the captain's state of mind vis-à-vis his ability to function as a Starfleet officer."

"Indeed." He sounded noncommittal.

"He ignored Admiral Janeway's orders and has escaped punitive action. It is my belief that that could lead to a sense of self-aggrandizement. He could start to believe that he can take whatever action he wishes, whenever he wishes, and ultimately endanger the entire chain of command. There is no telling where it could lead. If I allowed it, I would be failing in my responsibility as ship's counselor. I have no desire to see Captain Picard end up on a Klingon prison planet."

"I should think not. They *are* rather inhospitable."

"I see his decision to continue our course for Earth—to put his trust in the chain of command—to be a significant, positive step in his development as a human being and as a captain. I sincerely believe that those considerations outweigh attending to your plan of seeking out and reactivating the planet killer, a notion that is, at best, problematic, and at worst a . . ." She hesitated, then shrugged. "A flight of fancy."

"I can very much see why you would view it in that manner."

"Thank you. May I safely assume that this conversation will remain between us?"

"The captain will hear nothing from me." He paused. "However, I very much suspect he will hear something from you."

"Why do you say that?"

"Because we are, at this moment, en route to Epsilon Sigma V."

T'Lana, for possibly the first time in her life, was literally slack jawed. Then she realized it and forced her mouth closed. "When did we set course for Epsilon Sigma V?"

"Eleven seconds after the captain ordered it."

"May I ask why?"

"You certainly may. But I suspect the person to ask is your captain. I am sure that the conversation will be most . . . stimulating."

And he walked away.

- iii -

In the captain's ready room, Picard gave T'Lana a look that was not overabundant in patience. "I did it because I felt it was the best course of action, Counselor. There are many matters within your purview, but command decisions—particularly in time of war—are not among them."

"With all deference to time of war, Captain, such decisions, especially when they are related to matters of your mental health, are very much within my purview."

Picard's eyes widened. "Are you implying, Counselor, that I am not in my right mind?"

"No, Captain, but as we have seen before, when it comes to the Borg, you are not able to make decisions in a dispassionate manner."

"Counselor, you'll find that we humans tend to rely on our passions to determine what is important."

"And you will find, Captain, that that is what will forever limit your development as a race."

Picard did not appear any too pleased by that pronouncement, but T'Lana didn't especially care. "Counselor T'Lana, I know full well that your people tend to associate emotion with war. My people do not. We tend to focus on the positive aspects of emotion rather than the negative."

"Yet you were the one, Captain, who immediately cited the fact that we *are* at war to justify your decision."

"I am not obligated to justify my decision to you, Counselor, but if you're looking for justification, I believe you need look no farther than here." He turned his computer screen to face her and she was able to see for herself the valiant and ultimately short-lived struggle between Starfleet and the Borg cube.

Her face remained impassive, but she said softly, "Fascinating."

"I suspect you'll have an opportunity to see it again, close up and firsthand. If my obligation is to the safety of this crew and to protect the Federation, then I have to take whatever efforts are necessary to accomplish that. Reactivating the so-called doomsday machine and employing it as a weapon against the Borg may be the only thing that they are not expecting."

"Have you considered, Captain, that the reason they are not expecting it is because it is preposterous and ill-fated?"

"Then we'll just have to confound that, won't we."

"There is no 'we' involved here, Captain. I was not consulted on this decision. You have made it unilaterally."

"As is my prerogative. And your obligation as a Starfleet officer is to support my decisions."

"My obligation as a Starfleet officer is to support Starfleet . . . sir."

He looked at her askance. "What are you saying?"

"What I believe, Captain. I am incapable of saying anything else. If you find that disruptive or undesirable . . ."

"Of course not," Picard said firmly. "I count on you to be candid with me."

"I am pleased to hear that, Captain." She did not add that she didn't believe it for a moment. Instead she said, in as neutral a voice as she could manage, "I am quite certain that you will do what you feel is best for all concerned."

"That is true. And I am quite certain that I can expect you to understand why I do what I do."

"I do understand it, Captain. Perhaps better than you think." Again she did not add the further thought that was going through her mind: *better than you yourself understand.*

She walked out of the ready room, and her gaze fell upon Zelik Leybenzon. He was standing at the tactical station, as usual. It might have been her imagination, but she thought that he did not look any too happy. Then he looked back to her, and the moment their eyes met, she knew it was not her imagination at all. There was cold fury burning within his eyes, and T'Lana sensed that matters were reaching a tipping point. On the one hand, she had no desire to see what might wind up sending those same matters right over the edge.

On the other hand, purely from a behavioral point of view, watching things unravel due to Picard's own intransigence and recklessness could be . . . fascinating.

18

Starfleet Command—the Bunker

-i-

"THE BUNKER" WAS THE NAME LEFT OVER FROM hundreds of years ago, referring to a structure typically constructed of steel and concrete. Bunkers were usually small, secure locations where top military brass went to ride out enemy assaults.

The bunker to which top senior Starfleet brass had retreated was a far cry from those early incarnations. Three kilometers deep and eight kilometers wide, the bunker walls were constructed from castrodinium. If the entirety of Earth were blown to rubble, the bunker would be left floating, awaiting rescue. That, of course, assumed that there would be anyone left to rescue them.

Those thoughts crossed Edward Jellico's mind as he watched assorted Starfleet brass monitoring the situation of the oncoming Borg cube and the available fleet's attempts to try and impede it.

Jellico had no particular function in situations such as these other than to oversee what was happening. Considering that both offense and defense were being coordinated by some of the finest tactical minds that Starfleet had to offer, he knew they were in good hands. Technically he could take charge of the situation, but why would he want to?

He took a slow, controlled walk past the assorted arrays that charted every aspect of the current battle scenario. He knew that, even now, valiant starships were going head to head with the Borg cube . . .

. . . and losing.

Constant visual feeds were being provided by several observation vessels that had only one function: to maintain visual contact with the cube while staying far enough away not to be sucked in by the oncoming behemoth.

Jellico was having trouble believing what he was seeing.

A voice at his side said softly, "Having a flash of déjà vu, Edward?"

He glanced over and saw Admiral Alynna Nechayev standing next to him. He had known she was in the bunker with him but hadn't seen her until just now.

"No," said Jellico after a moment. "Actually, this is worse. Worse because this cube is making it look even easier than the last time . . . and worse because . . ."

"Kate Janeway is involved somehow?"

"We don't know that for certain."

"Don't kid me, Edward," Nechayev said with a touch of scolding in her tone. "I'm head of Starfleet internal security. Do you seriously think I wouldn't have read the reports of your discussions with Seven of Nine? She had some sort of 'insights' that Janeway has been delivered into Borg hands, and suddenly a massive cube is attacking us. Am I not supposed to put two and two together?"

"We don't," he repeated with conviction, "know that for certain. I'm going to hold out both judgment and hope until we know definitively."

"Who would have thought that Edward Jellico was an optimist?"

"Keep it to yourself," he said.

Their tone may have sounded light, but that was only to cover the concern that was pounding through them. They were watching good people, good ships falling one after another as the Borg cube kept moving implacably toward Earth. It had not yet reached the outer rim of the solar system, but unless something dramatic happened, that was inevitable.

The bunker continued to be a whirlwind of industry around them; they remained the eye of the hurricane. "Would you be out there?" Nechayev asked.

"Pardon?"

"If you had the choice: you could be here in a secure location, or you could be on the bridge of one of the ships fighting for your life."

"There. Out there," he said without hesitation. "You?"

"Absolutely."

"And yet we're here. Stuck on Earth as witnesses, unable to get our hands dirty. Here we are, admirals, and we have no say in our own fate."

"No one ever has a say in his fate, Edward. That's why it's called 'fate.'"

"If I believed that, Admiral, then everything we do here would be pointless."

Nechayev was watching ship after ship fall to the overwhelming power of the oncoming cube. "That may well be the case, Edward." She paused and then said, "We may need a miracle to survive this one."

"The *Enterprise* should be here soon," said Jellico. "Picard hasn't let us down yet."

"Hasn't let us down? This is all Picard's fault," Nechayev growled.

The comment surprised Jellico. "Is it?"

"Damned right. He had a means of disposing of the Borg right there, right in his hands, years ago. His people had developed a virus that they could have implanted into a Borg drone they'd captured. They could have used him as a carrier to infect the Borg. The entire race would have been obliterated."

"I remember that," Jellico said slowly. "As I recall, his defense was that he couldn't condone genocide. That if we simply annihilated an entire race, we'd be no different from them."

"We'd be alive and they'd be dead," Nechayev said. "That's sufficient difference as far as I'm concerned. I'd far rather be on the plus side of that equation. Wouldn't you?"

"True enough."

Fleet Commander Galloway approached them with obvious concern. "Two minutes until outer rim. We project that Pluto is directly in the cube's path. We're having the remains of the fleet regroup in Neptune's orbit to form a defensive line."

"Estimated time of arrival to Earth?"

"At current rate of speed, if the fleet is unable to stop them? Thirty-seven minutes."

Nechayev and Jellico exchanged worried looks as Galloway went back to the command post. "Evacuation procedures on the outlying worlds?"

"Almost finished."

"So at least some of our race will survive," said Nechayev.

The pronouncement was chilling. It was as if Nechayev was tacitly admitting that the defensive measures being taken by the fleet were doomed to failure. Jellico didn't comment on that as Galloway headed back to command central.

"At least there's nothing for them to assimilate on Pluto," said Nechayev after a moment. "The only planet in the system that doesn't have some fool colonists trying to turn hell into paradise."

Jellico looked up in surprise. "Planet? You mean dwarf planet."

"No. Planet. They changed it back again."

Jellico moaned. "Not again. This makes, what, the tenth time in the last three centuries? Can't they make up their damned minds?"

"I suppose they would if the 'they' didn't keep changing."

"My God, Alynna," Jellico said abruptly. "We're discussing matters of trivia while our people are dying by the thousands."

"What would you have us do, Edward?"

Jellico considered it and then admitted, "I've no idea."

"Welcome to the club that no one wants to be a member of."

They said nothing but instead headed toward command central where Galloway and the others were busy barking orders at the fleet. A proximity hologram was showing the Borg cube drawing ever closer to Pluto, hanging there dark and icy in the vastness of space.

"It'll go around it," Nechayev said, watching the cube approach the planet. "There's no reason for it to do otherwise. It's a ball of ice and rock."

"It doesn't appear to be doing so," said Jellico.

"Borg cube is on collision course with Pluto," confirmed Galloway. "Estimated time to impact, on my mark: forty-five seconds. Forty-four, forty-three . . ."

The countdown continued and, courtesy of the observation ships, they were able to see every moment of it.

"Perhaps they don't see it for some reason," suggested Jellico.

Nechayev was skeptical. "How could they not? They're on a damned collision course with it."

"Maybe they're blind to it because it's not technology based."

She considered that a moment. "That could be," she said slowly, although she didn't sound convinced.

"If that's the case, maybe we'll be lucky, and they'll collide with the thing and be destroyed."

"I have trouble believing this could end that easily," said Nechayev, but she did allow a small bit of hope to creep into her voice.

Galloway was counting down steadily. The constant flow of chatter had dwindled and now every eye was upon the bunker's main screen. The computer had placed graphic circles of red around Pluto and blue around the Borg cube that had transformed into red when the collision appeared inevitable.

"Five," droned Galloway, "four . . . three . . . two . . . one . . . impact."

Jellico wasn't certain what he was expecting to

see when the Borg cube came into contact with Pluto. Would the cube actually break apart, or would Pluto be slammed out of its orbit, sent flying away like a frozen billiard ball?

At first it was impossible to discern what was happening. It seemed that the two of them, Borg cube and planet/dwarf planet, were simply up against each other.

And then . . .

"Is that right?" Galloway was studying the readouts. The lieutenant commander in front of the station nodded in confirmation. "That can't be right," Galloway said, but it was more a weary protest of amazement than anything resembling a conclusion.

"What's happening?" demanded Jellico.

"Pluto is shrinking and the Borg cube is growing."

"What?"

"It's eating Pluto," Nechayev said in wonderment. "It's absorbing the sphere's mass; it's eating the damned world."

"That's impossible," said Jellico, knowing that it was in fact anything but.

The visual on the screen began to match what the instrumentation was already telling them. Pluto was becoming smaller and smaller, while the Borg cube was increasing exponentially.

It was a slow, painful process to watch as Pluto continued to shrink. The Borg cube swelled like a mosquito or a tick siphoning blood.

"How the hell is it *doing* that?" wondered Jellico.

"There's nothing technologically based . . . nothing . . ."

"It's mass," said Nechayev. "Matter. Matter that the cube is transforming into energy and back into matter again, along with the starships and the . . . bodies it's absorbed."

It took five minutes. Five minutes for the Borg cube, which had gained nearly a third in size by Galloway's estimates, to finish devouring Pluto.

"Well, at least that solves the issue of whether it's a planet or not," Nechayev commented. Jellico looked at her, appalled at the seeming callousness, and then saw beyond her deadpan observation to the barely controlled horror that was reflected in her eyes.

In short order, the cube also polished off Pluto's moons of Charon, Nix, Hydra, and Elysium. Jellico felt as if he were watching someone devour dessert mints after a sizable meal.

The Borg cube hung there in space for a long moment. The starships were ready to battle it, and Jellico felt sick at heart because he knew beyond question that they were not going to be able to stop it. Nothing was going to be able to stop it.

But as more time passed, the Borg cube continued to make no forward motion at all. "What's it doing?" Jellico said finally.

"Digesting, perhaps," suggested Nechayev. When she saw Jellico's look, she said, "I'm not joking. Perhaps it needs time to process the ingestion."

"Should we order the fleet to attack formation?" Galloway asked.

"No," said Nechayev immediately. "I suggest we wait and see."

"I concur," said Jellico.

They waited. And then they saw . . .

- ii -

There had been no mention of an incoming hail from comm central, no report that the Borg cube was endeavoring to contact them. The screens all over the bunker, including the main screen on the wall, simply went blank for a moment. Then they were replaced by an image so alien that, at first, Nechayev didn't understand what she was seeing.

It was the image of a woman with grayish-white skin and an array of tubing in her head. She was staring at them imperiously, as if she were some sort of royalty. The creature appeared vaguely familiar, but somehow . . .

"Oh, my God," said Jellico softly, and then Nechayev recognized her as well.

"Kate."

The creature who had been born Kathryn Janeway stared out from the screen. She smiled, but it evoked no human connection.

"Surrender," said Janeway. *"You have no choice. Certainly you must know that."*

"Can we reply to her?" asked Jellico.

"Negative," said Galloway. "It's one-way transmission only."

"Our terms are simple: Seven of Nine and Jean-Luc Picard. Give them to us and we will allow you to live."

With that pronouncement, the erstwhile Janeway blinked out of sight.

"Borg cube is holding its position," Galloway informed them.

"Contact the Federation Council," Nechayev said immediately. "Find out what they want to do."

"Find out . . . ?" Jellico looked stunned. "Find out *what*? You don't seriously believe the council will accede to this . . . this blackmail? We're talking about the Borg! The Borg aren't *really* going to bargain with us! They've no reason to! They're the damned Borg!"

"You know that. I know that. Chances are the Federation Council will know that," said Nechayev. "But if they act as if they're going to give in to the Borg, that could buy us time."

"It's insane!"

For the first time, Nechayev was on the verge of losing her temper. She pointed angrily at the screen and said, "*They ate Pluto!* I think we have to be prepared to throw all previous definitions of sanity out the window, Admiral!" She paused, pulling herself together, and then said tightly, "Get in touch with *Enterprise.* Find out where she is. I want to be able to report to the council that we are, at the very least, giving the *appearance* of providing the Borg with what they want."

"Picard is on his way."

"Do you know that?"

"Of course I—"

"Don't tell me that he's following the orders you gave him. Do you *know for a fact* that *Enterprise* is en route to Earth?"

Jellico looked ready to argue the point, but then said slowly, "I will verify her range to Sector 001."

"Do that. And if he's heading anywhere else but Earth, God help him . . . and God help us all."

19

The *Enterprise*

- i -

"WHAT CAN I DO FOR YOU, MISTER LA FORGE?" asked Picard.

Geordi La Forge sat opposite Picard in his ready room. Geordi had always been struck by the disconnect between the public perception of Picard and what he'd experienced in his own career with the captain. Stories of Picard had grown in the retelling so that he had, inexplicably, a reputation as a total hard-ass: impossible to reason with, difficult to talk to. That had never been Geordi's experience with him. Nevertheless, La Forge still felt some mild hesitancy to broach the subject to Picard, and obviously Picard sensed that hesitation. "Speak freely, Geordi. You've certainly earned the privilege."

"I'm concerned this mission to Trophy World may be a wild-goose chase," Geordi told him. "We've no guarantee that we can revive the planet killer . . . if we can, we've no guarantee we can control it . . . and if we can, we still don't know whether it'll be effective against the Borg cube."

"All of that is true," agreed Picard. "But I believe we do know that if we endeavor to attack the Borg cube without some manner of advantage, without something unexpected, we will fail in the attempt."

"No argument," said Geordi. "The thing is, I believe we may have something else unexpected that we can throw at them."

"And that would be?"

"Project Endgame."

"The virus." Picard drummed his fingers on the table. "The one that we were going to have Hugh introduce into the Borg."

"I know how you felt about the prospect of genocide, Captain. However, stopping the Borg cube—presuming we can find a way to infect it with the virus—doesn't automatically translate to annihilating the entirety of the Borg race."

"Frankly, Commander, it very much seems as if it's coming down to a choice of them or us. I vote for us."

It was a harsher position than La Forge had heard the captain take before, and he suspected he could intuit why. *It isn't your place to say anything about it.* But even as the thought crossed his mind, he blurted out, "It isn't your fault, Captain." Seeing the way Picard was looking at him, he suddenly wished he could retract the words, but since that wasn't an option, he continued, "You did what you thought was morally right."

"Morality applied toward an immoral race would seem to be a waste."

"Still . . ."

"I am not interested in seeing the human race die on the altar of my morality, Mister La Forge. But," he continued, "my understanding is that there is an inherent flaw with—or at least limitation to—Endgame."

"That's correct, sir." Geordi was relieved to move away from discussions of morality. "As designed, the virus would introduce a paradoxical mathematical construct into the Borg mainframe. Eventually it would dominate the entire matrix, drive out all other operational systems, and essentially cause the Collective to collapse upon itself as all its resources became consumed with trying to solve a problem that was insolvable."

"The problem being 'eventually.'"

"That's right, sir. As it currently stands, Endgame would require a hundred generations of replication to effectively wipe out the Borg. We obviously don't have that kind of time."

"If you're looking to me to provide a solution, I'm afraid I'm not going to be of much help."

"Honestly, Captain," Geordi hated to admit, "I'm stuck on this one as well. I've been reviewing all my notes on the project and I'm coming up empty. I was hoping that you might be able to approach Spock."

"The ambassador?"

"Before he was an ambassador, he was one of the greatest scientific minds the Federation had to offer. I thought if he came at it from a fresh perspective, he might be able to present a way in that I hadn't considered."

"Why come to me?"

"Because I didn't think it would be appropriate for me to approach him myself about a project that you didn't know I was working on."

Picard had to smile at that. "Mister La Forge . . . were you concerned about hurting my feelings?"

"Well, I . . ."

The captain raised a hand, stopping Geordi before he could speak further. "I will handle it."

"Thank you, sir."

Geordi stood and at that moment Commander Kadohata's voice sounded. *"Captain Picard, we're receiving a direct hail from Starfleet. Admirals Jellico and Nechayev. Do you want to take it in there, sir?"*

Picard and Geordi exchanged looks. "It might be advisable, Captain," said Geordi in a low voice.

But Picard shook his head. "Considering the

current situation, it would probably be best to be aboveboard with the crew in this matter. Commander Kadohata, I'll be right there."

"Aye, sir."

Geordi had the distinct feeling this wasn't going to go well.

He was right.

- ii -

Admirals Nechayev and Jellico were gazing out from the main viewscreen on the bridge and neither of them looked particularly happy.

Picard saw the background behind them. He didn't recognize it and suspected that they were inside the bunker. That would certainly be the logical place.

Jellico appeared shocked, while Nechayev merely looked like she was steaming. *"You're* not,*"* Jellico said slowly, as if Standard had suddenly become a second tongue to him, *"on your way to Sector 001?"*

"No, sir," Picard said carefully.

"Despite a direct order informing you to do so."

"That is correct, sir."

"May I ask where you are *going?"*

Picard had been prepared for that very reasonable question. Unfortunately, his answer was going to be anything *but* reasonable. "I feel it would be unwise to inform you at this time, Admiral . . . Admirals. I am concerned that the Borg may have found a way to monitor this transmission. To that end, telling you specifically where we are going would be counterproductive."

"Has it occurred to you that if that is the case, the Borg have just learned that you are not coming here as ordered . . . which would mean you may have doomed us all, since your returning to Earth is a condition upon which they will not attack us?"

"If the Borg believe that I am indeed returning, then they have no reason *not* to attack," Picard pointed out.

"They claim they will let us live if you are given over to them."

Picard tried not to let his amusement show and wasn't entirely successful. "And you believe that?"

"What I believe is irrelevant, Picard. This order comes directly from the Federation Council."

"They intend to serve us on a platter to the Borg?"

"What they 'intend' is not for you or me to question or second-guess, Picard. Now get your ass back to Earth immediately."

"With respect, Admiral . . . I cannot accommodate you at this time."

There was a deathly silence upon the bridge, and then Nechayev finally trusted herself enough to speak. All things considered, she sounded remarkably reasonable. *"I know that we have had disagreements from time to time, Captain,"* she said slowly. *"The business with the virus that could have eliminated the Borg . . . the incident on Dorvan V. I understand that you're a man of principles. An independent thinker. It is not easy for one of such views to fit into the mind-set of a Starfleet officer. You have done a creditable job thus far. As much as it pains me to admit, I have—on some level—admired you."*

However, thought Picard.

"However," she continued, her voice dropping an octave, *"that admiration has reached its end. There is too much on the line, too many elements to be considered, to permit what you are doing. I am telling you one last time: set your ship's course for Earth. Immediately."*

"Regrettably, I cannot comply."

"Very well. You are relieved of duty." Before the shock of those words could begin to settle in, Nechayev continued, *"Commander Worf, have Captain Picard escorted to the brig, assume command of the* Enterprise, *and set course for Earth."*

Everyone was dead still on the bridge for a long moment. Then, very slowly, very deliberately, Picard rose from the command chair, turned, faced Worf, and gestured for the Klingon first officer to assume command. Determined, he kept his face neutral.

Worf remained exactly where he was, in the first officer's chair. "I regret I am unable to comply, Admiral," he said.

"'Unable'?" asked a stunned Nechayev.

"Yes."

"For what reason are you unable*?"*

Worf scowled and then said, "My foot is asleep."

It was everything Picard could do not to grin.

"Commander La Forge," Nechayev said immediately, *"assume command."*

Geordi held up one arm and pointed at his eyes. "My implants are acting up. Can't see much of anything at the moment. Sorry."

Nechayev now focused on the ops officer. Kadohata did not look at Picard or Worf, but instead fixed her gaze upon Nechayev. *"Commander Kadohata,"* she said, emphasizing each syllable. *"How are you feeling?"*

"Fine, Admiral."

"Your feet? Your eyes?"

"They're fine."

"Anything else, perhaps? Trick knee? Bang your funny bone? Maybe you have the sniffles?"

"No, Admiral."

"Good. Relieve Captain Picard of command."

Still refusing to look in Picard's direction, Kadohata said, "With all respect . . . I cannot obey that order, Admiral."

Picard heard a sharp intake of breath behind him and suspected it was Leybenzon.

"It's always been my opinion, Commander, that it is impossible to disobey a command in any sort of respectful manner," Nechayev told her.

"My opinion as well, Admiral."

"Now listen carefully," Nechayev said, *"you—"*

And suddenly the image was gone.

That caught Picard by surprise. "Reestablish contact," he said.

"Unable to comply, sir," Kadohata informed him. "We're not receiving anything via any subspace transmission."

"Is the broadcast being scrambled?"

"Possibly."

"Another possibility," Leybenzon spoke up from tactical, sounding bitter and angry, "is that they're gone. That the Borg were listening in and, hearing that we weren't going to show up, blew Earth to hell and gone."

"I do not believe that," Picard said firmly. "The safety of Earth is as much something to hold over our heads as any other threat. They would not throw away that leverage so capriciously. They would have no reason to—"

"They don't need a reason! They're the goddamn Borg!" Leybenzon bellowed.

People didn't raise their voice to the captain of the *Enterprise,* particularly on the bridge, especially on the bridge. Leybenzon was glaring furiously at Picard, and Picard met the gaze unflinchingly.

"The fact that they are the goddamn Borg,"

Picard said slowly, "is precisely why they *would* need a reason. They are methodical. If their goal was to destroy Earth, Earth would be gone by now. Their goal is to obtain Seven and myself. They will try another means to do that. Destroying Earth will serve no purpose, nor will assimilating it. Not as long as there is a chance it can be used to get them what they truly desire: us."

"And you're willing to bet the survival of Earth—of the human race—on that."

"Yes," said Picard. Then, practically daring Leybenzon to say something else challenging, he continued, "Do you have anything to add, Lieutenant?"

Leybenzon appeared to have a great deal to say, but thanks to the icy glare that he was getting from Picard, backed down. "No, sir," he said.

"Good. Mister Stephens, maintain present heading. Increase to warp eight."

"Aye, Captain."

Picard slowly sank back down into his chair and then turned his gaze to Worf. The burly Klingon looked back at him. "Your foot is asleep?" he asked.

Worf shrugged. "It can be painful," he deadpanned.

Picard smiled at that, but even seated as he was with his back to tactical, he was sure he could feel Leybenzon's angry gaze boring into the back of his neck.

- iii -

In his office down in engineering, Geordi was going over the schematics for Endgame for what seemed the hundredth time. Then he became aware of someone entering and looked up, fully expecting to see Ambassador Spock standing there.

He blinked in confusion and surprise.

"I'm sorry . . . I . . . thought you were Ambassador Spock."

Seven of Nine stared at him. "Are you certain your ocular implants are functioning properly?"

"Yeah, I'm . . . I'm sure." He laughed, leaning back in his chair.

"Because I have never been mistaken for a Vulcan," and then she added after some thought, "or for that matter, a male of any species."

"I can believe that. I'm sorry, I meant to say that I was expecting someone else."

"Yes, Ambassador Spock. As you stated. To aid you in your attempts to streamline your weapon against the Borg."

"That's right." He was a bit surprised.

"It was the ambassador's opinion that I would be more suited for the task than he." She walked over to the side of his desk. "Is that it?"

"Yes, it . . ." Geordi suddenly felt self-conscious. "Look, I'm . . . I'm not sure if this is the best idea, or if maybe . . ."

"There is no one on this vessel more acquainted

with the Borg than I. I am the ideal individual to participate in this endeavor."

"That . . . that may well be, but I'm still not—"

She stepped back and eyed him curiously. "You are uncomfortable with me."

"Not uncomfortable."

"Is it because of my body? I am told that some males become preoccupied with imagining me unclothed and thus become unable to focus on other duties."

"No!" Geordi was taken aback. "Not at all! That . . . no! I wasn't imagining you unclothed at all! Not remotely! Not even close."

"Then I do not understand the problem."

"It's . . . well . . ." He forced himself to calm down. "It's . . . probably because you're a Borg."

"I am no longer a Borg."

"Okay, but you were, for a very long time. And the whole purpose of this virus is to exterminate your race. I'm concerned that it's going to be a problem for you to give this your all because of that."

"You are wrong in your belief. I was Borg. I am human. Whatever my past was, my loyalties are now to the race that I am. If the obliteration of my former race is the price of that loyalty, then I will gladly pay it. Does that answer all your concerns?"

It didn't, actually. But Geordi saw no reason to bring up the other thing that was preying on his mind. Instead he simply nodded and said, "All right, then. Let's get to work."

- iv -

Miranda Kadohata strode into her quarters and jumped back nearly two feet, putting her hand to her chest and gasping. Zel Leybenzon had been seated there, and the moment she entered, he was on his feet and snapping at her, *"You're no better than they are!"*

Kadohata did her best to recover from being so badly startled. As the door slid shut behind her, she said angrily, "You are damned lucky my husband didn't come in here first. He would have kicked your ass for disregarding basic privacy."

"You disobeyed a direct order!"

She stepped closer to him and said heatedly, "Head of security or not, *I* will kick your ass if you don't stop shouting at me."

Leybenzon looked ready to start shouting again but reined himself in. "You saw what he was doing," he said once he'd forced himself to drop his voice to an acceptable level. "The fate of the human race is at stake . . ."

"Don't be so melodramatic. There're humans on far too many worlds for us to be exterminated by the loss of Earth."

"Miranda!"

"Damn it, Zel, what did you *expect* me to do?" demanded Kadohata.

"Obey the order! Relieve Picard of command!"

"With Worf backing him up? And La Forge?"

"If you'd done as ordered, I would have handled Worf."

"Oh, would you have?" Kadohata asked witheringly. "Do you really think you would have? Look me in the eyes and tell me that you think you could have disposed of Worf. Well?"

Leybenzon looked as if he desperately wanted to make that exact claim, but he stopped short of doing so.

"Mm-hmm," said Kadohata. "That's exactly what I thought. Besides, is that *really* what you would have wanted? A pitched battle on the bridge? And while you were busy doing that, La Forge would have been standing there at the engineering station. He could have done God knows what to the engines—shut them down, whatever—while you were busy having your head handed to you by an angry Klingon. The result would have been you in the brig, very likely me right there beside you, and the *Enterprise* would be on its present heading. What would be the benefit of that, hmmm? Well? You were standing here in my quarters, waiting to ambush me with accusations. The least you can do is answer my question."

Leybenzon muttered something under his breath.

"I'm sorry. I didn't quite catch that."

"I said," he repeated a bit more loudly, "I see your point."

"Well," she said, slightly mollified, "I suppose

that's the closest to an apology I'm going to get from you, you big idiot."

"So . . . so that's it?" he asked. "Picard flies in the face of not one, but two admirals, leaving Earth hanging in the balance, and we're just . . . just going to take it?"

"I never said that."

"Well, then . . . ?"

She took his hand and sat down opposite him. "How many people working security were here before? As opposed to those who came in with you."

"About a quarter predate. The rest came in when I did."

"Quickly, quietly, speak to those officers whom you're absolutely positive you can trust. Have them, in turn, feel out those whom we're less certain of. You need to determine, in short order and to a certainty, which of your people are loyal to Picard as opposed to loyal to Starfleet."

"All my people are loyal to Starfleet. And to me. Even the ones who were around before I was put in charge."

"You'd best make damned sure that's the case. Because otherwise this is going to go very badly."

"What 'this' are you referring to?"

"Obviously, Zel, we're going to obey orders. And if that means taking command of the *Enterprise* over the captain's wishes—over his metaphorical dead body—then that's what we're going to have to do." She paused. "What? The way you're looking at me . . ."

"I'm just wondering whether you had all of this in mind when you initially refused to take a stand against him, or if you're just saying this now. Were you planning ahead at all?"

The chime sounded at her door. Kadohata said to him, "See? At least some people know how to wait for permission to enter. Come!" she called.

Counselor T'Lana entered. Never demonstrative, she nevertheless looked even more grave than usual. She glanced from one to the other and then asked, "You summoned me, Commander?"

"Yes."

T'Lana did not hesitate. "This would relate, I assume, to the prospect of mutiny."

"It's not mutiny," Kadohata pointed out, "if all you're doing is obeying orders."

T'Lana considered that, then nodded. "That is true."

"You're going to help?" asked Leybenzon.

She glanced at him and said mildly, "Naturally. It is the logical thing to do."

- V -

Outside Kadohata's quarters, Lieutenant Jon Stephens listened to the entire exchange, shook his head, and sighed.

"Yup. This was inevitable."

Then he shrugged as if it had nothing to do with him and started to walk away . . .

And stopped.

Ambassador Spock was standing there, facing him.

They said nothing, merely assessed each other.

Then Stephens walked away without a word. Spock watched him go and then stared at the door to Kadohata's quarters. He stood there for quite some time.

20

The Borg Cube

IN THE HEART OF THE BORG CUBE, TWO AP-proached his queen. He saw that she was smiling. She typically did that when she was contemplating absorbing sentient beings. He suspected that this was no exception.

"You heard the transmission between Earth and the *Enterprise*?" he inquired.

"Of course," said the queen. "I was the one who ended it, after all. I saw no point in letting it continue once we had learned what we needed."

"They did not say where they were going."

"It was not required that they do so," replied the queen. "The transmission itself was all I needed. With the connection established, I was able to scan the *Enterprise*'s database. While they were busy discussing the chain of command, I was studying their navigation records. I know precisely where they are headed."

"If you had access to their computer system, why not simply trigger it to self-destruct?"

"My presence there was passive only. I could not actively interact with their computer; they have too many barriers in place to allow such tampering. At least," she added, "for the time being."

"If they are not returning here, then shall we assimilate the rest of the solar system?"

"In time," said the Borg queen. "As long as Earth exists, sooner or later Picard and Seven of Nine will come here to try and effect a rescue. Why remove their incentive to do so?"

"If Seven and Picard do return here at the behest of the Federation, will you truly allow them to live, as you stated?"

"Yes," said the Borg queen, and then added, "I simply didn't specify for how long."

Then she smiled to herself in anticipation of what was to come.

She was about to become a mother.

True, she wasn't glowing, as pregnant women were wont to do. But she was going to attend to that in short order.

21

The *Pride*

GRIM VARGO'S FATHER WOULD HAVE BEEN ASHAMED.

Vargo could practically hear his father shouting in his head: *What the hell do you think you're doing? Didn't I teach you anything? You shouldn't be anywhere near this!*

And yet he'd had to come. He'd had to see it for himself.

He'd charted the path of the Borg cube once it departed and, after sending out the emergency signal in as many directions as he could think of, he'd thought long and hard before sending the *Pride* flying after the cube.

He had no intention of trying to fight the thing. That would be insane. At least he was willing to cede *that* much to all his father's lessons. There was no profit whatsoever in getting involved in a futile firefight with a vessel that could annihilate him without the slightest effort.

Above all else, though, Grim Vargo remained a human being. And if this was fated to be the last stand of the birthplace of humanity, then Vargo wanted to be there to see it.

He had remained cloaked in invisibility, keeping a careful distance from the Borg cube, undetected. Since he'd moved far slower than the cube, it had taken him time to catch up. All during the trip, he'd been convinced that he was going to arrive there too late. So he was pleasantly surprised ("pleasantly" might actually have been too strong a word) to arrive on the scene only to discover that the Borg cube was hovering nearby Pluto while an armada of vessels remained a safe distance away, keeping an eye on it. Some sort of standoff, perhaps, which gave Vargo hope that maybe . . .

"Wait a minute," he muttered, double-checking the cube's location. "Where the hell *is* Pluto?"

His scans quickly verified what he had already concluded, much to his horror: Pluto was nowhere to be found. Neither Pluto nor its moons. The Borg cube, however, was measurably larger than the last time he'd seen it.

Vargo was quick to put the facts together, and the conclusion he'd come to stunned him.

"The bastards ate Pluto," he gasped.

From that point on, there was nothing to do but monitor the situation. He kept the engines on standby, since the cloak tended to be a drain on energy. He wondered what plan, if any, Starfleet had to deal with this disaster.

He sat and watched the monitor, waiting for something to happen. Hours passed, and at one point he nodded off. He had locked his ship's sensors onto the cube and set the alarm to inform him if it moved.

The alarm started howling, startling him so violently that he fell out of his chair. He hauled himself up and looked at the screen.

The Borg cube had departed from its stationary point so quickly that there hadn't been time for the remaining members of the fleet to react. It had simply accelerated with such velocity that one moment it was hovering in place of where Pluto had once been and the next it was barreling right through the line of ships that had been stitched together to try and impede it. The cube could have gone above or below or around the defensive line, but it was as if the ships weren't even worth the cube's time. Instead it plowed right through the heart of the phalanx. This time it didn't even bother to absorb the ships; it hit them full speed, causing the vessels that were unfortunate enough to be in the way either to be knocked spiraling out of the way or just shatter from the impact, despite their shields.

"Gods," said Vargo. Even as he watched the destruction that the cube had left in its wake, he fired up the engines and started following the cube . . . remaining, naturally, at a safe distance, since he had no desire to attract the thing's attention. He cruised around the fleet, which was still largely in disarray thanks to the cube's unexpected departure through the heart of its forces.

"Whoa! Damn!" Vargo shouted, as he veered his ship quickly to avoid floating chunks of debris. A large piece of metal with a registry number spun past him and he realized it was the remains of a saucer section.

The cube hurtled through the solar system, Vargo on its tail. He felt a growing sense of helplessness and frustration, and did all that he could to ignore the latter. Helplessness was fine; frustration could possibly lead him into making a Very Bad Mistake that he would never regret later because there would likely be no later for him.

He followed as the cube drew closer to Earth. The home planet of the human race sat there, defenseless. Vargo knew that there was ground-based weaponry that Earth could unleash upon an invading force, but he also knew without question that it would prove useless in the face of the Borg's superior force. His onboard log was recording everything that the monitor was displaying.

He wondered if the cube would slow down and absorb Earth, as it apparently had already done with Pluto, or the *Thunderchild,* for that matter. Or instead was it simply going to smash the planet apart? The Borg cube was damned near as big as Earth; that certainly seemed a possibility.

Then he realized that it wouldn't even be necessary for the cube to do that. As soon as something that large got within range of Earth's gravitational field, the presence of the object alone would be enough to wreak havoc. After all, if something the size of Earth's moon had an influence on the tides, what kind of damage would something as big as the Borg cube inflict upon the blue-and-green sphere? Vargo was no scientist, but he had to imagine that the answer would be anything from massive global flooding to seismic stress that could crack the planet like an egg.

"It's done. It's over," he said in a hushed voice. Never before had he wished this hard that he had someone to share his vessel with, someone he could talk to. Grim Vargo typically didn't mind being alone; actually, he preferred it. But this day, this moment in time, the last moments that Earth would ever know, he despised it.

He waited for the inevitable impact, or at least for the Borg cube to get close enough to inflict such damage upon Earth's structure that the planet might actually break apart right in front of him.

The Borg cube passed Mars' orbit, headed straight for Earth. Vargo held his breath.

The cube veered off.

Vargo couldn't believe it.

He couldn't believe even more what he saw next.

22

The Bunker

JELLICO HAD FACED DEATH BEFORE. HE'D JUST never faced it on a global scale.

That's what he believed he was about to experience as the Borg cube bore down upon them. As it drew closer, as it approached the point where its very presence would be sufficient to inflict cataclysmic damage upon Earth, Galloway was shouting orders for the planetary defense grid to open fire on the incoming vessel. Jellico knew it was an exercise in futility, but if they were going to go down, then damn it, they would go down fighting.

To his surprise, he felt a hand insinuated into his. He looked to his left and saw Nechayev standing there. Of all the things he'd witnessed in the past hours, this gesture may well have been the one that stunned him the most.

Nechayev squeezed his hand once and said quietly, "No one should die alone."

"Everyone dies alone."

Alynna nodded. "True," she admitted.

"Change in aspect ratio!" came a shout from the monitor station.

Jellico immediately released Nechayev's hand, and both of them headed over to the station. Galloway was already there. "To what degree?" he demanded.

"It's veering off! New course charted to 318 Mark 4 . . ." There was a stunned pause. "They're heading right into the sun."

"Janeway," breathed Jellico. When all eyes turned to him in confusion, he said, "Don't you see? She's exerting her influence on the cube. They didn't manage to turn her completely. Her humanity is causing her to make the cube commit suicide rather than harm us!"

"Maybe. Or maybe they're planning to absorb the sun."

"*Absorb the sun?* Is that even possible?"

"At this point, Admiral," Nechayev said grimly, "I don't think we can rule out anything as being impossible when it comes to the Borg."

They continued to watch as the Borg cube headed straight for the sun. As large as it was, it was a dwarf in comparison to the heart of the solar system. It drew closer, seemingly dwindling in size, and then . . .

"It's gone," said Galloway. "They went right in. Never even slowed."

"Monitor all solar readouts. See if there's any change in radiation levels, the corona . . . sunspot activity, anything," said Nechayev.

"Is there a possibility they're planning to launch solar flares at us?" asked Jellico, but then he answered his own question. "No, that's ridiculous. If they wanted to destroy us, there're far less elaborate ways."

Long minutes passed, and then came the shout: "Target reacquired!"

They looked up at the screen.

"Oh, my God," said Jellico.

23

The *Pride*

GRIM VARGO HAD SEEN MUCH IN HIS LIFE, BUT HE had never seen anything like this.

He'd watched the Borg cube hurtle headlong into the sun, but not for a moment did he believe that that was the end of it. There was simply no way this was going to end that quickly, that easily.

Whatever it was he had expected, though, it didn't begin to stand up to the actuality of what he was witnessing.

The Borg cube tore out of the sun, and it was gargantuan. Larger than Earth, gigantic and blazing hot, a cube-shaped fiery star, burning with nuclear fire ripped from the heart of the sun itself. If the damned thing had come anywhere near Earth, or any planet, for that matter, it would have shredded the planet like tissue. Instead it went straight up, up being relative, of course. In the cold of space, in the airlessness of the vacuum, Vargo imagined he could actually hear the flames roaring.

Then the cube began to shudder violently, and for half a heartbeat he thought that he was going to witness a miracle. That perhaps the cube had indeed attempted something beyond even its capacity, and it was going to self-destruct from the stress to which it had subjected itself.

The smaller ship, the *Einstein,* had been following in its wake. The ship was staying a safe distance away, certainly not having the ability to pull away from the sun if it got too close. Vargo wondered why the Borg vessel hadn't bothered to absorb the *Einstein* by this point and came to the conclusion that there was no reason to. It no doubt served the cube as a useful scout vessel. Besides, everyone on board the science ship had no doubt been "Borgified" by this point anyway.

Something emerged from one face of the cube. Then from another face, and another.

Vargo had once seen footage of seahorses giving birth. The stupid little creatures had spat out their young by the dozens from their bellies, sending them tumbling into the water around them.

That was what Vargo felt as if he was seeing now. Out of each face of the cube, something was being ejected. Each of the "somethings" was a blazing ball of fire, incandescent, a miniature star, with some unidentifiable form within. Then, in seconds, each of them cooled off, and Vargo saw now what they were.

They were starships in every sense of the word, birthed from the fiery energy of an actual star.

The general outline of the vessels was evocative of a traditional starship, but the exterior was not remotely the gleaming white and silver that Vargo knew all too well. Instead each of them looked like a smaller version of the cube itself, with the familiar elaborate latticework design. They were not, however, as large as typical starships. They were bigger.

Much, much bigger.

Six of them, one from each face of the cube, hanging there in space. They remained that way for a minute as if stabilizing themselves . . . getting used to being "alive" . . . and then two of them peeled off and headed away from the cube. They went in the opposite direction of Earth, instead leaping into warp space and departing the Sol system as quickly as they could.

The reason was obvious to Vargo: they had been dispatched to go find something and either bring it back or destroy it utterly.

Whatever it was, Vargo was relieved that it wasn't him.

24

The *Enterprise*

- i -

SEVEN OF NINE WAS ABOUT TO WALK OUT OF HER quarters, only to discover two security guards standing there. She looked from one to the other, trying to determine exactly why they had shown up. All the possibilities ran through her head in seconds, and she was forced to one ineluctable conclusion.

"You are idiots," she said. "Summon me when you are prepared to take me to the brig."

She walked back into her quarters. She could have tried to warn Picard, but she assumed that communications had been severed and so didn't bother.

- ii -

Beverly Crusher was just starting her workday when a security officer, Lieutenant Brennan, strode into sickbay. She was in her office, going over personnel records and seeing who was due for his or her regular checkup, and by startling coincidence she had just pulled up Brennan's file when he walked in. She blinked in surprise. "How did you know?"

He looked confused, as if he had expected her to say something, but that wasn't it. "How did I know what?"

"That you were due for your physical."

"I didn't."

"Well, then, this is . . ." She stopped as she realized that she had no idea what it, in fact, was. "All right, then, why are you here?"

"I've been ordered to take up position here. There may be a problem."

"A problem?" Beverly got to her feet, instantly concerned. "What sort of problem? Does the captain know?"

"He will, very shortly."

"What is that supposed to mean?"

He didn't answer. He looked as if he wanted to, but he said nothing.

Suspicious, Beverly Crusher tapped her combadge. "Sickbay to bridge." When no response came, she hit it again with growing concern. Then she looked up at the security guard and suddenly realized that he wasn't the least bit surprised that her combadge wasn't functioning.

"What the hell is going on?" she demanded.

"I'm afraid I can't tell you at this time."

"You realize I outrank you."

"I'm under orders, Doctor."

"And I issue orders, Lieutenant."

"With all respect, Doctor, not right now . . . and not to me." His voice sounded apologetic, but there was no trace of apology on his face. His features were hardened and everything in his body posture told her that if she tried to walk around him, he would physically put her right back in her chair.

This is not going to be a good day . . .

- iii -

A security team showed up at Ambassador Spock's quarters. They rang the chime and waited for a response. None was forthcoming. Glancing at the others, the leader stepped forward and triggered a security override on the lock. They entered quickly, not wanting to take any chances: Spock was a Vulcan, and Vulcans could not be underestimated.

In this case, Vulcans also could not be located. The security team tore the quarters apart, but Ambassador Spock wasn't there.

- iv -

Geordi La Forge glanced at his chronometer and wondered where Seven of Nine was. They had arranged that they would meet down in engineering at 0800 hours sharp. He was there, ready to continue work on Endgame, but she was nowhere to be seen. That was very unlike her.

"La Forge to Seven of Nine," La Forge called out, expecting the ship's comm system to route him directly through to Seven's quarters. It was so automatic for him to receive immediate responses to hails that he was visibly startled when he heard nothing back from Seven. "La Forge to Seven of Nine," he repeated and still got nothing in reply. "Computer, status of comm system."

"Comm system functioning normally."

"Why is Seven of Nine not replying?"

Geordi had not actually addressed the question to the computer. Instead he was wondering it aloud. The computer, however, did not distinguish a rhetorical question from a direct one and promptly responded, "Comm system to individual designated Seven of Nine is blocked."

"Blocked!" He couldn't understand it. "Who blocked it?"

"Lieutenant Zelik Leybenzon, utilizing Security Protocol 276."

"That's ridiculous! La Forge to bridge."

Nothing.

"Computer," he said slowly, "is my comm channel blocked as well?"

"Affirmative."

Behind his desk, Geordi stood. Just as he did so, a security team appeared, grim faced, silent.

"Would one of you care to tell me what's going on?" demanded Geordi.

None of them did.

- V -

Picard gave a brief smile in greeting to Worf as the Klingon stepped into the turbolift. He had learned long ago that first thing in the morning was not the time to try and engage Worf in any sort of routine chitchat. Worf was not, as the saying went, a morning person.

Instead, Picard kept it businesslike. "My understanding is that we will reach Epsilon Sigma V in just under forty-seven hours."

"Yes," said Worf.

That was terse, even for Worf. Picard turned to the Klingon first officer and said slowly, "Commander, I understand that this must be difficult for you . . . knowing that other vessels are in the midst of a battle for survival, while we are—"

"Not?"

"If I did not believe that this was the best way to help Starfleet, I would not be undertaking the endeavor. Ambassador Spock—"

"—is a Vulcan."

Picard looked at him suspiciously. "Do you have a problem with Vulcans, Number One?"

"I seem to," he admitted. "I do not do well with a race that is so . . . inscrutable."

"You mean you like to have some hint of what they're going to do next."

"Correct."

"So you can defend yourself properly."

"Yes."

"Worf," Picard said with a smile, "it was fine while you were head of security to think of everything in terms of combat. I think you'll find, however, that you do not necessarily have to frame all of your interactions with others in a strategic manner."

The door to the bridge slid open and Picard strode out. The moment the tuborlift doors closed behind him, everyone on the bridge stood and faced Picard. Everyone except Stephens, who sat at the conn station and looked resolutely hangdog.

Picard sensed tension practically radiating from Worf. He couldn't blame him. Something was clearly wrong, and he had a feeling he was about to find out what. He was also aware that Leybenzon had stepped in behind them. He had two security men with him, standing on either side. Neither had his phaser drawn, but their hands were hovering near them.

Kadohata had her hands behind her back. Standing off to the right was T'Lana. Naturally she gave no hint of what was going through her mind. Was it smug satisfaction? Sorrow? Disdain? Impossible to tell. Several other bridge officers were also on their feet, and they all looked nervous but determined.

"Captain Picard," said Kadohata in a formal tone, as if she were reading a list of charges at a proceeding. "You have been issued an order to head to Earth, an order that was presented by two ranking Starfleet officers and represents the direct request of the Federation. I am asking you now, formally, if you intend to obey that order."

"And if I'm not?" Picard said slowly.

"I am asking you now, formally, if you—"

He cut her off. "No. I'm not."

"Then by order of Starfleet, and under the authority issued me by Starfleet Command, I am hereby relieving you of duty."

"This is mutiny!" Worf thundered.

"Obeying the orders of superior officers is not mutiny, Commander," said Leybenzon.

Worf took a step toward Kadohata, his fists clenched.

Not for a second did Picard believe that Worf was actually going to attack her. She was half his size and unarmed. He'd break her in half. If nothing else, Worf would consider it dishonorable to go after her.

Leybenzon, however, obviously didn't know that. Suddenly his phaser was in his hand and he said, "Stop right there, Commander!"

Everything happened very quickly from that moment.

- vi -

A truism had floated around the *Enterprise* for some time, having originated in holodeck simulations: *Never shoot Worf. Never even try. You'll just make him angry.*

Leybenzon had apparently never heard it. People would tell him about it afterward, but that would do him very little good.

The security chief had always been impressed by just how formidable looking Worf was. However, he'd also always been of the opinion that someone that large could be taken down without much difficulty since muscles were all fine and good, but speed would always trump muscles.

He had no idea just how fast Worf was. He discovered it, though, when it seemed as if Worf was merely looking in his direction, and all of a sudden his phaser was flying out of his hand, knocked away by a casual swat from Worf that was stunning in its velocity.

Worf took one step forward and smashed his fist into Leybenzon's face.

- vii -

"Worf, no!" shouted Picard.

Worf didn't hear him. His blood was pounding in his ears, his fury thundering and blocking out anything else.

The truth was that Worf had been walking a fine line emotionally for some time. He had taken on the position of first officer, but only after considerable hesitation. He had felt conflicted, believing that he wasn't a good enough officer to warrant such a position of trust. He had been struggling with those principles and had not managed to come to any sort of definitive conclusion. He'd wished with frustration that Deanna were still around. Not only was she a trained counselor, but they had developed a close relationship. Granted, it had ended badly, but still, of all the original crew he'd served with, she was the only one he really felt he could open up to.

But she was gone, and in the place of ship's counselor was that bowl of dead *gagh,* T'Lana, who had taken an instant dislike to Worf and thus far had managed to build herself up only to determined tolerance.

He had never felt more alone than he did these days, and that loneliness had been causing his frustration to build to dangerous levels.

This pushed him over the edge.

Leybenzon went down as if he'd been constructed of cardboard. Again Picard was shouting, *"Worf! Don't do this!"* Had Worf heard him, he would doubtless have obeyed his captain's orders. But he didn't hear him, for he was overcome with a sort of warrior madness that compelled him to do one thing and one thing only: eliminate any and all threats to his commander.

One of the other security guards, Meyers, actually

managed to get a shot off. The phaser blast, set to stun, struck Worf in the chest. The Klingon staggered back toward the other security guard, Boyajian. Boyajian made a tactical blunder that nevertheless came out of reflex. Rather than shoot Worf a second time, he moved to catch Worf, who appeared to be about to collapse to the floor.

It never occurred to Boyajian that any normal being could withstand a point-blank stun blast.

His brief display of gallantry was sufficient to cost him dearly. Worf shook off the effects of the phaser shot just as he fell into Boyajian's arms. Meyers's phaser never wavered from its target, but it didn't matter. The instant he came into contact with Boyajian, Worf grabbed him by the throat and upper chest and yanked forward. Boyajian flipped up and over and crashed into Meyers.

He saw from the corner of his eye that Leybenzon, blood gushing from his nose, was scrambling forward toward one of the fallen phasers. Worf moved toward it. He could have reached to pick it up. Instead he brought his booted foot slamming down and crushed the phaser, rendering it useless. Sparks flew from it, the ruined weapon's gasping protest.

Leybenzon yanked his hand away just in time; if he'd been a split second slower, Worf would have crushed his fingers. Credit Leybenzon with determination: he lunged forward, throwing his arms around Worf's knees, trying to knock him off balance. It didn't come close to working. Rather than falling, Worf simply reached down, grabbed Leybenzon by the back of his uniform shirt, and yanked him to standing. He snarled into Leybenzon's face, and the veteran security chief actually blanched.

"Now you die," Worf told him, and no one could have said at that moment if Worf would truly have killed him or not.

They never had the opportunity to find out.

Worf caught a glance of something out the corner of his eye, a hand coming in. He had only a heartbeat's warning, and he moved quickly enough that had the hand been wielding a blade or some other weapon, he would have managed to get out of its way. But instead the hand simply clamped on to Worf's shoulder.

Worf had an instant to realize what had happened and enough time to growl, *"ghuy'Cha'."* That was the last thing Worf remembered before the world went black around him.

- viii -

T'Lana saw the look of pure fury on Worf's face, but naturally she was mentally several steps back from the emotion of the scene. So she perceived it in a sort of distant, neutral fashion. She kept her hand firmly clamped upon Worf's shoulder, worried that he might find some way of fighting off the nerve pinch. She needn't have concerned herself, as it turned out. Worf said something in his native tongue that she very much suspected was not intended as flattering, and then he slumped to the floor. When he hit, it made a sound like a bag of boulders.

"Thanks," grunted Leybenzon, who was busy helping his team to their feet.

T'Lana turned to Picard, who was staring at her in what seemed to her almost a pitying fashion. "Are you satisfied with the outcome, Counselor?" he asked sarcastically.

"I did not desire this, Captain. None of us did. We are doing what we feel is right for Starfleet."

"I had hoped it would not come to this."

"You brought it upon yourself, Captain," Kadohata spoke up.

"I did what I believed had to be done."

"As are we," she replied. "We all want what's best for the Federation. We're just of differing opinions on how to go about that."

"As captain of the *Enterprise,* I would have thought that my opinion on that topic would have taken precedence."

"Not in this instance, no." With a sigh, as if this were the most difficult thing she had ever done, she said, "Mister Stephens, set course for Earth."

"I can't do that," Stephens said.

T'Lana did not react with shock because naturally she was who she was. Kadohata, however, looked coldly furious.

"Mister Stephens," she said, her building anger threatening to overwhelm her. Her voice became even more clipped than it typically was. "I thought we had been over this. I thought that, whatever personal loyalties you may have to Captain Picard, you were willing to set them aside in favor of loyalty to the chain of command and to the needs of the people of Earth. You've picked exactly the wrong time to try and take a stand against me. If you won't set course for Earth, then I will have you relieved and put someone else in charge who's willing to do his damned job."

Stephens just stared at her as if she hadn't spoken.

Kadohata looked to Leybenzon, who simply shrugged. The security guards, meantime, were grunting under Worf's weight as they tried to pull him enough to standing that they could maneuver him into the turbolift.

"Mister Stephens, set course for Earth," she repeated.

"I. Can't. Do that," he replied.

At which point, T'Lana realized what was going on.

So, apparently, did Kadohata. "Can't . . . or won't?"

"Funny you should ask. The navigation computer has shut me out. It won't respond to my trying to implement a new heading."

"Shut you out?"

The turbolift hissed open and Ambassador Spock stepped out just as Worf's heavy body was slipping from the grasp of one of the security guards. Without a word, Spock caught the falling Klingon and lifted him upright with no visible display of effort. "I take it," he said calmly, "that the mutiny has already occurred. Humans do tend toward impatience."

T'Lana couldn't believe what she was hearing. Neither, obviously, could Kadohata. "You . . . *knew* about this?" she demanded.

"I regret that I overheard your discussions regarding your dissatisfaction with the captain's action."

Kadohata looked stunned. T'Lana had to credit her, though: she rallied quickly. "Computer," she called. "As per direct orders from Starfleet, I, Commander Miranda Kadohata, have assumed command of *Starship Enterprise.* Acknowledge."

"Acknowledged," the computer replied readily. That much was to be expected: the ship had a record of the recent conversation with Admirals Jellico and Nechayev, and was able to reference it.

"Release command of navigational system to me."

"Unable to comply."

"I am ordering you to override any command lockouts instituted by Captain Picard."

"Unable to comply."

T'Lana saw coloring flush under Kadohata's jawbone. It was Leybenzon, however, who turned to Picard and snapped, "What did you do to it?"

"What did you do to it, *sir,*" Picard coolly corrected him.

Leybenzon looked none too happy, and T'Lana had no desire to see what the security officer might do next. So she took it upon herself to intervene and asked, "What did you do to it, sir?"

"Nothing," replied Picard. "I'm no computer expert."

T'Lana didn't require a map to be drawn for her. "Ambassador Spock, however, is." She looked toward the Vulcan. "You reminded me of it yourself, when you assumed control of the *Enterprise* in the matter of Captain Pike."

"A wise man once said that there is no future, only the past endlessly repeating itself," Spock replied easily. "In this instance, it is impressive how sophisticated computer systems have become since my time as an officer . . . and yet how much has remained exactly the same."

"*You* locked this vessel on its present course?" demanded Kadohata.

"That is correct."

"Release control immediately," Leybenzon told him.

Spock gazed at him as if he were a new form of fungus. "My captain and best friend—quite possibly the only human I ever truly considered friend—gave me that same order once. I did not accede to his wishes in that situation. May I ask what leads you to believe I shall accede to yours?"

"Because the fate of our world is at stake," replied Leybenzon.

Spock raised an eyebrow. "Your world, perhaps. Not mine."

Leybenzon looked as if he was ready to lash out, but he wisely chose not to. T'Lana was relieved, if for no other reason than she suspected Spock could dispatch the security chief without too much difficulty, and there was only so much humiliation that Leybenzon should have to endure in the course of one shift.

"Ambassador," T'Lana began. Then she stopped as she ran everything she could possibly say in this situation through her mind . . . and came up with absolutely nothing useful or persuasive.

She felt as if Spock had a window into her head, because he merely said, "Very wise," as if anticipating that she had chosen not to continue the conversation because she had figured out that it would be useless.

Kadohata clearly couldn't believe matters had gone so completely wrong. "There must be a way we can overcome whatever lockout he's done on the navigational system."

She turned to Picard and said, "Do you anticipate that this will prompt me to put you back in charge, sir?"

"I *am* in charge," Picard replied. "That much remains clear. The only question before us is whether you're willing to acknowledge that."

"Lieutenant Leybenzon," Kadohata finally said, "escort the captain and the ambassador to the brig. Put the rest of the senior staff in with him. We'll do what we can to turn the ship around."

"You will fail," Spock said confidently, "but it is your time to waste."

"Call us when we arrive at Epsilon Sigma V," Picard called out as they were escorted at phaser point into the turbolift.

"Will do, sir!" called Stephens.

Kadohata fired Stephens a disgusted look as the turbolift doors closed. Stephens promptly withered in the face of it and returned to trying to take the *Enterprise* off its current course.

"That," sighed Kadohata, "did not go as planned." She looked to T'Lana. "Any thoughts?"

None that would be considered useful. But she'd been asked, so she said, "We may as well return control of the vessel to Captain Picard now and save ourselves time and effort."

"That isn't very useful."

T'Lana sighed.

25

The Bunker

THE REMAINING FEARSOME STARSHIPS THAT HAD been spat out from the cube, numbering four in all, ringed the Earth. Jellico, Nechayev, and the others had discussed the prospect of summoning the balance of the system's defenders to engage the Borg starships. Ultimately it had been decided that this wasn't the best way to proceed. Matters were at a standoff. There had been no further communication from the Borg cube, but neither had there been any manner of attack on Earth.

The consensus from the Federation Council was that, although things appeared to be at an impasse, it would be unwise to assume that they were going to remain that way.

Starfleet was already doing everything it could.

Distress beacons had been sent out across subspace, and every armed vessel in the sector—and even beyond—had been recalled and was on its way to try and provide some manner of defense. The council, on the other hand, had decided that more needed to be done.

When word had come down as to what was being discussed, the admiralty couldn't believe it.

"They want to *negotiate* with the Borg?" asked Jellico, stunned. "Are they insane?"

"No. They're diplomats," replied Nechayev, who looked no more sanguine about the notion than did Jellico. She paced a corner of the bunker, shaking her head. "We've advised against it, but there's pressure from some of the member worlds that the step should be taken."

"It's obvious why they would," said Jellico. "They're concerned that the Borg are going to come after them next. So they figure that if some sort of accord can be struck, then they'll be safe."

They had a clear view on the main monitor of the starships that were grouped around Earth, an omnipresent reminder of the Borg's presence. The Borg cube continued to remain a safe distance away, for which Starfleet was grateful

"How soon?" he asked Nechayev, who was fixedly watching the screen.

"They're dispatching the ambassador right now."

"Which one?"

"Lucius Fox."

Jellico knew the name immediately. Fox and his

ancestors had served the Federation in various ambassadorial capacities for as far back as Jellico could recall. Lucius was the latest in the long line of distinguished gentlemen and gentlewomen who had dedicated their lives to bringing a disparate galaxy together.

Fox definitely had his work cut out for him this time, though. The Borg cube had ignored all hails that had been sent its way ever since they had demanded that Picard and Seven be brought to them. The two Borg ships had departed with no explanation offered, although Jellico had an uncomfortable idea of exactly where they'd gone off to. They were, he suspected, heading toward wherever Picard and Seven were, discerning their location somehow based on the transmissions they had received. Were that the case, and Earth was being kept around to serve as a lure for Picard and Seven, then Earth's time might really be running out. If the *Enterprise* was outgunned and dispatched by the Borg vessels, then Earth would have served its purpose.

Earth would be assimilated.

Or absorbed.

Or destroyed.

Jellico shook off all such morbid thoughts and focused again on the immediate situation. With the Borg queen unresponsive, Fox had no choice but to proceed into space and hope that he could somehow make direct contact. It was an incredibly risky move, and Starfleet had recommended strongly against it. But Fox had been determined to undertake the challenge, and the Federation had overruled the admiralty. In recognition of the council's authority, Starfleet had agreed to send a small escort along with Fox's vessel. It was more symbolic than anything else, because the Borg had already proved their superior power in pitched battle with Federation vessels. Nevertheless, form and decorum dictated that someone be sent along. Consequently, when Fox's runabout moved through the atmosphere, two escort vessels were alongside to accompany it.

From the relative safety of the bunker, Starfleet brass watched with collective breath held as Fox's runabout moved toward the Borg starships. For a short time, Jellico actually thought they were going to allow Fox's vessel to go through. But then they drew closer in to one another, and Fox's ship slowed to a halt. The escort ships did likewise.

Long minutes passed.

"Are they communicating with the Borg vessels?" Nechayev asked.

"Impossible to tell, Admiral," reported Galloway. "All our secure lines are being scrambled by the Borg. We've no idea what they're saying, or even if anything is being said at all."

"This stinks," muttered Jellico. "This stinks to high heaven."

More time passed, but no one in the bunker relaxed for even an instant. There was much pacing and drinking of coffee, but otherwise the facility lapsed into silence.

Then, much to Jellico's shock: "We're receiving an incoming hail from Ambassador Fox," said Galloway, who looked no less surprised than Jellico was.

"Directly to us?"

"No, sir. The Federation Council is on the same receiving beam as well."

"Put it on."

The image of the Borg vessels was replaced by a smiling visual of Ambassador Fox. Jellico would have assumed that Fox had been assimilated if not for the fact that he had not come directly in contact with the Borg or their queen, the tragically unfortunate Kathryn Janeway.

Obviously feeling the need to get right down to business, Fox—his round face suffused with pride—said, *"I have been in direct communication with the Borg queen. I have provided her assurances that the UFP has no hostile intent toward her or her species. That the Borg's aggressive actions toward the Federation have no basis in reason, and that if the Borg are interested in petitioning the Federation for membership, I will be pleased to aid them in that endeavor."*

"He's got to be joking," said Jellico in wonderment.

"I am pleased to say," Fox went on, a broad smile plastered across his face, *"that I have received assurances from the Borg queen that there will be no hostile action taken against Earth, the Federation, or any of its member worlds. I have to say that this*

is the best of all possible outcomes. Clearly, there will be . . . peace in our time."

"I have to say," said Nechayev, "I was not expecting that."

Fox, nodding as if acknowledging applause that only he could hear, opened his mouth to speak once more . . . and suddenly was jolted forward. He had only enough time to let out a terrified scream, and then the image of the ambassador's vessel vanished.

"They're opening fire!" shouted Galloway.

The Borg-created starships had indeed opened fire, but their target was not anything on Earth.

Instead, phaser blasts from all four ships converged with pinpoint precision upon the ambassador's runabout. It was, to put it mildly, overkill. The runabout was defenseless; a single one of the ships could have disposed of it. All four together was an obvious demonstration: to show that the Borg were united in purpose and in formidability.

The runabout erupted and disappeared in a burst of flame that was instantly snuffed out in the vacuum. The escort vessels tried to run but failed utterly. Seconds later the burning remains of the escort ships were likewise nothing more than random hunks, nearly pulverized by the assault.

There was dead silence in the bunker.

"*That,*" said Nechayev with surprising calm, "was what I was expecting."

She turned to Jellico, who felt a cold shock that she could remain this detached. Giving voice to his astonishment, he said, "How can you remain so calm?"

"I don't have a choice. Do I? Do we?"

Slowly, Jellico nodded. "No. We don't."

She looked back to the screen. The ships had moved back to their stations. Far in the distance of the dark, the Borg cube remained.

"It looks like we're going to need another ambassador," she said.

26

The *Enterprise*

- i -

"SPOCK! DAMMIT!"

Kadohata slammed her fists in futility on the navigation controls, causing Stephens to jump back, startled. Her angered curse cut across the bridge and brought silence upon it. Spock wasn't there, but the shout was loud enough that he might well have been able to hear it.

T'Lana wasn't surprised. Along with Stephens and the top people they had on the ship when it came to cybersystems, they had been working for hours trying to get the navigation system back under their control. Nothing had worked, and the frustration was beginning to get to Miranda.

Aware that all eyes were upon her, she composed herself through sheer force of will. Lieutenant Tom Mortenson, the computer wizard from down in engineering, was standing next to her, looking as irritated as she. Mortenson was tall and slender, with small tufts of brown hair clinging to the sides of his otherwise balding head. He walked around to the other side of the conn station as if regarding it from another angle might provide a clue as to how to proceed.

"What are our options at this point?" asked Kadohata.

"Well," said Mortenson, "we could try a reboot of the central computer core. But the computer's not designed for such cold shutdowns. It'll take a day or more to get it back up and running. Typically such procedures are undertaken while in drydock. In this case, we'd be dead in space. We'd be completely vulnerable to whoever or whatever shows up."

She shook her head. "Unacceptable. What else? What else can we do to stop us from continuing on our present heading?"

"We could shut the engines down. That'll take us out of warp. Then we're not heading toward Epsilon Sigma."

"But we're not heading toward Earth either." She drummed her fingers on the console. "I have to think," she said abruptly and turned away. She headed into the ready room. After a minute, Leybenzon started to go in after her, but T'Lana was already moving. She fired a glance that froze him in his tracks as she entered the ready room.

She had expected to find Kadohata behind Picard's desk. She was mildly surprised to see that that was not the case but then decided in retrospect that it was only logical. Kadohata was standing, resting her hand on the top of the desk, staring down at it as if she were going to discover great truths reflected in its shiny surface.

"What?" asked Kadohata, her voice flat and inflectionless. "Do I look like I need counseling?"

"Yes," T'Lana said without hesitation.

Kadohata didn't look at her. Instead she continued to stare at the desktop.

"Dammit!" she suddenly exploded again, and this time she pounded the desk repeatedly. T'Lana was taken aback but gave no outward sign. Within seconds the fit of fury had passed and Kadohata had once again pulled herself together. Then, very softly, in a voice that was a complete contrast to her fury of only moments before, she said, "What the hell have I done?"

"What was necessary. You should not doubt that."

"My commanding officer is in the brig because of me. A commanding officer whose strategies are required reading at the academy. How am I not supposed to doubt that?"

"Very well, then," said T'Lana. "Doubt if you must. But know that you did what needed to be done, at a time when those whom he trusted betrayed that trust by not doing what was necessary."

"And what happens now?" She gestured vaguely. "This ship is heading toward Trophy World. We're on this . . . this quixotic quest of his, whether we want to be or not. Once we get there, then what?"

"Perhaps at that point we can take back command of navigation. The vessel will have arrived at its destination . . ."

"Do you really think that's going to be the case?" She sounded sarcastic, and T'Lana knew that Kadohata was as aware of the answer to that question as she herself was.

"No," admitted T'Lana. "The ambassador would have thought too far ahead. There will undoubtedly be some further step required to reassume command of the *Enterprise,* and as long as the captain or the ambassador does not implement it, we will likely be in the same predicament we are now."

"This is crazy," said Kadohata. She shook out her hand, clearly having done it some damage during her short-lived emotional outburst. "We're a starship. How did this happen?"

"When Ambassador Spock is involved, anything is possible."

"Thank you," she said bitterly. "That's exactly what I wanted to hear."

"I have many talents," T'Lana replied, "but telling people what they want to hear is not one of them. I am able to tell them only what I believe they should hear. More often than not . . . they do not like it."

Kadohata took that in and then said, "All right. What do you believe I should hear?"

T'Lana told her.

She didn't like it.

- ii -

Worf rubbed his shoulder in irritation. Solicitously, Beverly Crusher said, "Do you need me to take a look at that?" The look of annoyance he gave her spoke volumes and she promptly tried to find something else in the brig to look at.

Picard, La Forge, Spock, and Seven of Nine were loosely grouped around, standing or sitting depending on individual preferences. There wasn't enough seating room in the brig for all of them to sit at one time, so they took turns. The only one who never sat, who seemed to have no need of doing so, was Spock. He simply stood to one side, staring off into space, his hands clasped in a relaxed manner in front of him.

The Klingon turned to Spock and said, "That paralyzing grip . . . is there a counter to it?"

"A counter?"

"Every blow that exists has a countermove to prevent it. Is there some manner in which I can counter that Vulcan paralyzing technique?"

"Yes."

"And that would be . . . ?"

"Do not allow a Vulcan to put his or her hand on your shoulder."

Worf glowered. "Thank you," he grunted.

Geordi, who was one of the people sitting for the time being, rested his head on the wall behind him. "I wish I knew how long we've been in here."

"Eleven hours," said Seven of Nine.

"Nineteen minutes," Spock added.

She glanced at him and then finished, "Thirty-seven seconds."

"Forty-eight," he corrected her gently.

She considered it and then shrugged, obviously not feeling it was worth the effort to dispute.

Worf heard her coming before he saw her. He knew he would forever recognize her footfall. Sure enough, T'Lana walked up to the brig, standing on the other side of the field, gazing in with that typical arrogant attitude of hers. Miranda Kadohata was standing next to her. Both of them were trying to look all business, but Worf was sure that he could see at least some fear in Kadohata's eyes. Damned right she should be afraid. Worf was ready to stuff her into the nearest Jefferies tube the moment he got his hands on her. As for T'Lana, she would meet a very different fate. In Worf's imagination, she was spread-eagled and staked on top of a fire ant hill.

Picard regarded them for a moment and then said, "Are you here with the wine list?"

"I hear they have a superb merlot," Crusher told him.

"I want to release you, Captain Picard," Kadohata said.

"Do you. How very kind. And the others?"

"All of you."

"Good. By all means, release us. It will be . . . entertaining," said Worf. He cracked his knuckles and it made a sound like boulders being split apart.

"It is a poor matter for ship's morale for things to be as they are," said T'Lana.

"You should have thought of that before you aided in usurping my authority."

"Your authority was not usurped. It was revoked by Starfleet," Kadohata reminded him. "I was acting on their authority. If I had to do it over again, I would do the exact same thing."

"As would I, so it appears we are at loggerheads," said Picard.

"It can be solved, but I need your word."

"My word?"

"Yes. I need your word that you will defer to my authority as acting captain of the *Enterprise.* That if we release you, you will serve merely in an advisory capacity."

"And in return?"

"In return, we will allow the *Enterprise* to proceed to Epsilon Sigma V."

"How generous of you," said Picard, and he smiled in a manner that looked positively wolfish. Worf found it comforting. "Particularly when one considers the fact that we are going to Epsilon Sigma V whether you want us to or not."

"Not necessarily . . ."

"Yes," Spock spoke up. "Necessarily. If you were capable of overriding my sabotage of the computer, you would have done so by now. You would not be here, speaking to us. The logical conclusion is that you are endeavoring to make the best of what you perceive as a bad situation."

"How else are we supposed to 'perceive' it?" demanded Kadohata.

"As the only solution."

"Your generous offer is rejected," Picard told them. "You have taken responsibility for this ship. I am not particularly inclined to accept your 'handouts.' If you wish to return full command of this vessel to me, I might—*might*—consider keeping you on in your current capacities. Not tremendously likely, I admit, but it's the best you're going to receive from me."

"Keep them *on*?" Worf made no effort to keep the disbelief from his voice.

"We can't allow that, Captain. You have to be willing to defer to our judgment. To—"

Picard interrupted her. "This conversation is ended," he said briskly.

Kadohata was about to try and keep talking, but T'Lana touched her gently on the forearm as if to say, *This is pointless.* Shaking her head, Kadohata walked away with T'Lana right behind her. Neither cast a backward glance.

"Definitely," Worf muttered. "Ants. Hungry, angry ants."

No one in the brig knew what he was talking about, and he made no effort to explain.

- iii -

The doomsday machine hung in space in front of them.

Everyone on the bridge had, at one time, heard about it or read about it in Starfleet Academy. Everyone knew how Commodore Matt Decker had valiantly given his life in the line of duty to put an end to the monstrous machine. But aside from Stephens, none of them had ever actually taken the time to visit the so-called Trophy World. Its reputation as a tourist attraction was considered by many Starfleet officers to be a disincentive.

Faced with the reality of the legendary device, however, it was still a daunting moment. Looking like the horn of plenty from hell, it was a vast, cone-shaped deactivated robot, kilometers long. Its maw, when the machine was functioning, was alive with a ball of energy burning so furiously that it looked as if the thing were powered by an actual sun.

There were a number of other famous derelict ships hovering around Epsilon Sigma V. They were not technically "orbiting," since they were not falling around the planet. Instead they were kept in place via geostationary devices attached to the hulls. But the doomsday machine was by far the largest.

A lengthy silence pervaded the bridge as they gazed at it. Finally Stephens spoke up: "The crew of this *Enterprise* took on something ten times that size?"

"Yes," said Leybenzon.

"And we have *them* locked up in the brig?" When no one replied immediately but instead just glared at Stephens, he shrugged but offered nothing else.

"Has the computer unlocked navigation controls?" asked Kadohata, knowing the answer before she asked the question. She was not seated in the command chair; instead she had retained her usual position at ops. Leybenzon had told her she should really be taking center seat, but she had just given him a look and didn't otherwise respond.

"No, Commander," said Stephens. "We're still locked out."

"One has to admire Ambassador Spock's thoroughness," T'Lana observed.

"We don't have to admire a damned thing," Leybenzon snapped. He came around the tactical station and approached Kadohata. "Look, let's stop dancing around the obvious. I'll say it if no one else is willing to. There's no reason we can't force Picard to—"

"*Captain* Picard," Kadohata said quietly. "Or simply 'the captain.'"

Leybenzon looked as if he wanted to argue it but instead simply said, "There's no reason we can't force Captain Picard to cooperate."

"Force him?"

"Anyone can be persuaded of anything if you're willing to exploit his weak point."

"What would you suggest?" asked Kadohata, sounding mildly amused despite the seriousness of the situation. "That we threaten to torture Beverly Crusher if he doesn't release ship's controls to us . . . ?" Her voice trailed off and she saw the look in Leybenzon's eyes. Slowly she rose from her station and faced him. "That *is* what you're suggesting, isn't it."

"I'm not suggesting we actually *do* it . . ."

"So we use it as a bluff? Lieutenant, that idea alone is repulsive enough."

"Furthermore," T'Lana spoke up, "he will call the bluff."

"Fine. Then we don't make it a bluff."

"Lieutenant!" Kadohata was shocked. "What the hell is wrong with you?"

Leybenzon didn't back down. "We're talking about the future of our race! The fate of our planet! I don't know about you, but I'm willing to do whatever it takes in order to ensure the safety of both! And if you're not, then what the hell is wrong with *you*?"

Kadohata was ready to respond in anger, but she checked the impulse. She put her hands to her face, calming herself, and then she said, "All right . . .

this is what's going to be. We're not going to torture anybody. We're not going to kick everyone loose either. But since we're here, and we can't do anything about it, then we try to accomplish something with our presence. Send a security squad to the brig." She headed for the turbolift. "You have the conn, Stephens."

"Where are you going?" asked Leybenzon, sounding annoyed that he hadn't been asked to come along.

"To try and save our world," Kadohata shot back as the turbolift doors swished shut behind her.

- iv -

The security team was waiting when Kadohata arrived. Knowing something was up, Picard and his officers were all on their feet. Picard had that same insufferably smug expression on his face as he'd had before, as if he was certain that everything was going to come out exactly the way he wanted it to and all that was required was waiting for that to happen.

Kadohata said nothing at first, then she turned to the nearest guard and, putting a hand out, said, "Your phaser, please."

He gave her an odd look but, without hesitation, handed over his phaser.

"We've arrived at Epsilon Sigma V," she informed them. "The planet killer is hovering twenty thousand kliks to port. The navigation systems have still not been released from the computer lock. I assume that is your doing, Ambassador?"

Spock inclined his head.

"Fine," said Kadohata, knowing ahead of time that would be the answer. "Here's what's going to happen: we're going to lower the force field. Ambassador Spock, Commander La Forge, and Seven of Nine will be released. They will be allowed to take a shuttlecraft and head over to the doomsday machine to see if they can activate it. If the three of them endeavor to take the shuttle in any direction except toward the planet killer, we will use the tractor beam to haul them back in, throw them back in the brig, and then we all sit here and wait to hear that Earth has been destroyed. And won't we all feel special about that. Now . . . when we lower this field, I expect all of you to remain exactly where you are except for those designated to come forward. Anyone who tries to rush us, the security guards will phaser you into unconsciousness before you get half a step. As for you, Mister Worf"—she made a show of deliberately dialing up the power level on the phaser she was holding—"if you move so much as a centimeter, I will bring you down." She leveled the phaser directly at him and held it with both hands. "As the officer in temporary command of this vessel, I don't want this responsibility to fall upon anyone but me. Your Klingon hide may be surprisingly resistant to stun setting, especially when you're in full warrior mode. I suspect, however, that your molecules will separate as quickly as anyone else's." She had been keeping her voice flat, but a bit of emotion slipped in and she almost choked as she said, "I swear, Worf, I'm not kidding around. If I have to use this, it's going to take everything I've got not to turn the phaser around and fire it at myself afterwards. But then Leybenzon will take command, matters will proceed as they currently are, and you'll still be gone. So please, I'm begging you, keep your big feet planted where they are."

She felt drained after saying it all. And even with that threat hanging in the air, Worf *still* looked to Picard to see if that was acceptable. It was unreal, the amount of dedication these people had to him. Kadohata felt a swell of jealousy, because she suspected that—no matter how long she served, and even if she got a ship of her own—she would never command that degree of loyalty.

"Do as she says, Number One," Picard said slowly. "All of you . . . do as she says. This time, Commander, your terms are acceptable to me."

She wanted to say *Thank you, Captain.* Not only that, she wanted to tell the security team to lower their weapons, turn command of the ship back over to Picard, and forget this entire sorry incident had ever happened. She knew that was impossible, though. She had undertaken her course for good reason, and she had to stick with it no matter what the outcome.

The force field was lowered and, very slowly, Spock, La Forge, and Seven walked out of the brig. Each of them took care to stay out of the direct line of fire between Kadohata and Worf. Worf glowered at her; if looks could kill, she would have been long dead.

She was relieved beyond her ability to express when nothing untoward happened and the force field was snapped back into place.

"Good luck," Picard said to the three of them. Then he turned to Kadohata and said, "Good luck to you as well."

"You're wishing me luck?" She didn't know whether to laugh at that or not. "I took control of your ship."

"And with it all the responsibility that entails. It's a terrible burden, isn't it? You don't have to answer. But you and I both know it."

Yes. Yes, we do.

She said nothing. Picard simply nodded as if he knew what was going through her head.

Hell, he probably did.

27

Shuttlecraft Spinrad

- i -

AMBASSADOR SPOCK HAD TAKEN IT UPON HIMSELF to pilot the shuttlecraft toward the planet killer. This provided Geordi and Seven more time to go over the specifics of Project Endgame.

They had been doing so while they'd been cooped up in the brig. After all, reasoned Geordi, what else did they have to do to keep themselves occupied? It had been problematic, though, since Geordi didn't have any of his research or notes in front of him. Now that they did, having transferred all the research to the shuttle's computer from the engineering database, he watched as Seven went over all the specifics. He marveled at the focus she displayed: nothing short of a quantum torpedo detonating in her ear seemed capable of distracting her.

"We are overthinking this," she said finally. Geordi was sitting at a research console, with Seven standing behind him. "We are endeavoring to devise a way to speed up the virus, and it is unnecessary."

"Then how do we solve the generational problem? We can't wait around for a hundred generations of Borg—"

"We do not have to. Rather than reconfigure the virus, we reconfigure the collective mind of the Borg."

Geordi looked up at her, confused. "Run that past me again?"

"It is unnecessary for us to change the virus itself. We need to change the way the Borg react *to* the virus. The manner in which the virus is currently designed, it must wait until sufficient Borg resources are devoted to solving the geometric puzzle it presents. The fact that it does so gradually is where the problem lies. We must present the virus to them . . ."

The ambassador spoke up from the helm. ". . . in terms so plain and firm as to command their assent."

"Exactly," said Seven. "It is logical that a Vulcan would find the most precise means of expressing it."

"Actually," said Spock, "the word choice was Thomas Jefferson's. A human." He glanced back at Seven. "Your race has produced some eminently quotable individuals."

Geordi nodded. "Okay. So what you're saying is that we introduce the virus to them in such a way that, rather than insinuating itself slowly into the mainframe, we cause the Borg mind to make it top priority." The chief engineer smiled. "In the early days of computers, they had a term for it: a 'spambot.' A piece of rogue programming that pushed out everything else in a computer and forced it to focus all available resources on whatever the spambot was trying to introduce."

"That is correct. By turning Endgame into the modern-day equivalent of a spambot, we can force the Borg collective to prioritize it even above its greatest priority of all: assimilation."

"But how?"

"That," admitted Seven, "is the challenge."

Geordi leaned back in his chair and stared at the geometric patterns playing across the screen—the infinitely twisting, insolvable patterns that could theoretically terminate the entire Borg uni-mind. He was aware of Seven literally breathing down his neck as she gazed at the patterns. "Very elegant," she said. "Attractive yet destructive. A formidable combination."

"I'm sorry," Geordi said abruptly.

Seven clearly didn't follow. "Sorry about what?"

"I was . . . reluctant to work with you on this. But it had nothing to do with you," he added hastily. "It's because . . ." He paused, then pushed forward, "It's because when I look at you, I see her."

Seven looked puzzled, but then understanding

dawned on her. "The other female Borg. Reannon."

"Yes," he said. "The one who . . . she took her own life. Because I wasn't able to do what was necessary to make her want to live again. To live as a human." He shook his head. "All this time, I've tried to tell myself that it was because it was impossible. That since she'd been part of the Borg for so long, there was just no way to recover her human identity. But here you are, and you're in one piece, and alive, and yes, you have implants, I can see that, but you're still human just the same and content with that."

"I have a human aspect," Seven replied, "but within, I remain Borg. I do not know the details of your time with this Reannon individual. Nevertheless, the failure was not yours but hers. Her inability to balance both sides of her essence. I accept all that I am. In fact," she said slowly, "that is how we are going to go about doing what needs to be done."

Geordi shook his head. "I'm not following."

"There is a 'back door code' that can be utilized to provide direct access to the Borg core," said Seven. "It is how the queen is able to focus the entirety of the Collective's attention on an immediate threat. Otherwise it would be too unwieldy for the collective to cope when something untoward presents itself."

"And how do we get this back door code?"

"We do not. It cannot be fed into the Endgame virus. It is too thoroughly ingrained into the Collective's core."

"Well, then, I don't . . ."

Then he saw the look in her face, and he realized.

"No," he said immediately.

"It is the only way," she replied.

"You're suggesting . . ." He couldn't believe he was saying it. "You're suggesting we feed the Endgame virus into you . . . you allow yourself to be assimilated by the Borg . . . and in doing so, you'll be the one who serves as the carrier."

"If the planet killer proves to be of no use, then that will remain the sole alternative presented us," she said, sounding quite reasonable about it. "We will return to Earth, and I will turn myself over to the Borg as they have requested. Once I am assimilated, their destruction will be all but assured."

"They want you *and* the captain," Geordi reminded her. "While they're busy assimilating you, what's going to happen to him? If he's assimilated as well, then the virus will destroy him, too."

"If we are assimilated and the virus does not destroy them, then they will annihilate Earth. You know this as well as I."

"This is exactly how we were going to use Hugh."

She tilted her head. "Hugh?"

"Hugh was a Borg who was with the *Enterprise* for a short time. He was the original means we were going to employ to utilize Endgame. We were going to return him to the Borg collective with Endgame implanted within him . . ."

"And thus destroy the Borg."

"Yes."

"I was wondering how you originally intended to implant the virus. Well, now you will have the opportunity to do precisely as you originally intended."

"And lose you."

"The needs of the many, Commander La Forge," Seven said slowly. "If you do not wish to cooperate with the downloading of the virus into my cortical implants, then I shall undertake the endeavor myself. I would prefer not to do so; I believe your aid will make the process more efficient, less prone to error. It is up to you."

Geordi didn't reply immediately, weighing all the options before them. Finally, reluctantly, he nodded. He stood, gestured for her to sit down, and said, "Prepare for download." Even as he prepped the computer, he turned to Spock. "Ambassador, let's hope to hell that this planet killer is everything it's cracked up to be. Because what I'm doing right here is Plan B, and I have no desire to upgrade it to Plan A."

"I concur," Spock said gravely as he piloted the *Shuttlecraft Spinrad* toward the yawning chasm that was the entrance to the doomsday machine.

- ii -

Spock was intrigued.

All of the readings that he had taken of the planet killer had been from outside the vessel, in the comparative safety of the *Enterprise.* He had never had the opportunity to explore the interior. There had been no need: once the thing was dead, there were other matters for the *Enterprise* to attend to.

Spock was not one to feel regret over decisions he had made and priorities in his life. But if he were to feel regret about something, failing to spend extended time investigating and exploring the doomsday machine would certainly qualify.

At first, upon entering the device, the darkness was so complete that even the ship's monitors couldn't compensate. It almost seemed that the darkness was an entity unto itself, rather than the mere absence of light. Furthermore, the interior seemed to be resistant to the *Spinrad*'s sensors. Spock had experienced that in the first go-round but had chalked it up to the machine's hull being constructed of pure neutronium. Now, though, they were inside the thing and they were still having trouble. He was certain the vessel didn't possess some sort of active machinery that was causing problems. The fact that it wasn't generating any sort of energy readout precluded that. So it had to be something else, and the only thing that occurred to Spock was that the material itself from which the machine was constructed was somehow thwarting their instrumentation.

It was not, however, able to do so indefinitely, especially with Spock, Geordi, and Seven all working together to refine the images they were receiving.

Spock watched this new generation of engineering and scientific experts with quiet admiration. The technology and knowledge they displayed made the scientists and engineers of Spock's time seem primitive, almost quaint in comparison. Spock was fully aware that Montgomery Scott had survived to this era. He wondered how much difficulty the fabled Scotty, a miracle worker of his time, felt trying to make adjustments to a new time. Spock had made no effort to contact him and wondered why that was. Could it be that such contact would be . . . painful in some respects? Spock certainly hoped not. He wanted to believe that he had sufficiently divorced himself from such emotions that they were no longer remotely a consideration.

"I think I got it," said Geordi, and the blackness of the screen gave way to an enhanced visualization of their surroundings.

Geordi let out a low whistle.

The initial glimpse of the interior of the doomsday machine made it seem, just for a moment, as if they were surrounded by a hundred identical shuttlecrafts. That, of course, was not the case. Instead it was quickly evident that the machine's interior was entirely crystalline. Everywhere they looked there were interconnected spires that made the ship appear to have been fashioned entirely from ice.

"It's just the way the captain described the bigger one to me," said Geordi.

"You did not view the interior yourself?" asked Spock.

Geordi shook his head. "The captain did. He, Deanna Troi, Guinan, and Data. I was aboard the *Enterprise* dealing with another crisis."

"They do seem to come in sizable quantities," Spock observed.

Seven turned to Geordi. "The larger vessel was habitable within?"

"Yes."

"Then we must find a way to it. Our current whereabouts are open to space and hence will not sustain us."

Geordi La Forge nodded in agreement, and under his and Seven's careful guidance, the shuttlecraft began to probe for some signs of a central control area that would support them.

As this happened, Seven was studying the readouts, and something akin to recognition flickered across her face. Spock, keenly attuned to emotions since he tended to study them so closely in others, asked, "Is this familiar to you in some manner?"

Seven nodded slowly. "I recognize this technology."

"The theory is that it was created by the Preservers," Geordi told her.

"If that is the case, then they imparted the technology to another race, because I have seen this before. It was a race that was assimilated by the Borg centuries ago."

"What was its name?" asked Geordi.

Seven shrugged. It looked surprisingly odd to see such a human gesture from her. "Species 038. Once a race is assimilated, names are meaningless. They are part of the Collective. Nothing else before that matters. They are Borg."

"But I don't understand. How could you recognize it if it was assimilated hundreds of years before you were born?"

"Because I once shared all knowledge of all Borg technology. Everything that is assimilated becomes part of the 'mainframe' of Borg intelligence. As a Collective, we are all integrated into that mainframe. What they know, I know."

"I don't remember seeing anything crystalline in any Borg vessel I've ever encountered," said Geordi.

"No. There has not been. But that is not the aspect of the technology that the Borg utilized."

"What was?" asked Spock.

"The aspect that allows machine mind and living mind to bond on every possible level. That will result in 'living machinery,' as it were. The machinery bonds on a physical, mental . . . even spiritual . . . level with its operator. In a manner of speaking, you are looking at the very technology that enabled the Borg cube to take over Kathryn Janeway and transform her into the new queen."

"Damn," whispered Geordi.

Seven returned her gaze to the screen. "I will say this, however: now knowing the design and construction of this vessel, it lends support to your theory, Ambassador. I readily believe that all instrumentation available to you at the time would have told you that the planet killer was dead. You perceived no energy readouts, no indication that the power core was functional. But there are multiple stages to death in human beings: the heart may give out, but as long as the patient is not brain-dead, then he remains technically alive."

"You are suggesting," said Spock, "that this vessel had some sort of living pilot."

"Perhaps not 'living' in any sense that you and I would understand, but yes. Theoretically, when the *Constellation* detonated within the heart of the machine, the power core shut down not simply because of the power of the explosion but also because the intense radiation from the explosion annihilated the being who was within. Without a mind to guide it, the ship effectively died."

"Meaning that if a new mind is brought in to guide it . . ."

She nodded. "The planet killer could live again."

- iii -

Seven of Nine looked at twenty-seven reflections of herself dispassionately.

It had seemed forever until the shuttle had finally detected an interior, enclosed chamber that had a breathable atmosphere. Once they had found it, they had used the transporter aboard the *Spinrad* to beam themselves over. This was a calculated risk; Geordi had rigged the shuttle's comm system to respond to his command and lock on to beam them out if an emergency arose. However, there was no way of knowing if the planet killer might somehow interfere with that transmission. In fact, Spock had informed them that the planet killer had blocked their transmissions to Starfleet when they had first encountered it, so it definitely had the technological capability to make sure that the three of them didn't return. But none of them had any desire to remain behind, particularly Geordi, who made no secret of the fact that he regretted not having the chance to explore the larger planet killer and wasn't going to pass up this opportunity.

So they had all beamed over, Geordi putting his faith in the shuttle's recall system. Spock hoped that La Forge was not making a catastrophic mistake, but he was philosophical enough not to dwell upon it since the decision had already been made.

La Forge and Seven were moving slowly through the vast caverns that constituted the heart of the doomsday machine. Spock took it all in. He found it difficult to believe that he was walking around in what was essentially a gigantic dead machine. Instead he felt as if he were walking the surface of another world. The air was breathable, as the sensors had indicated, but it had a stale odor to it. The surface upon which they were walking required them to move carefully, for it was as crystalline as anything else around them. It was a bit disorienting to see mirror images of oneself wherever one looked. James Kirk had once made reference to a savage parallel universe in which he and several other crewmen had been trapped as being a "fun house mirror" version of their own sphere. Spock had not known what that referred to but had, naturally, done the research. He was beginning to feel as if he was likewise in a fun house—minus, of course, the fun.

Geordi had a tricorder out and was carefully studying the results. "I'm not seeing any sign of energy levels," he said, his voice echoing in the stillness. "I can see why everyone believed it was dead."

"If Seven of Nine's supposition is correct, then reactivating it remains a possibility," said Spock. "It is our first, best hope of attacking and defeating the Borg."

There were tall, crystal pillars everywhere. Spock placed his hand against one of them and found it cold to the touch but not so cold that it seemed frozen. Geordi stepped in next to him, still checking the readings of his tricorder. In a low voice, he asked, "Have you given any thought as to what we do if we can't get this thing up and running? For that matter, how much time do we spend here before we give up?"

Spock considered it a moment and then said, "Seventeen hours."

Geordi looked taken aback. "How did you come up with that number?"

"Purely arbitrary. I do not truly believe that any answer I could have provided would have proved relevant or of use, and so I selected an answer at random. Would you prefer if I chose a different response?"

Smiling, La Forge shook his head. "That won't be

necessary, Ambassador." Then he checked around and got a look of concern. "Did you see where Seven got off to?"

"I did not."

La Forge tapped his combadge. Seven was wearing one as well, so there should have been no reason that they couldn't communicate with each other. "La Forge to Seven."

"Seven here. I think you should see this."

"I'd love to. What 'this' are we talking about?"

"I'll keep my signal open. Track it."

Geordi promptly ran the comm signal through his tricorder and started walking. Spock followed him, continuing to take in everything around him. They were threading their way through a maze of crystal columns, but Spock was charting their path in his head with ease. That way, if the tricorder failed for some reason, he'd be able to lead the others back.

They maneuvered their way around several more of the pillars and then they saw Seven standing near the tallest column they'd yet seen. In fact, as near as Spock could determine, it was the only one that stretched from the floor to the cavernous ceiling hundreds of meters above.

Seven was gazing intently at it. "Do you see it?" she asked. "My ocular implants enable me to perceive it. Commander La Forge . . . ?"

Geordi leaned forward. Spock was aware that La Forge's eyes were more than they appeared, with lifelong blindness overcome by technology. The Vulcan knew that certain things gave him an advantage over humans, but he had to admit that humans were coming up with enough gadgetry to close that gap.

"Some sort of faint residue," said Geordi after studying it for a short time. "Like something discorporated."

Seven nodded. "I believe it was whatever had been previously operating the planet killer."

Spock knew that they had received no life readings from the doomsday machine when they had first encountered it. But certainly the ship's hull and interior makeup could easily have thwarted their sensory apparatus.

"It was living," La Forge asked, "within the crystal? In a sort of suspended animation?"

"That would be my conjecture," said Seven. "But it was unable to protect the machine from the massive amount of radiation unleashed by the *Constellation.* Once the guiding mind died, the crystal either ceased to preserve it . . . or else was unable to."

"And it is your belief," Spock said, "that another mind can reactivate the machine?"

"It is conjecture at this point, but it does seem possible."

Spock considered that a moment and then said, "It seems only logical that we test that conjecture."

He started to move toward the central crystal but was surprised when Seven of Nine stepped into his path, facing him. "I am aware of your intention, Ambassador," she informed him.

"Are you?"

"Yes. You intend to perform a mind-meld with the crystalline entity that forms the core of this vessel. In doing so, you intend to blend your personality with the biotechnology that constitutes this vessel's essence."

"That is correct."

"I would advise against that."

"And why," Spock asked slowly, "would you do that?"

"Because I understand this technology far better than you. You may have, from time to time, brought your mind and thoughts together with another. I, by contrast, have spent the majority of my life as part of a collective. By the standards of Vulcans, you are accomplished in your mental prowess. By the standards of the Borg, you are an amateur."

Spock raised an eyebrow, which was his default response. "I have been called many things in my career. That is not one of them."

"Then you have experienced something new." She paused and then said, "Ambassador, in order to understand this biotechnology—in order to control it—you must be prepared to commit to it with both body and soul. You are, quite simply, too old. Too set in your ways. Your mind is not flexible enough. If this device is still functional, the clash of your personality and what it will impress upon you will literally shred your cerebral cortex. It would be irresponsible of me to stand by and permit that to happen."

"And you would put yourself forward as a viable alternative?"

"You know, I'm standing right here," Geordi spoke up. "And I'm not exactly a slouch when it comes to understanding this type of technology. If anyone is going to—"

"I have decided," said Seven of Nine, and before either of them could say or do anything to stop her, she stepped forward and threw her arms around the crystal column.

"Seven! Wait!" shouted Geordi.

She did not do so. Instead she closed her eyes and placed her face directly against the crystal, pushing her cortical implant against it so that it was in direct contact. It was obvious to Spock what she was doing: she was endeavoring to force the machine—if "machine" was remotely a word that could be used to describe it—to take notice of her, explore her, and accept her as a viable pilot.

Geordi started forward, but Spock placed a hand on his arm and brought him up short. La Forge looked startled at the strength that Spock effortlessly displayed.

"Allow her to do what needs to be done," Spock said.

Long moments passed. Spock had no idea what they were waiting to see, but that didn't stop him from patiently waiting to see it.

Seven's eyes remained closed. Her breathing slowed.

All was silent.

And then, very slowly, her eyes opened to slits.

"Anything?" she asked.

"Nope," said Geordi.

She pulled her head back and stared in annoyance at the crystal.

"I believe," Spock said, "that this may be an appropriate time for a colorful metaphor."

28

The *Enterprise*

- i -

"OH, SHIT," SAID LEYBENZON, AND THEN LOUDER, "*Commander!* Hot contact on long-range scanners! Two vessels bearing down, moving at warp nine!"

"What sort of vessels?" asked Kadohata, getting to her feet and crossing to tactical. "Hostile?"

"I don't know. Readings are all over the place. They have the ion signature of starships, but I'm getting biologic readings that are consistent with a Borg cube."

"Go to Red Alert," snapped Kadohata. "Man battle stations." Without thinking, and for the first time since she had assumed command, Kadohata went to the command chair and sat in it. She leaned forward, gripping the armrests.

The doomsday machine continued to hang dead in space, and Kadohata cursed Picard for getting them into this situation in the first place. If they'd headed back to Earth, at least they'd have other Starfleet vessels backing them up. Granted, it might not do them any good, but it would have been far preferable to the sense of solitude they currently had.

Space twisted and warped directly in front of them, and two ships dropped out of warp space. "Are those . . . *starships*?" Kadohata asked in confusion. "What *are* those?"

"They were starships," Stephens spoke up. "Now they're Borg ships. Look at them; it's obvious."

Leybenzon realized that Stephens was right. They were not only Borg ships, but they looked far more formidable than typical starships. The tactical readouts of the ships' weaponry indicated that one of them could annihilate the *Enterprise* unless the *Enterprise* was extremely lucky. Two of them dropped the odds of survival nearly to zero.

Then Leybenzon was surprised to see a telltale light blinking on his board. "They're hailing us," he said, unable to keep the astonishment from his voice. The vessels had arrived weapons hot and seemed ready to open fire the instant they'd targeted the ship. Now they wanted to talk? They were Borg. What the hell could they possibly want to talk about?

"Put them on," said Kadohata.

The screen shifted and the image of a Borg appeared on the screen. He appeared to have been Asian in his previous existence, but now he—

"No, no," Kadohata whispered. "I know him. That's Captain Matsuda of the *Thunderchild*."

The Borg drone did not appear to register what she had just said. Instead he said in that flat, emotionless voice that the Borg typically displayed, *"I am Nine of Eighteen. You will produce the units Picard and Seven of Nine."*

"This is Commander Miranda Kadohata of the *Enterprise*. We will produce neither Picard nor Seven of Nine until you make clear your intentions."

"They're firing!" Leybenzon had barely enough time to shout out a warning before a blast from the nearer Borg starship hammered across the *Enterprise*'s bow. The vessel shook as if a cosmic hammer had just leaped into existence and slammed across the saucer section.

Leybenzon couldn't believe it. A single shot had already knocked down shield capacity by 30 percent. What in heaven's name had been done to those ships? What sort of weaponry were they packing?

The former Captain Matsuda gazed at them blandly from the screen. *"That should clarify our intentions. Produce Picard and Seven of Nine immediately."*

"Borg vessel, stand by," said Kadohata, and the screen blinked out. She turned to Leybenzon. "Get the captain. Get the whole damned command staff up here, now."

"Commander," Leybenzon protested, "I don't—"

Kadohata didn't bother listening to what else he had to say. "Bridge to security!"

"Security, Meyers here."

"Release Captain Picard and the rest of the command staff. Ask . . . tell Captain Picard to report to the bridge immediately."

Meyers hesitated only a moment. *"Aye, Commander."*

Kadohata tilted her head back and met Leybenzon's angry gaze. "Don't say it, Lieutenant."

His jaw twitched, for he was indeed aching to say everything that was on his mind. Instead, with considerable effort, he kept it to himself.

- ii -

Hearing the Red Alert klaxon sounding, T'Lana was heading as quickly as she could toward the turbolift that would take her to the bridge. Just as she arrived, she heard a voice behind her call out, "Hold the lift."

She couldn't quite believe what she had just heard.

She turned and saw, to her shock, Jean-Luc Picard and Worf striding toward her. A security guard was following them, but he looked a bit confused, as if uncertain what he was doing there or what had just happened. It was Picard who had snapped out the order to her. T'Lana, who had already stepped into the lift, stood there frozen, making sure to keep it where it was. Worf and Picard stepped in and Picard said, "Bridge." As the doors slid closed, he turned to her and said as casually as if nothing had happened, "You *were* heading to the bridge, I take it?"

T'Lana nodded numbly. She was all too aware of Worf standing less than a meter away, glowering at her.

"This is . . . awkward," she said slowly.

"Really. I assume your extensive training in counseling informs you of that?"

"Captain—"

"I suggest whatever it is you're thinking, Counselor, you break a lifetime of habit and—at least for the time being—keep it to yourself. Do I make myself clear?" When T'Lana didn't reply immediately, Picard turned a blistering stare upon her and repeated, "Do I make myself clear?"

"My apologies," T'Lana said slowly. "I had assumed the statement was rhetorical. Yes, Captain, you make yourself clear."

"Excellent."

The doors slid open and Picard stepped out onto the bridge. Kadohata was at the ops station, keeping her distance from the command chair. Picard strode straight toward it as if it was where he was supposed to be by divine right. T'Lana remained in the turbolift for a moment, trying to comprehend what had just happened, and then she heard Worf's low voice near her ear.

"Fool me once . . ." Worf then moved past her. He bumped her aside as he did so, his right shoulder colliding with her upper arm. She had the very strong suspicion it was not an accident. She rubbed herself where he'd struck her but remained, as ever, stoic.

"Status report," Picard said briskly.

Leybenzon hesitated, and Picard turned toward him. "I am not accustomed to repeating myself, Lieutenant," he said.

Shaking off his momentary paralysis, Leybenzon cleared his throat and said, "Two starships that appear to have been . . . assimilated by the Borg. Approximately four times larger than standard starships, with proportionately more formidable weapons array. We've taken one hit already that knocked shields down to seventy percent. Engineering is endeavoring to restore them to full power, but it is doubtful shields can be maintained in the face of further attacks."

"Can we outrun them?"

"Unlikely. They were moving at warp nine when they arrived, and—it's only a guess—but I suspect they could probably move even faster. We are in communication with them at the moment. They have demanded to see both you and Seven of Nine."

Picard considered his options for a moment. There did not appear to be an abundance of them. "Put them on screen," he said.

"I'm reasonably sure," Kadohata spoke up, "that the Borg speaking on their behalf is . . . was . . . Captain Matsuda."

"Of the *Thunderchild*? Damn," Picard said under his breath.

T'Lana felt that she was witnessing a phenomenal display of emotional control. Here was Picard, whose authority had been usurped by the very people to whom he was now issuing orders. She knew that Leybenzon was steaming over at tactical, but even he was falling into old patterns of obedience.

She was also aware that Worf hadn't taken his eyes off her. What did he think, that she was going to attack him for no reason? Then it occurred to her that, as far as Worf was concerned, he'd *already* been attacked for no reason. He simply did not see Picard's insubordination and refusal to obey direct orders from Starfleet as a reason for an assault. To him, it was all terribly arbitrary, and his guard was going to be up for the foreseeable future. She supposed she could understand his thought process, even if she thought it was a bit narrow-minded.

The image of the being who'd identified himself as Nine of Eighteen appeared on the screen. If Picard was taken aback by what he saw, he did a superb job of hiding it.

"Locutus of Borg," said Nine of Eighteen.

"Not anymore," replied Picard. "Not ever again."

"You are wrong. You will be assimilated."

"*You* are wrong. We will defeat you, as we always have and always will."

"We have evolved. We are Borg. You will be assimilated. Show us Seven of Nine."

"No." Picard gave no indication that he couldn't do so even if he wanted to, that she was aboard the doomsday machine.

"You will show her to us. You will both return to the Borg."

"You can return to the Borg cube and let them know that you have failed in your attempt. Neither Seven nor I will turn ourselves over to you."

"Your resistance is not only futile, but foolish. Surrendering to us is your only chance to save your vessel."

"If I believed that, I would do so in a heartbeat," replied Picard. "But I do not think for a moment that you intend to do anything other than try to assimilate everyone and anyone who is in your way."

He is stalling for time. He is waiting for La Forge, Seven, and the ambassador to pull some sort of miracle from the depths of the planet killer. The realization went through T'Lana's head and she wondered just how long he could possibly keep Nine of Eighteen talking. Considering that the planet killer was still showing no signs of life, but instead was hanging there in space displaying all the activity of a dead moon, she didn't think it was going to be long enough.

"The queen does not desire your destruction," said Nine.

"Then you would appear to have your hands tied."

"No," said Nine. *"She does not desire your destruction . . . but she does not desire your freedom even more. If you will not be assimilated . . . you will die."*

"Their phasers are locking on!" shouted Leybenzon.

"Evasive maneuvers!" called Picard. "Target the saucer section of both vessels and open fire!"

29

Doomsday Machine

- i -

WHEN THE SURGE CAME, SEVEN OF NINE WAS caught completely off guard.

She had been leaning against the crystal column and was about to step away from it when a sensation that was both new and familiar hammered into her. She gasped and her body became paralyzed. Even though she had been seeking the contact, her survival instinct told her to pull away. She was unable to do so. Her hands felt as if they were glued to the column.

"Seven!" shouted Geordi, but she didn't hear him. His single voice was crowded out by what seemed the thousands in her head. Thousands of

voices, but all of them speaking as one. It was different from what she had experienced within the Borg collective, however. In that instance, the unified voice of the Borg spoke in a flat, uniform manner. Here, though, the voices spoke in a sort of harmony, as if one speaker had recorded his voice over and over again, but in different pitches, so that they blended together into a seamless whole.

And they sounded angry.

You are Borg. You are what we were created to destroy.

I was. I no longer am.

We sense you. We sense them. We have slept for so long. Others have come to us, probed us, violated us. We have remained silent. Hidden. Afraid. We had forgotten our purpose. You have reminded us. They have reminded us.

They?

An image suddenly presented itself into Seven's mind. It was two vessels that looked very much like Borg cubes except molded into the shape of starships. They were closing in on the *Enterprise,* which was desperately trying to pull back, get some fighting distance. The Borg starships were preventing that. Seven had no idea of just how much time the *Enterprise* had left, but she suspected it wasn't all that much.

They have come. They have come and we can hide no longer. You have come, and you would invade us. You are they whom we were designed to destroy.

Not anymore.

You reek of them. Your thought processes are theirs.

I am what they have made me. But I have transcended that. Moved beyond that.

You tell yourself that. We do not believe it. You seek to hurt us. We will hurt you.

Seven screamed as pure mental feedback washed through her brain. The One Voice—for that was how she had come to think of it—was trying to batter her away, both physically and emotionally.

I am not going to hurt you. I want to help you. I want you to help us. I want to aid you in doing what you were designed to do.

You seek to assimilate us. You are Borg.

I want to destroy the Borg. They threaten the race that spawned me. They must be stopped.

We will stop you.

Seven of Nine, whose internal clock was hyperprecise, lost track of time. She could have been interacting with the One Voice for seconds or minutes or centuries, for all she knew. She felt as if her head was exploding. She was being barraged with images, but they were coming at her so fast and furious that it was impossible for her to distinguish one from the next. The doomsday machine, which had slumbered for so long, seemingly dead, without a guiding mind through which it could focus its energies, was rousing from its coma. It was then that Seven realized their extreme danger. It was possible that this machine, this biorobot, this creature that was a perfect synthesis of technology and biology, could assume complete control of her mind. Rather than be a collaborator, she could wind up being—irony of ironies—assimilated by the planet killer. Were that the case, it could exploit her mind and transform her into a mere shell of herself while simultaneously using her brain to power itself.

Unless she gained control of the situation, she might well be unleashing yet another unstoppable force upon the galaxy. A force that would no doubt have learned from its past mistakes and not allow itself to be dismantled the way it had last time.

And then something brushed past her mind, something that was not originating from the One Voice. She sensed Spock's presence. There was no articulation of words, nothing beyond a calming influence that she didn't even know she needed but was grateful for receiving.

It was like providing her an anchor in the midst of a buffeting tornado. Steadying herself, she thrust her mind back into the maelstrom of the One Voice.

I am as dedicated to stopping the Borg as you are.

You cannot prove that. You—

I can. Survey my cerebral cortex. Probe the implants that are there. Witness the virus contained within, designed specifically to destroy the Borg.

For a moment the whirlwind of mental fury lessened. It was enough for her to catch her mental breath. She could sense the machine doing exactly what she had instructed it to do. Her instinct was to recoil, to pull away, but she fought the impulse because she had to give herself over to it, no matter how intrusive it felt to her.

This will destroy the Borg?

That is the intent.

In order to implement it, you will give yourself up to assimilation so that it can occur.

If need be.

Self-sacrifice is your plan?

It is the secondary plan.

And the first?

You.

- ii -

Geordi watched as Spock stood next to Seven, his fingertips lightly on her face. He desperately wanted to ask what Seven was saying: she'd been muttering in a low voice as if she were in deep conversation with someone. At least she'd calmed down from moments before when she'd been screaming as if in agony. He'd never seen anything like it. All the strength had gone out of her legs and she'd sagged against the crystal. Yet she was being kept up by her hands alone, as if they'd formed some sort of powerful suction attachment to the column.

Spock had taken it upon himself to intervene. Geordi remembered what Seven had said about Spock's mind possibly being overwhelmed by whatever sort of mental prowess was behind the planet killer. Spock had assured Geordi, though, that he was proceeding with caution. Rather than a full-blown mind-meld, he simply brushed his thoughts against Seven's, steadied her so that she could cope with whatever it was that she was facing. He had said that he would probe no farther than that, for fear of literally shredding the poor woman's consciousness.

Now Seven had regained her feet, and although she was not outwardly acknowledging Spock's involvement, she was focused once more upon her task. Her breathing had slowed back to normal, and she didn't seem like she was under assault anymore. Satisfied at this turn of events, Spock tentatively removed his hands. He remained near her, however, waiting to see what would happen.

She continued her muttering. Geordi caught Spock's eye, but Spock simply shook his head. The message was clear: even with his acute hearing, Spock couldn't discern the specifics of what she was saying. It was simply too slurred, too under her breath. For all Geordi knew it wasn't even coherent words.

Then she said something that he did, in fact, understand: "You."

"You what?" asked Geordi, wondering if she was addressing him and needed him to do something.

That was when Seven's hands melted directly into the crystal.

At first Geordi didn't understand what he was seeing. It happened so quickly, so unexpectedly, that he thought something had gone wrong with his ocular apparatus. Then he realized and, with a cry of alarm, started forward.

Spock turned and said, far more sharply than Geordi had ever heard him speak before, "Stay where you are."

The surface of the crystal was rippling like the surface of a pond. Seven moved forward, sinking into it, first up to her elbows, then her shoulders and head. Geordi couldn't understand how something could be solid one second and liquid the next, and wondered if the substance was more like mercury than crystal. In the time that it took for that thought to cross his mind, Seven was completely enveloped by the crystal.

"She'll suffocate!" Geordi said. Dashing past Spock while ignoring his cautions, Geordi grabbed at the column. His hands banged up against solid crystal.

"She will not suffocate," Spock said confidently.

"You can't be sure of that!"

"No. But I can be reasonably sure."

"Reasonably?"

Seven was frozen inside the crystal. Geordi reached for his phaser.

"That will not be necessary, Commander."

It was not Spock who had spoken to him.

Geordi stopped in midmotion and slowly lowered his hand.

Seven of Nine was standing outside the crystal. Her body was still inside, but there was what Geordi assumed to be a hologram of her less than a meter away from him. Just to make certain, he reached out. Sure enough, his hand went right through her.

"Seven?" he asked in a low voice. "Are you all right?"

"Yes. I am being perfectly preserved."

Geordi would not have thought it possible that Seven's voice could be even more inflectionless than it already had been, but he was surprised to discover that he was wrong. Whatever humanity had been present in her before seemed stripped away. Instead there was a monotone that made the *Enterprise* computer voice seem positively garrulous.

"I have," she continued, "made contact with the core mind of the planet killer."

"And . . . now what?" asked Geordi.

"Now," she said, "we go to work."

30

The *Enterprise*

JEAN-LUC PICARD WAS RUNNING OUT OF IDEAS.

The *Enterprise* had been engaging in evasive maneuvers while laying down as much firepower as it could muster. It was, at best, a stalling tactic. The Borg starships swung around to either side, cutting off escape, while peppering the *Enterprise* with a series of blasts that seemed designed to pound away at its shields.

"They are toying with us," said Worf, and Picard had to believe that the Klingon had assessed the situation correctly. The strength of their firepower seemed such that, if they so chose, they could obliterate the *Enterprise* with just a few shots. The fact that they were failing to do so indicated to Picard that they were taking their own sweet time.

But why?

"They're waiting for us to surrender both myself and Seven of Nine," Picard concluded, bracing himself in his command chair as the *Enterprise* shuddered from another blast. "They're delaying until the last possible moment. They want to make sure they have either captured the both of us . . . or destroyed us both. And I have no idea which one they'd prefer. Bring us around, hard to starboard!"

The starship swung right and seconds later let loose with another phaser barrage. The blasts danced across the surface of the nearest Borg starship and were no more effective than any of the previous shots had been.

"Shields at thirty percent and dropping!" Leybenzon informed them.

"Damage to Borg starships!"

"Minimal!"

"Sir, we have no choice," said Worf. "We must depart the area at once."

"They can outrun us," Picard reminded him. "Plus, if we take them out of range of the planet killer . . ."

"It's not going to work, Captain!" Leybenzon shouted. "You disobeyed Starfleet orders on this wild-goose chase, and it's—"

Before Picard could interrupt him, Kadohata

turned at the ops station and shouted, *"Zel, shut it!"*

Taken aback by the fury in her voice, Leybenzon immediately lapsed into silence, save when it was necessary to give an update on just how badly the *Enterprise* was getting the stuffing kicked out of it.

The ship's resources were dwindling rapidly. Picard ordered all power to be fed through to the forward shields and Stephens desperately maneuvered the ship around to try and keep that bolstered defensive grid between themselves and the Borg starships.

Then the *Enterprise* was struck again, shuddering violently. Picard was nearly thrown from his seat by the impact.

"Port deflector gone! Aft phaser bank down!" shouted Leybenzon over the screeching of the alarms.

We have no choice. Picard knew it was a desperation move that likely was not going to work, but he couldn't see any way out. "Mister Stephens, plot us a course out of here! Emergency warp! On my mark, enga—"

The closest Borg starship was crushed.

One minute the ship was bearing down on them, and the next it was being smashed in. Something had struck it, a beam so powerful that it had trampled the Borg's shields and the Borg along with it. It hung there, helpless, sputtering in space, and then another blast lanced through the Borg starship, blowing it into a thousand pieces.

The remaining Borg starship angled around to face the source of the blast. The screen shifted and there they saw, to their astonishment, the doomsday machine coming around and taking aim at the other Borg vessel.

"I'll be damned. They did it," said Picard.

The Borg starship fired at the planet killer, a direct hit. The phasers bounced harmlessly off the machine's neutronium hide. The planet killer returned fire with a blast that Leybenzon informed them was, according to sensors, pure antiproton. The Borg starship, struck amidships, flipped over backward. It tumbled through the void, spinning like a pinwheel. The planet killer adjusted its positioning and cut loose with its antiproton beam, erupting from the maw of the machine like a fountain of lava from a volcano. The Borg starship never had a chance. The beam cut through the hull, sawing the starship in half. It blew apart, flying violently in two different directions. Picard watched as Borg drones tumbled out into space, flailing about. The doomsday machine cleaned up after itself, firing two more blasts that effectively incinerated all trace of the Borg. Only a few random scraps of the ship remained floating.

Leybenzon let out a slow, astonished whistle. It was hardly the appropriate response, but Picard couldn't fault him for it: he was thinking much the same thing. Picard had known going in that the entire plan was a pipe dream at worst, a long shot at best. But even he, who had been hoping against hope that the doomsday machine might help level the playing field, had trouble believing it had worked that effectively.

"Astonishing." He paused and took a deep breath. "Mister Leybenzon, attempt to hail the planet killer. See if—"

Then they saw on the screen that the planet killer had slowly pivoted on its axis and was now facing directly at them. The roaring fireball within told them that the power of the device had been rekindled. The device's near century-long rest had obviously done it good.

"Oh, bugger," said Kadohata.

Picard was about to order evasive maneuvers when Seven of Nine appeared on the bridge, directly in front of Lieutenant Stephens. What seemed briefly odd to Picard was that Stephens appeared to react to Seven's abrupt entrance a half second before she actually appeared, but he had no time to give that oddity any further thought. "Seven!" he exclaimed.

"You will doubtless be attempting to contact the away team," Seven informed him. "I am saving you the effort. As you have seen, we have activated the planet killer."

Picard rose from the command chair. He crossed quickly to Seven. "How did you come here? Transporter . . . ?"

Then he noticed that she was casting no shadow.

"You're not here. Not really," he said, slowly realizing. "It's a projection. The same way that Delcara did. My God, Seven . . . have you *merged* with that device?"

"What did you *think* would happen, Captain?"

"I thought . . . I hoped that with the combined knowledge of yourself, Mister La Forge, and Ambassador Spock, you would somehow be able to activate it in a manner short of . . . of giving yourself over to it. Doing that destroyed Delcara . . ."

"From my understanding, her own obsessions destroyed her. I have no such obsessions, no vendetta to pursue. I feel obligated to ask you, Captain, whether standing around and discussing the fine points of my command over the planet killer is truly the most effective use of our time. The Borg queen is certainly aware that two of her 'children' have been destroyed."

"Yes. Yes, of course," said Picard, knowing that what she was saying was correct. "Mister Stephens, set course for—"

"That will not be necessary," Seven of Nine said. "The planet killer can travel far faster than the *Enterprise,* for a longer period of time. I will simply take you in tow."

"Wait—"

"There is no time to wait. We must destroy them, Captain." Her voice dropped. "We must destroy them all."

She blinked out.

Abruptly the *Enterprise* was yanked forward. "Tractor beam's got us!" shouted Leybenzon. "Stronger than any I've ever seen!"

"Well, Lieutenant Leybenzon," said Picard grimly, "Commander Kadohata, Counselor T'Lana, it appears you're going to get your wish. We're about to go home."

The planet killer hurtled into warp space, and the *Enterprise* followed.

31

The Borg Cube

THE BORG QUEEN HAD NO IDEA WHAT TO THINK, how to react.

Part of her wanted to screech in fury at what she had just sensed. Another part—a very small, very minor, very irrelevant part—crowed in triumph and was quickly silenced.

Ultimately, she had no reaction at all. She simply stood in the heart of the Borg cube, processed the information, and then her thoughts went out to the Borg collective:

They are coming. Get ready.

32

Doomsday Machine

ALTHOUGH THE COMMUNICATORS HAD FUNCtioned within the body of the doomsday machine itself, Geordi La Forge had been unable to reach the *Enterprise.* It appeared that the subspace interference that the doomsday machine generated was an unavoidable part of its makeup. So he and Spock were effectively on their own.

It wasn't that they didn't know what was happening. The holoimage of Seven of Nine had informed them of her meeting with Picard and of the fact that the planet killer was now tearing through space at high warp speed, hauling the *Enterprise* along like so much baggage.

What still remained a mystery to Geordi, in

terms of not knowing what was happening, was the condition of Seven herself.

Ambassador Spock was off exploring other parts of the device. Geordi was a bit frustrated, because he had wanted to discuss with the Vulcan at length just what they should do about the current situation. Spock, however, seemed disinclined to participate in the discussion. Instead, he displayed a laissez-faire attitude that threatened to drive Geordi to distraction. Seven had just been possessed by a massive alien vessel and Spock didn't seem to care about that in the least. Geordi knew full well that Vulcans were unemotional, detached. That was just their way. Still, even given that consideration, Geordi found it infuriating that Spock didn't seem interested in *doing* anything about the situation. Instead Spock had simply said, "Matters must be allowed to run their course," and walked away, apparently considering the topic closed.

Geordi was using his tricorder to monitor Seven's vital signs. He was beginning to think, though, that he was wasting his time. Since the moment she'd been taken over by the crystal column, nothing had changed. In fact, it was unnatural the way that everything about her was remaining exactly the same. Her heart rate, pulse, all her vitals remained rock solid to the point of impossibility. There was not the slightest variance in any of it.

Hours had passed this way. Hunger gnawing at him, Geordi had returned to the shuttle and gotten something to eat. He had barely tasted it going down and ate only half of it, just enough to attend to his stomach's gnawing cravings. Then he had returned to Seven's side and remained there, a bridesmaid to her frozen bride.

"Seven!" he finally called. "Seven . . . can you hear me?"

"Yes."

He jumped slightly, because she had chosen to materialize behind him. He turned to look at her and was startled to realize that in her holoimage of herself, the implant had vanished from above her eye. She looked fully human. Her demeanor, however, seemed less so. Her gaze was locked forward. She seemed to be looking at Geordi and yet through him at the same time, as if she knew it was expected to look at someone when you were talking to him but didn't want to bother actually *seeing* him.

"I was . . . concerned about you," he said.

"There is no need." Flat. Indifferent.

"I'm actually thinking there is a need," he told her. "I'm worried about what can happen to you in the long term with this . . ."

"The long term?" She did not appear to understand.

"Yes. The long term. You need to . . ." He paused, then started again. "You need to realize that this thing . . . this condition of yours . . . it's only temporary, right? That once we've returned to Earth, destroyed the Borg, saved humanity . . . this thing is going to let you go, right?"

"Let me go?"

"Yes! Let you go! Allow you to separate so that you're Seven of Nine again instead of being part of this . . . this killing machine."

"It is not a killing machine," she said. "You do not understand. You cannot hope to. It is a device of peace."

"How can you say that?" He took a step toward her, his voice trembling with urgency. On some level he knew that what he was doing was dangerous, even stupid. Everything hinged on Seven being able to steer this device and control it so that it could be used against the Borg. But Geordi was afraid that an unseen clock was ticking down. That the longer she was bonded with this thing, the less chance they'd have of being able to recover her from it. "A device of peace? It's designed to destroy!"

"As is your starship," she reminded him evenly. "You purport to be a vessel of exploration. Of peace. But you have weapons that render you indistinguishable from a vessel of war."

"We have them only to defend ourselves!"

"And we are designed to defend not only ourselves but also our entire galaxy. If you must carry the formidable weapons array that you do merely to protect your own lives, how much more formidable must my weaponry be if all known life depends upon my ability to protect it?"

"But the *Enterprise* was designed to accomplish so many things. This machine is designed only to destroy."

"Do you think we are unaware of that?" she asked. "Do you think we do not wish it was otherwise? We are what we are."

"You keep saying 'we.' There is no 'we,' Seven. There's you. And there's the planet killer. Two separate entities. That's what concerns me: that you're losing sight of that."

"What does one born blind know of losing sight of anything?"

She did not say it with any malicious intent. It was simply a disinterested comment. Nevertheless it stung slightly, but Geordi pushed aside his feelings. "What I know is this," he said, keeping his voice neutral. "You've spent most of your life being part of something else. Having no free will of your own. And maybe . . . maybe it's like having an addictive personality. You have to stay away from those things that you know are going to do you damage because you can't control yourself when it comes to them. So here you are, and you've just merged your personality with whatever the AI is that's driving this ship. And I'm saying you have to be careful, because to you, having your own personality being subordinate to some larger intelligence is far more familiar to you than living independently of it. Maybe being blended with the planet killer is more solidly in your comfort zone. No need to make decisions or deal with people on a human-to-human basis. No having to worry about your pesky own identity. You just turn yourself over to the hive mind, step back, and enjoy the ride. And I don't want that for you."

She appeared to be focusing on him for the first time in the conversation. It gave him cause to feel that he was getting through, but instead she said to him, "You do not know me at all. What you know is Reannon. The Borg woman you lost. Who took her own life despite your best efforts to reclaim her. You are not concerned about losing me. You are concerned because you lost her. And you feel that if you can 'save' me in some manner, then that will expiate your previous failure to some small degree. Understand this, La Forge: we do not care about your conscience, your life force, or your need to cleanse both. We care about the Borg. We care about destroying the Borg. All else is irrelevant. And now, if you will excuse us—or even if you will not—we need to free the *Enterprise* of our tractor beam so that it may deal with the other ships."

She vanished, leaving Geordi no time to wonder about anything except what "other ships" she was referring to.

33

The *Enterprise*

- i -

THEY COULD HAVE GONE INTO THE CONFERENCE lounge or the captain's ready room. He could even have had them arrested and tossed into the brig.

Instead Jean-Luc Picard faced his accusers on the bridge, out in the open, with the intraship comm on so that the entire ship's complement could hear.

The *Enterprise*'s status wasn't going to be changing in the very near future. They were heading for Earth at top speed, courtesy of the planet killer. It would be a few hours yet before they arrived. But matters were still extremely tense, and that could not be allowed to continue.

"So," said Picard. Instead of at his command chair, he was standing at the front of the bridge, looking at his crew. To their credit, they were making eye contact with him, rather than looking away. "It seems we have a unique situation. Usurping control of a starship from its commanding officer is, by any standard definition, mutiny."

"Klingons kill for mutiny," Worf rumbled.

"Number One," Picard said sharply, bringing the meeting back on track. "As I said, by standard definition, mutiny. However, you were ordered to undertake your course of action by Starfleet Command. So on that basis, you were simply doing what you were expected to do under the oath you took as Starfleet officers. Which, I expect, you thought I was not doing. Correct?"

"Yes, sir," said Kadohata.

"As was I. Because the part of the oath that I was attending to was protecting the United Federation of Planets. I was doing that the best way I knew how, and in this instance, I felt that—yes—I knew better than Starfleet. Considering what we have seen of the planet killer's capabilities, is there anyone who feels that that belief was unfounded?"

No response.

"What I have not lost sight of," said Picard, slowly walking from one side of the bridge to the other, "is that, ultimately, we are all on the same side. Do not misunderstand: when you did what you did, I was furious beyond my ability to express.

I, who consider myself first and foremost an ambassador of goodwill, would have gladly lined up the lot of you against a wall, assembled a firing squad, and given the order to pull the trigger. However, the longer I have considered the situation, the more I have resolved that you were motivated not by a lust for power or command but because you truly felt you were doing what you were morally required to do."

"To say nothing of the fact that you were prepared for our doing so and thus minimized the effectiveness of our actions," pointed out T'Lana.

"Yes, there is that," Picard acknowledged.

"Captain, if I may," Kadohata said slowly, "I wish to make it clear that I take full responsibility for what happened. If there is to be . . . retaliation, I, as the ranking officer—"

"I have said nothing of retaliation, Commander. The simple truth is that I have not decided how this matter is best addressed. In point of fact, if it went before Starfleet, there is every reason to believe your actions would be commended. That does not concern me. What concerns me is the here and now. I cannot have a crew that is bristling under my command. On the other hand, you were chosen for your positions because you are the best. Nothing that I have witnessed in the past several days has persuaded me otherwise. So what it comes down to is this: do you believe that you can set aside your recent feelings and actions and obey me in the coming actions without hesitation? Because I will not be second-guessed again." He paused. "Well?"

Very slowly, Miranda Kadohata said, "I serve at the captain's pleasure."

Picard nodded and then turned to Leybenzon. He waited.

Leybenzon sounded far more strangled when he spoke, but he likewise said, "I serve at the captain's pleasure."

"I serve at the captain's pleasure," echoed Stephens, and the words came from the other members of the bridge crew.

"No."

The word was firm and harsh, yet said without undue emotion, as Picard could have, would have, expected.

T'Lana was standing and facing Picard. "What you did was wrong. What we did was right. The fact that events have turned out in a manner that appears to support your actions is irrelevant. To swear fealty to you, to say that I will obey your orders, is to imply that I somehow find your actions acceptable. I refuse to do so, even in the smallest manner. You are unfit for command, Captain Picard. You have aggrandized yourself above the chain of command, above every reasonable course of action that a Fleet officer should take. Those who support you in any manner are simply acting as enablers to your delusions of infallibility. Furthermore, I believe that everyone here feels exactly the same way." She gave them a sweeping, contemptuous look. "They simply lack the resolve to say so. In any event, I will not be a party to it. Do with me as you will."

"Very well," Picard said. "Mister Worf, would you be so kind as to escort Counselor T'Lana from the bridge? See that she is confined to her quarters."

"Not the brig?" asked T'Lana with a raised eyebrow.

"I don't believe," Picard replied, "that tossing you in the brig would be dignified. Do you?"

She didn't answer.

T'Lana headed for the turbolift, Worf right behind her. "Keep your hands at your sides and where I can see them," he warned her.

She fired him a contemptuous look as the lift doors closed.

Suddenly Leybenzon called out, "Captain! Long-range scanners are detecting other vessels . . . eight! All Starfleet!"

"Borg influenced?"

"Too soon to say."

Picard's heart sank. He wasn't looking forward to battling more starships, nor was he going to be sanguine about watching the doomsday machine annihilate more shiploads of former humans. "See if you can get through to the planet killer. Inform Seven of Nine—"

"I am already aware."

Once again Seven of Nine's image had appeared on the bridge with no warning. Picard was startled but managed not to give any outward display.

Without waiting for Picard to speak, Seven continued, "I am disengaging you from my vessel's tractor beam."

"That is much appreciated."

"I suggest you do not delay overlong in discussing the current situation with them. Certainly the Borg queen knows we are coming. We do not wish to accord them even more time."

"True."

"Furthermore, if these vessels endeavor to impede our mission, we shall be forced to destroy them."

Picard's blood ran cold. *"What?"*

"Speak quickly to them," said Seven and vanished.

"*Destroy* them?" said Kadohata.

There was no time for Picard to dwell on what Seven had just said. Instead, even as Leybenzon reported that the vessel had indeed been released from the hold that the doomsday machine had upon it, eight ships of varying size dropped out of warp space within proximity of the *Enterprise.* One ship, however, a *Galaxy*-class vessel, immediately caught Picard's eye. Partly that was because it was at the point of the V-formation in which the ships were flying, and partly because somehow . . . Picard was halfway expecting it.

"Lead vessel is hailing us, Captain."

"Can't say I'm surprised. On visual, Lieutenant."

A moment later, a familiar visage appeared on the screen. It was that of a strikingly handsome man with black hair, purple eyes, and a vicious-looking scar down the right side of his face.

"Captain Picard. Not dead yet?"

"Not for want of trying, Captain Calhoun," replied Picard. "And you?"

"The same," said Mackenzie Calhoun, captain of the *Starship Excalibur. "You on your way to Sector 001?"*

"Yes. You?"

"Yes, indeed. Just happened to run into a few friends on the way back. You appear to have also."

"You've spotted the planet killer, I take it."

"Kind of hard to miss. We noticed it's hanging back a distance."

"Necessary. When one is in proximity to it, it scrambles subspace communications."

"I see. Did you just stumble over it?"

"Not exactly. More like a detour to Epsilon Sigma V."

"Ah. That makes sense. Did you see the gift shop?"

Picard sighed. "No. We didn't get to it."

"Your loss. I take it that's on our side?"

"For the moment."

Calhoun caught something in Picard's tone. His eyes hardened even as he kept his voice in the same conversational manner. *"I see. Are you suggesting there's a time limit involved for that alliance?"*

"I'm suggesting that perhaps we'd best proceed to our mutual destination at all possible speed."

"Understood," said Calhoun, all business. That was the thing about Mackenzie Calhoun—he had an odd, sometimes even off-putting style, but when the crunch came down, he was as good as any captain in the Fleet and better than many. *"I had been operating as coordinating officer of our little fleet here, but with you on board, obviously I defer to your authority."* He paused and added, *"Commodore."*

"It's 'captain,' Mac."

"You're in command of a squadron of more than one vessel, Jean-Luc. My definition says that makes you a commodore. And my monumental ego won't permit me to defer to someone who doesn't outrank me."

"As I recall your service record, you don't tend to defer to individuals even when they do outrank you."

"Consider this special circumstances, Commodore. We await your orders."

"Very well. All ships: This is the . . ." He paused and then, with a small smile, said, ". . . acting commodore. Prepare to go to warp eight, continuing course for Earth."

"Don't forget to say 'engage,'" Calhoun cautioned. *"It's just not the same unless you say 'engage.'"*

"Make it so."

"Damn you, Picard, you tricky bastard," said Calhoun.

The armada, now numbering nine plus the

formidable planet killer, headed into warp space, moving toward Earth as quickly as possible.

- ii -

Having secured T'Lana in her quarters, and making certain that security guards would be standing outside at all times, Worf was preparing to leave when T'Lana said, "This must be very satisfying to you."

Worf looked at her, uncomprehending. "I do not know to what you are referring."

"This. My being restricted to quarters while your captain does whatever he wishes."

"He is *your* captain as well, whether you prefer that to be the case or not."

"Still, I am quite certain this situation appeals to your sensibilities. I mean, ultimately, you have won. Is that not all that matters? You have won and I have lost."

"When you pushed the captain out of power, Counselor, all of us lost. If we save Earth, defeat the Borg, all of us win. You benefit. We all benefit." He looked at her for a moment. "You took an instant dislike to me. From the moment we met, you held me in contempt."

"I did not hold you in contempt. I simply did not trust you. I did not feel you were fit for the position that you had been given."

"Nor did I. On the other hand, I never questioned whether you were fit for your position. Yet here we are."

"Yes. Here we are. Tell me . . . could you do it, Worf?"

"Do what?"

"Tell your captain that what he is doing is wrong? Refuse to do what he wanted?"

"Why would I?"

"One never knows until it happens."

He gave a contemptuous snort, the very notion absurd to him.

They stared at each other for a long moment and then, very softly, almost as if she were afraid to hear the answer, T'Lana asked, "What will become of me, do you think?"

"Become of you? I do not understand."

"I am curious," she asked, "if you are going to kill me."

Worf was utterly taken aback. "Kill you."

"I know that you would like to. I participated in a coup that you were unable to halt. While doing so, I rendered you insensate. Certainly your sense of honor feels violated. On that basis alone, I should think you would want to exact some measure of vengeance."

"I do."

"It is my experience that Klingons have little to no restraint in how they conduct themselves. However their passions drive them, that is the direction in which they go."

"I see."

"On that basis," she continued, "you would have no reason to resist the urge to kill me yourself."

Worf appeared to be considering it. "You are correct," he said at last. "However, there are all types of vengeance. Killing you would simply support all of your suppositions about Klingons . . . and about me. I think it far greater justice that you live with the knowledge that you have completely misjudged the captain, and me, and all those in the command crew who supported him. I think you should live with it for as long as possible. As I recall, Vulcans are fairly long-lived. Several hundred years." When she nodded, he continued, "I believe several hundred years' worth of punishment is an appropriate sentence for rendering me unconscious and turning against your captain." He headed for the door, paused, and added, "Of course, I can always kill you later. One never knows with Klingons."

He walked out, the door sliding shut behind him.

"No," said T'Lana, "one never does."

34

The *Pride*

GRIM VARGO WAS BORED OUT OF HIS MIND. IN fact, he briefly considered ramming his vessel into the Borg cube just to have something different to do. It would be suicide, but still . . .

"Get out."

Vargo let out a yelp. He'd been sitting in his chair, dozing, waking up every so often to see that the Borg cube was still there. The four remaining Borgified starships were stationed at four points around Earth, clearly ready to open fire. The *Einstein* was maintaining a slow orbit around the cube, like a moon. Nothing much had happened since those vessels had blown the living crap out of those Federation ships that had endeavored to approach the Borg cube.

So it was understandable that, when Seven of Nine appeared out of nowhere in the middle of his vessel, Vargo was so startled that he pitched over backward from his chair and once again hit the floor. He tried to scramble to his feet but wound up instead on his knees, leaning on his chair and gaping. *"Where the hell did you come from?"*

"That does not matter now. Get out of the system while you are still able."

He squinted at her. "Am I dreaming this? Are you really there?"

"No to the first, yes to the second, but only in a manner of speaking."

"A manner of—"

"We do not know why you are still in the vicinity."

"Neither do I." There was something wrong, something different in her voice. A sort of vibrato, as if many voices that all sounded like hers were speaking as one. "I guess . . ." He stood, and he couldn't believe he was saying the words as he did so. "I guess I was hoping you'd come back. I wanted to see you. I . . ." He put a hand to his head, his eyes wide in astonishment at what he was saying. "Gods. That sounds so—"

"If you are about to profess love, you are ill timed."

"*Love!* Lady, I don't—"

"Depart. Now. You will not see us again."

"You can't tell me what to do! And why are you talking in plurals, *Ann*!"

She stared at him as if she was very far from him on a number of levels. "We are not Ann. We are Seven of . . . the One. Leave. No further warnings."

She vanished.

There, in space, hidden beneath a cloak of invisibility, Grim Vargo shook his head and tried to figure out what in the hell was going on.

That was right before there was massive weapons discharge all around him. He had no idea why or how, but it all seemed to be originating from behind him. Then he saw the Borgified starships turning away from Earth and coming right toward him.

He was squarely in the middle of a crossfire.

"Oh, hell," he said.

35

The Bunker

"DISPATCH YOUR STARSHIPS TO ENGAGE THE Borg."

Admiral Jellico was drinking a cup of coffee when Seven of Nine appeared before him. He was so startled that he blew a mouthful of it right at her . . .

. . . and through her.

Other officers, seeing the intruder, gaped in shock as they approached her. Seven of Nine paid them no heed. "You have a number of vessels on station at the outer rim of the solar system," she continued, as if popping in out of nowhere in holographic form was the most routine thing in the world. "Dispatch them to engage the existing Borg vessels immediately."

"But why?" asked Nechayev.

"Because we are going to be arriving within minutes. Once we are there, the Borg queen will have no reason to continue to allow Earth to exist. The orbiting vessels will either open fire upon Earth to destroy it, or else Earth will serve as a hostage. Neither is permissible."

"Who's 'we'?"

"A fleet led by Commodore Picard."

"Commodore—" Jellico looked in confusion at Nechayev. "Did I miss a memo? Who promoted him?"

"Mackenzie Calhoun," said Seven.

"Oh. Well, figures." Jellico sighed. Then, all business, he asked, "How are you doing this? This holographic projection from such a distance, outside a holodeck . . . it's beyond our technology."

"There is no more time. Do as I have instructed. Commodore Picard cannot tell you to do this himself because transmissions will likely be monitored by the cube. She cannot monitor us, however. We are shielded from her."

"How?"

"By the One. Act now." With that, Seven of Nine blinked out.

They all looked at one another. "Do we trust her?" asked Jellico.

"I'm not sure how we don't," replied Nechayev, and she turned to Galloway. "Emergency subspace to the fleet: Code 9."

"Code 9, aye."

Code 9 was a very simple term: it meant attack

the enemy immediately, no questions asked. It was something reserved for when it was believed that the enemy was monitoring subspace messages.

At warp speed, the ships hovering in the outlying section of the solar system would be there within a minute.

"We may," Jellico said softly, "be witnessing the end of the world."

"We may," agreed Nechayev. Then she paused, met Jellico's eyes, and said, "Care to put a hundred credits on the side, just to make it interesting?"

Jellico didn't hesitate. "You're on." Then he wondered belatedly if he'd just bet for or against the human race.

36

The Borg Cube

THE BORG QUEEN DIDN'T BELIEVE WHAT SHE WAS seeing.

The foolish starships were barreling toward Earth. They were making a direct run at the Borg starships that she herself had birthed. They weren't even waiting to get in range of the Borg; they simply began firing. Phasers, quantum torpedoes, full barrages from all ships, at all angles.

The Borg starships, their shields already up, turned to meet their assailants. They hurtled forward, returning fire, outnumbered but not remotely outgunned.

"What fools these mortals be," said the Borg queen.

And then the awareness of military tactics that belonged to Kathryn Janeway made her realize what was happening.

She had lost her link to Seven of Nine. She knew that they were on their way because of the actions that had been taken against her two vessels. She had felt their deaths stabbing into her consciousness. The loss of life was of no consequence to her; she was outraged that she had been deprived of valuable drones.

It was obvious upon reflection: Picard and Seven must be almost there, and the oncoming starships were being sent in to draw off her own creations from Earth.

No matter. She could dispose of Earth handily enough from the cube itself.

Or maybe she'd just eat the damned thing.

Yes. Yes, that sounded the best way to go.

"Break orbit," she informed the *Einstein.* "I have matters to attend to."

The small vessel did as it was instructed, and the Borg cube began to move slowly, ponderously, toward Earth.

37

The *Enterprise*

THE *ENTERPRISE*, TAKING POINT IN THE SMALL but determined armada, blew past Jupiter with the rest of the ships howling on her tail.

Picard had the comm links open to the entire squadron, allowing for simultaneous transmission. "Steady," he warned the other ships. "We're coming within range."

"We have visual," came Calhoun's voice from the *Excalibur,* and then, *"*Grozit, *look at the size of that thing."*

He knew immediately what Calhoun was reacting to. The initial attack force was furiously battling four Borg-spawned starships that were identical to the ones that had assaulted the *Enterprise.* Despite the size differential, the smaller starships were proving a formidable challenge for the far larger ships. They had adopted a hit-and-run strategy that was working perfectly, diving in quickly, firing, and then getting out of the way as the Borg starships worked to determine which way to look first.

In the meantime the massive Borg cube, which had initially been hanging back, was slowly approaching Earth.

Picard immediately saw the danger.

"We have to cut past the Borg starships; we need to get between the Borg cube and Earth."

"No. You do not."

Seven of Nine—or, as she had referred to herself, Seven of the One—appeared once more on the *Enterprise* bridge, like a wandering ghost. She stood next to Picard, looking at the monitor screen. "We will come at the Borg cube from the other side. You attend to the Borg starships. We shall focus on her."

"On it," Picard said sharply. "You mean on it, the cube."

"No," Seven corrected him. "This is between us . . . and the queen. If we destroy her, we destroy them. And we will."

"Seven, if you destroy the queen . . . you've destroyed Kathryn Janeway. You need to find a way to capture her . . . to free her from—"

"Commodore, we must assume that Kathryn Janeway is dead. Her conversion to the queen was no simple assimilation. Now there is only death for the Borg. We will destroy them. We will seek them out and make them all pay. Forever."

"Seven!"

It was too late. Seven of Nine had vanished.

Before Picard could react to that, Leybenzon called out, "Estimated fifteen seconds to range of Borg starships!"

Picard forced himself to focus on the job at hand. "Picard to fleet. Two-by-two formation. Prepare to engage."

"Good luck, Commodore," came Calhoun's voice.

"And to you, Captain."

The *Enterprise* and her fleet closed with the Borg starships and opened fire.

38

Doomsday Machine

INSIDE THE HEART OF THE PLANET KILLER, GEORDI La Forge was going out of his mind with frustration.

He had no idea what was happening, no idea where the Borg cube was, no idea of the details of the battle. Spock was standing next to him, looking at the immobilized form of Seven of Nine still trapped within the crystal.

Geordi could, however, hear the distant sound of the machine's powerful antiproton ray being unleashed. "What's happening out there!" Geordi demanded. Frustrated, he pounded on the crystal. *"Seven!"*

"Perhaps attempting to distract her is not the wisest course at this time," Spock suggested.

La Forge knew that Spock had a valid point, but that didn't stop him from punching the crystal one more time in frustration. In doing so, he succeeded only in hurting his hand, and he shook it furiously to get the numbness out of it.

Seven of Nine's holographic form appeared next to him. "What is it, Commander La Forge?"

"What's happening out there?"

"We are battling the Borg."

Geordi waited for her to elaborate. When she didn't, he said impatiently, "Okay, *and* . . . ?"

"We are attacking the Borg cube while the *Enterprise* and the other ships attack the Borg-created starships."

At least Geordi was aware of the other elements that had come into play since Seven of Nine had apprised him of them earlier. Still, there seemed to be a hell of a lot going on, and here he was stuck inside this giant floating cone . . .

But he couldn't bring himself to leave, for he was certain that if he did, he wasn't ever going to see Seven of Nine again. He would lose her, just as the captain had lost Delcara, and he himself, Reannon.

Besides, at this point, it wasn't as if going outside would be the smartest or safest move.

"What's our status?"

"The Borg cube is attempting to fight back. It will not succeed. We will destroy it. And then," Seven continued with an air of confident satisfaction, "we will seek out the others and destroy them."

"No," Geordi said emphatically. "No, Seven . . .

you can't. Don't you see? That's the thing you have to avoid. Once this is done, you need to come back to us. To cut loose from it . . ."

"Why?" Seven was genuinely puzzled. "Why would we want to leave this behind? Leave this power, leave this sense of unity? We belong here."

"No! Dammit, Seven, listen to me! You are a human being, an individual! You can't just turn your back on that!"

She looked at him with a vague sort of pity. "You do not know us. Do not pretend to know us."

"It's not 'us'! It's you and them! They—!"

"This is pointless," she said brusquely. "And you need to leave."

Geordi folded his arms. He knew it made him look like a petulant child, but at that point he didn't care. "I'm staying right here. We're both"—he indicated Spock—"staying right here."

She stared at him and said nothing. For a moment Geordi felt as if he'd won a great victory. That feeling lasted until he heard a familiar sound and became aware of the fact that the world was dissolving around him. He tried to shout in protest but it was too late as he suddenly found himself back inside the shuttlecraft, Ambassador Spock having materialized at his side.

"Dammit!" shouted Geordi as he crossed immediately to the transporter controls. "How the hell did she do that?"

"I would surmise that, in her joined state with the biotechnical mind that is intertwined with the—"

"Ambassador, no offense, but never mind. I was already figuring it out myself. I just need to—"

Geordi had barely enough time to smell something burning, and suddenly he leaped back as sparks flew from the control board. He quickly extinguished the fire, but it was too late, the damage done. Wonderingly, Geordi said, "She blew out the transporter circuits. How the hell did—never mind," he said quickly, anticipating Spock coming up with a detailed answer. "We're trapped in here. We can't get out."

"Yes, that would seem the reasonable definition of 'trapped in here,'" Spock agreed dourly.

Geordi considered his options and realized there were none. Even the monitor wouldn't do them any good; inside the doomsday machine, they were deaf, dumb, and—of course, he thought bitterly—blind.

39

The *Enterprise*

THE STARSHIP SHUDDERED VIOLENTLY AS A PASSing blast from the nearest Borg starship clipped the main hull.

"Shields holding but weakened!" Leybenzon shouted.

They were faring better than were other ships. Two starships had already been blown to bits. Two more were crippled and had tumbled away, unable to fight. The *Excalibur* was taking more than its share of punishment but was still in the thick of battle. Unlike the other vessels, *Excalibur* was a mutt of a craft, starship technology melded with both low and high tech that enabled it to make daring, high-speed maneuvers that would have torn apart any other vessel attempting them. In the case of *Excalibur,* it often seemed as if the will of its captain was holding the damned thing together.

"Heading two twelve mark seven!" Picard called out. "Bring us around and target the nearest vessel! Fire at will!"

The phasers cut loose at the closest Borg starship, which was busy firing in another direction entirely. Picard was horrified to see it blow the nacelle clear off another vessel, the *Freedom,* which spiraled away from the conflagration like a crippled bird.

The doomsday machine, meantime, was hammering away at the Borg cube. The bridge crew watched in amazement as the two gigantic alien vessels engaged in life-and-death combat. The doomsday machine blasted at the Borg cube, blowing huge, gaping chunks of it into space. But as fast as the Borg cube was wounded, it regenerated itself. Picard had never seen anything like it. Where in the world was it getting the mass to replace the sundered pieces with—?

Wait.

"Kadohata! Is the cube . . . shrinking?"

Kadohata ran a scan on it and nodded grimly. "Yes. It is. The thing's eating itself in order to survive."

It was the only thing that made sense. The more the doomsday machine smashed it apart, the faster it sent pieces of itself to shore up the sections that had been damaged. One had to admire the dedication to maintaining perfect geometry.

"Crap!" Stephens suddenly shouted even as, without being told to do so, he yanked the *Enterprise* hard to starboard. A giant piece of flaming wreckage hurtled past. Picard knew instantly that it was another piece of one of the ships in his rapidly dwindling armada. The other Starfleet vessels that had already been in position when Picard and company had arrived were battling just as aggressively . . .

. . . and losing just as badly.

40

The Borg Cube

PICARD WAS NEAR. SO VERY NEAR. THE BORG queen could sense the presence of the *Enterprise*. It was frustrating to have him so near and yet so far. She was instructing the Borg starships to go easy on the *Enterprise*. She had every intention of holding him out for last, of absorbing the starship and then scooping him out like cream rising to the top.

But closer still was Seven.

She had no sense of her, but she knew Seven was there, in that hideous contraption, pounding away at her, smashing apart entire sections of her. The monstrosity was tearing gaping holes in the midst of the cube, and it was everything the queen could do to repair the damage.

"All right," she said both to herself and to the entirety of the Collective, "this has gone on long enough."

She reached out, bent time and space, and shunted.

41

The Bunker

THE BRAIN TRUST OF THE ADMIRALTY WATCHED with growing hope as a horrifying ghost from the past, the doomsday machine, repeatedly ripped into the Borg cube. Every time another huge chunk of the cube went tumbling away into space, Jellico had to fight the urge to cheer. Yes, granted, the cube seemed to be repairing itself with unbelievable speed, but he was becoming convinced it was just a matter of time.

"We should never have doubted him," Nechayev said in wonderment, and then quickly added, "You didn't hear me say that."

"Say what?"

"Exactly . . . oh, no. *No, dammit, no!*"

Jellico, who had been looking away briefly from

the viewscreen, turned back to see what it was that she'd reacted to.

Seconds earlier the Borg cube had been directly in front of the doomsday machine. Suddenly . . . it wasn't. The cube had jumped behind it before the less maneuverable doomsday machine could react.

"Tractor beam!" shouted Galloway. "It's put a tractor beam on the planet killer!"

The doomsday machine struggled furiously in the grasp of the Borg cube, but it was quickly becoming evident that the cube was more powerful. Slowly, inexorably, the Borg cube began to drag the doomsday machine backward. The planet killer was helpless to extricate itself with its powerful antiproton beam capable of firing only out the front.

The Borg cube was going to absorb the doomsday machine, and there was absolutely nothing anyone could do.

42

The *Enterprise*

"WE HAVE TO DO SOMETHING!" PICARD CALLED OUT, seeing the danger that the doomsday machine was in. "Stephens! Plot a course around—"

"No, sir."

It was Worf who had spoken. Picard looked at him, astounded. "*No,* Number One?"

The *Enterprise* shuddered, another glancing blow. Leybenzon called out another diminishment of the shields. Worf ignored it. "It is a poor tactical move, Captain. We are coordinating the fleet and cannot engage on another front. Furthermore, if we get within range of the Borg cube, we will be drawn in as well. If the planet killer cannot resist the tractor beam, we have no chance. I believe it is only the fact that the Borg queen has not yet captured you that the Borg starships are holding back. If we depart the immediate area, the rest of the ships will not stand long."

Despite the chaos of all that was going on around them, Picard waited a long moment before he said—never looking away from Worf—"Mister Stephens, belay previous order. Bring us around at"—he glanced at the battle grid before him—"four nineteen mark one. Aft torpedoes, fire."

Worf let out a slow breath.

They continued to fire on the Borg vessels, but nothing seemed to be getting through. "Enterprise, *you seeing this?"* came Calhoun's voice. *"We're having no luck against their shields."*

"So we take them on one at a time," Picard said sharply.

The *Enterprise* whipped around and, coordinating an attack, had the bulk of the ships concentrate their fire on a single Borg vessel while the remaining starships fought to keep the others at bay.

And Picard fought to keep his despair at bay as well.

43

Doomsday Machine

SEVEN OF NINE APPEARED IN THE *SHUTTLECRAFT Spinrad* and the look on her face was as distant, as inscrutable, as ever. Geordi, who was still attempting to rewire the transporter despite all odds, wasn't even surprised when she appeared. Instead he simply stood and waited for her to speak.

"You have to leave," she said.

"No."

"You have no choice. We have been outmaneuvered. We are being pulled in. We will be absorbed. We will have to implement the virus. The Borg will not survive. You will not survive. You must be gone."

"Seven, wait—"

To his surprise, she reached up and put her hand where his face was. Naturally she didn't come into contact with him, but if she had been able to, she would have. "You are sweet. We had . . . we were forgetting humans could be sweet. We were forgetting what sweetness was. We will . . . miss it . . ."

"Seven!"

Seven vanished, and suddenly the shuttlecraft was violently thrown backward. Geordi, not remotely prepared for it, was sent crashing forward. He slammed his head against the main console and slumped to the floor, unconscious, a fearful gash across his forehead. Spock, keeping himself balanced with astonishing precision, moved to Geordi and knelt next to him, ripping cloth from his sleeve and using it to stanch the blood.

The interior of the doomsday machine hurtled past them at blinding speed. Whatever inner fire had existed to power the antiproton beam had been extinguished. Suddenly, just that quickly, the shuttlecraft was in space, spinning away from the planet killer. Spock quickly brought the main viewscreen online.

The doomsday machine had already been pulled halfway into the Borg cube. The cube was clearly growing, its mass increasing as the planet killer's surface gradually merged with that of the cube. The surface of the Borg cube began to ripple, to swell, taking on the properties of the planet killer. As fast as it had been regenerating before, the surface was rapidly acquiring the same sheen as the planet killer had borne. It was absorbing the properties of neutronium, becoming even more impervious than it had been before.

"Fascinating," Spock whispered.

44

The *Enterprise*

EVEN AS HE CONCENTRATED ON THE BATTLE BEfore him, Picard watched in mounting frustration as the planet killer succumbed to the power of the Borg cube. He saw that the thing was becoming bigger, more powerful, acquiring the impervious exterior of the doomsday machine.

It was at that point he realized that he had basically made matters far worse by bringing the planet killer to Earth.

He had made a terrible mistake, and the result was that the Borg were going to be empowered by it.

Kadohata was looking at him. He waited for her to say what he knew she would say.

She surprised him.

"You did what you had to, sir. I respect that,"

she told him before turning back to her station.

Picard, despite the dire situation, actually smiled. But it quickly vanished as he watched the futile struggle of the doomsday machine. He kept waiting for a miracle to occur, for it to break free somehow.

No miracle came.

It had happened slowly at first, but the more the cube drew it in, the less capable of fighting back the planet killer became. Bit by bit it disappeared and soon, all too soon . . .

It was gone.

45

The Collective

SEVEN OF THE ONE, FORMERLY SEVEN OF NINE, *feels herself being pulled in. She knows this is the time, there will be no other. The One that pervades her cries out to her, begs her not to leave it, but it feels itself slipping away. It is losing all sense of itself, being absorbed into the Collective, and it fights, oh how it fights. But it is too much, this Collective, and Seven of Nine, formerly Seven of the One, comes to understand why this planet killer, this so-called doomsday machine, was only the prototype. The technology was sound, the mind was in the right place, but it was simply not powerful enough to stand up to the unfettered fury of the Borg Collective.*

Seven gasps. She has no idea how she gasps, for she no longer has any sense of her body, her lungs, her anything. She has been sundered from the One, and unfamiliar emotions rampage through her. She wants to laugh and cry and scream and sob both in frustration and gratitude. The "wanting," however, is not remotely the same as feeling the need to do so. Consequently she is able to clamp down on her emotions, hold them in check because they are simply not what Seven of Nine is about. Instead her focus should be, must be, upon dismantling the threat of the Borg. She is capable of doing so, for she knows that the virus still lives within her. She has kept it pressed close within her, and as long as her mind exists, so too does the virus. Now she has no choice. Plan B has become Plan A. The doomsday machine has failed, and so she must unleash the Endgame and, via the back door code, send it plunging deep into the Collective.

She does so.

It collides with a firewall and is halted in its tracks.

The mind of Seven of Nine cannot comprehend it, cannot even fully believe it. Something has blocked the virus, prevented it from burrowing deeply into the Collective and doing what needs to be done. This is impossible. This isn't fair.

Fair? Oh, Seven, when did "fairness" enter into this?

She is there. The Borg queen. She is right there with her, not meeting physically . . . there is no physically here. This is a true meeting of minds.

Seven gazes at her, into her, through her. She is terrible to behold and yet Seven loves her unconditionally. She has no idea how much of that is due to the influence she is already exerting as the Borg queen, and how much is her devotion to her mentor, Janeway.

"Kathryn . . ."

There is no Kathryn Janeway. There is only the Borg. You are Seven of Nine. You will be assimilated . . . absorbed . . .

"No. I am Seven and I will be free, and I will take you with me. I will rescue you."

You do not believe that. I know you do not. You have no secrets from me. You know as well as I that Kathryn Janeway is a thing of the past.

"Then how did you know?"

Know . . . ?

"How did you know of the virus? How did you know to block it before I could insinuate it into the mind of the Collective?"

We utilized Janeway's memory. We have assimilated her knowledge so that we were aware of the virus's existence and prepared for it. But that does not make us Janeway. It simply makes Janeway raw material for us, no different from anything else. We are Borg.

Seven of Nine knows this is the case.

Seven of Nine refuses to accept it.

She is in the Collective, the heart (if not the soul, for the Collective is a soulless entity) of the Borg. The Collective is shaped by the will of the queen. It is what she says it is, accomplishes what she desires to accomplish.

None can stand against her there. None can oppose her.

But Seven of Nine is unlike any other being in the galaxy. She has strode both worlds, that of the Borg and of humanity. She has inhabited both spheres for far longer than Kathryn Janeway has. The Borg queen, when all is said and done, is still new to this. No drone would ever think of challenging.

Seven is no mere drone.

Seven is no mere anything.

She feels the weight of the Collective bearing down upon her, trying to absorb her into it, to tell her who she will be and how she will serve the Borg. She pushes it away. The move is unprecedented, and the Borg queen is surprised.

How did you do that? You should not have been able to. You will not continue to do so. You will be worn down. You will be assimilated. It is your destiny to return to us, dear Seven of Nine. You . . .

"No."

The word catches the Borg queen off guard.

"No," *Seven says again, and she feels emotion swelling within her. This time she does not disconnect herself from it. This time she welcomes it, because it separates her from the herd. She can feel the Collective recoiling from it, as if it were a disease. She hurls her free will at it as if lobbing bombs.*

"No. I refuse. I have free will. Your belief in the inevitability of my destiny pales in comparison to my determination that that will not happen. I control my own fate, not you. You cannot play God with me."

There is no playing here, Seven. I am your God.

"You are wrong. You are a parasite, nothing more. You have taken possession of Kathryn Janeway, and you will return her."

She is gone.

"She is within you. I can sense her, crying out. You know she is there. You sense her as well. You attempt to deny that which is within you. I know that feeling. I have done it any number of times myself. But we both know that it is living a lie. You have tried to supplant Kathryn Janeway, but you have failed. You have done everything you can to blot her out, but I am here now, and I will pull her free of you."

You can do nothing but submit to the will of the Collective. Resistance is futile.

"No. This is futile. This existence is futile. It means nothing. We are nothing. You are nothing. 'Collective' is right. It is a collection of other races' personalities and achievements, and we have pretended to mold it into a society all our own, but it is nothing. It is a sham. It is a house built upon a foundation of sand, and I will destroy that house now. I will destroy it with the aid of Kathryn Janeway. Kathryn, reach out to me . . ."

She pushes through the Collective. She senses the minds of the Borg coming at her, a swarm of ants endeavoring to overrun a lion. They try to pull her down through sheer numbers. She will not be bowed. She will not be broken.

The Borg queen is there, right there in front of her, her face twisted into a sneer of confidence. More drones swarm upon her, and even more, and Seven of Nine pushes them aside. This is no physical battle but instead purely mental, and every time she thinks she is about to be dragged down, a new thrust of willpower propels her. The Borg queen's sneer fades into uncertainty. She redoubles her efforts, and the contest of wills heightens. She is doing everything she can to beat back Seven of Nine, but Seven will not be deterred. Meter by weary mental meter she draws nearer, nearer, and now the Borg queen is approaching desperation. She tries to back up, but Seven forces her to remain where she is. Her will is dominating the Collective. It will not, cannot, last. Seven knows this. The minds of more and more drones are piling upon her with every second, and if she stops for even a moment, that will be the end of her.

She feels herself starting to fall, and the Borg queen's look of worry momentarily becomes one of triumph. Triumph of the will. That is all the spur that Seven needs, the pure determination that the black-clad bitch simply will not succeed. Seven lunges, stabbing forward with the mental equivalent of her fingers, and they spear directly into the Borg queen's face.

"I have your assimilation right here," *Seven snarls.*

The Borg queen, the living personification of the cube, tries to push her away, but Seven has sunk her fingers into her face, into her mind. She probes deeply, piercingly, furiously, and she senses rather than sees the consciousness of Kathryn Janeway. It is howling for release but too submerged within the Borg collective to fight its way free.

"Kathryn, reach out to me . . . see what they have done to you." *Seven stretches out her fingers as if reaching across a vast chasm.* "They have taken your face . . . your identity. They have presented themselves to the world as you, but they are not you. I know you. I know you for what you are. I know that you are fair and just and the most human woman who has ever lived, and you would not want to exist this way. You cannot let the Collective win. You cannot let the world's last memory of you be as some sort of thing."

The Borg queen is fighting back. The personality of the cube rallies and Seven of Nine suddenly realizes that she is spent, she has nothing left, she is going to lose . . .

And Kathryn Janeway sees it. Kathryn Janeway sees the plight of her close friend, this woman she has come to care for so deeply, and Kathryn Janeway howls at the injustice of it.

Kathryn Janeway takes her final voyage and strikes home.

She is freed for only a split second, but it is enough time to punch a hole in the firewall that the Borg queen has erected against the virus. Endgame, like a thing alive, swarms through, striking deep into the Borg collective.

And the voice of Kathryn Janeway sounds in Seven's head.

"Thank you, Seven," *she says, and it is both despairing and uplifting, and then Seven of Nine screams as she is ripped clear of the Collective. Not ripped . . . pushed. She hears the alarmed scream of the Borg queen and the triumphant, furious howl of Kathryn Janeway, and then everything spirals away.*

46

The *Enterprise*

"LOOK!"

It was Leybenzon who shouted it, but they all saw. They weren't sure what it was they were seeing, but they all saw.

The Borg cube was losing its shape.

No one on the *Enterprise* had ever heard of or seen the old Earth toy called a Rubik's Cube. If they had, they would have been reminded of it by what they were witnessing now.

The Borg cube was twisting back around on itself, entire sections swiveling around, trying to imitate some sort of bizarre geometric shape.

"The virus," Picard said with growing excitement, rising to his feet. "It's the virus. It's permeating the entirety of the Borg consciousness. The whole of the Collective is trying to re-create an imaginary geometric shape that can't exist in the real world!"

The Borg starships were doing likewise. They endeavored to reconfigure themselves. They spiraled toward one another, hoping to combine into some semblance of a shape that simply could not be imitated. The Borg refused to accept that as a reality. If it existed in any realm—even that of the imagination—then it had to be assimilated and reconfigured into the reality that was the Borg.

The Borg cube was unable to maintain its cohesion. Neutronium might well have been able to shield the Borg from any attack that came from without. It was powerless against an attack from within, though, as its very molecular structure began to split apart. Atomic explosions erupted all along the surface. The Collective was unaware, devoted only to the overwhelming impetus to solve this unfathomable geometric progression.

The influence of the virus reached its breaking point . . .

. . . and it broke.

The Borg starships flew apart in all directions while the Borg cube imploded. It crumpled in on itself, then expanded, and then contracted once more as it shook violently.

Despairing, desperate, Picard was calling over the comm unit, "*Enterprise* to La Forge! *Enterprise* to Ambassador Spock! *Enterprise* to Seven of Nine! Come in!"

"*Enterprise, Spock here,*" came a surprisingly laconic voice.

Even as he watched the Borg cube in its death throes, Picard felt relief sweeping through him. "Ambassador! Are you all present?"

"Negative. Mister La Forge is with me, albeit injured. Seven of Nine was absorbed into the Borg cube."

Picard's heart sank. His mind raced, trying to determine some way to rescue her.

It was too late.

The Borg cube shredded, smashing itself to pieces.

The threat was gone. So were Seven of Nine and Kathryn Janeway.

47

The Sun

SEVEN OF NINE HAD A GREAT DEAL TO THINK about as she drifted toward her death.

Still immobilized in a sheath of crystal that kept her impervious to the ravages of space, she wondered why it was that she had survived the destruction of the Borg ship.

She had touched Kathryn Janeway's mind, touched her life force, right before the Borg cube had self-destructed. The fact that such ephemeral things had still existed, hidden deep within the Borg collective, gave her hope for herself. She had occasionally wondered, when she had been disposed toward deep personal spiritual examination, whether she still had a soul at all—presuming such a thing existed. Or had the Borg simply destroyed it and she was some soulless creature in the shape of a human?

But she had recognized the essence of Kathryn Janeway's soul, deep within the Borg collective. She didn't know how she knew that's what it was . . . but she did. And because she felt as if she had connected with it, she was convinced that she, too, had a soul.

Or maybe not. Hard to know for certain, and she didn't trust anything that couldn't be quantified.

The sun loomed before her. She wondered how close she would get before she could feel heat from it. She wondered if she would tumble all the way to the surface. Just how durable was this crystal encasement, anyway?

Her mind wandered. Why, indeed, had the Borg queen called to her and only her . . . just as, in the previous situation, the Borg had called to Picard but not to her? She supposed she would never know for certain. Perhaps in Picard's case, it had been due to proximity. He was much closer, so he sensed it. In her case, it was because of her close connection to Kathryn Janeway. That could indeed be it. It had been sort of a psychic SOS, detectable to Seven because of their relationship and to no one else.

Hell, maybe it was divine intervention. God. Wasn't that the all-purpose explanation that some humanoids used when they didn't truly understand why things happened? God's will. God's plan.

A quaint and ephemeral concept, this God thing. But perhaps it warranted further study.

That was when she realized she wasn't going to have the opportunity to undertake it. She certainly hoped someone else saw the potential and embarked on the course of study on her behalf.

I am sorry, Kathryn. I am sorry I was unable to save you. Thank you for saving us.

She wondered if she would encounter Kathryn Janeway again after she died and was actually mustering interest in finding out when the world dissolved around her.

Before she knew what was happening, Seven of Nine found herself sprawled on a floor, having fallen because her legs were unable to support her weight. The crystal was gone. Someone had actually locked onto her vital signs and beamed her directly out of the crystal and into . . .

She looked up. She couldn't believe it.

"Welcome aboard the *Pride.* I was scavenging for souvenirs from the destroyed Borg cube and stumbled across you. So . . . did you miss me?" asked an entirely too cheerful Grim Vargo.

48

San Francisco

- i -

THE MEMORIAL SERVICE FOR KATHRYN JANEWAY was mobbed. It was also, of course, orderly. These were Starfleet personnel, after all.

Picard had never had the opportunity to meet most of the crew of the *Voyager.* There was one resolute-looking fellow with strange tattoos on his face who looked as if he was trying with all his might not to break down. Seven of Nine was standing next to him. She was resting her hand lightly on his forearm.

Hard to believe that she had survived. It was nothing short of miraculous. And that some independent ship operator was in the neighborhood and salvaged her? It was astounding.

Various Starfleet personnel made speeches extolling Janeway's bravery, her determination, her dedication to Starfleet and its ideals. As memorial services went, it was one of the more impressive ones that Picard had attended. It seemed to him that he had attended far, far too many in his lifetime.

Why? Why was he still here when so many others who were just as worthy as he had passed on before him?

Well, maybe it just hadn't been his time yet.

"Destiny." The word floated back to him, unbidden. If "his time" was something that could genuinely be pinpointed, then he'd been wrong. No matter what he did, he really was part of some grand game, a mere piece to be played rather than a player.

He didn't want to believe it.

But Kathryn Janeway was gone, and he didn't want to believe that, either.

But she was.

It had been her time.

Destiny.

- ii -

"It's insane. You realize that, don't you?" asked Jellico.

Seated across from his desk, Admiral Nechayev said, "No disagreement here."

"Who the hell came up with this idea, anyway?"

"Actually, Ambassador Spock."

Jellico moaned. Spock's reputation preceded him by several parsecs. If he suggested something and made an argument for it, more often than not, the sheer weight of his endorsement was enough to get it done.

Nechayev shrugged. "He's trying to convince the admiralty that it is 'only logical.'"

Jellico stared at the memorandum on his screen, still finding it hard to fathom. "A proposal for a new General Order: 'In the event of suspected Borg incursion, Captain Jean-Luc Picard, after properly informing Starfleet, is to be allowed to act in whatever manner he sees fit to thwart said incursion without censure or threat of countermanding. Said General Order to be considered retroactive to . . .' This is nonsense. This has to be shot down, quickly and quietly."

"The ambassador has proposed a compromise."

Jellico sighed. "Of course."

"No charges to be levied against the captain or the crew."

"Have you reviewed the log of the events with his crew seizing control of the ship?"

"Yes," said Nechayev. "What I find impressive is that the key individuals in charge of the insurrection have stated a desire to remain aboard the *Enterprise,* and Picard concurs. He believes trust can be rebuilt. The only person on the ship who has requested a transfer is the counselor, T'Lana. She wants out, and Picard also wants her gone."

"Fine. In that case, she stays."

Nechayev didn't think she'd quite heard him right. "Excuse me?"

"I want at least one person on that damned ship who's going to keep getting in Picard's face."

"Bull, Ed. You just want to keep her there because you're pissed off about the ambassador's suggestion."

"Damned right."

She considered it and then nodded. "Okay. I can respect that. But Ed, if we don't agree, she is going to resign her commission."

"Fine."

- iii -

Jean-Luc Picard and Mackenzie Calhoun stood in front of the memorial for Kathryn Janeway. It was a tall, gleaming pillar with a light burning atop it.

"She was quite a woman," said Picard. "She will be missed."

"I know." Calhoun paused and then asked, "What kind of memorial do you think I'll get? When I die heroically, I mean."

"You? You'll have a bugle on a pedestal that emits loud and discordant notes at random intervals to startle passersby."

Calhoun considered that. "I like it," he decided.

Picard extended a hand. "It was good working with you again, Mac, if only for a brief time. We should try getting together when we're not all teetering on the edge of galactic disaster."

"What fun would that be?" He shook Picard's hand.

"Oh, by the way," said Picard. "That former crewman of yours, Stephens, rather odd, I have to say. But I think he'll work out."

Calhoun gave him a confused look. "What are you talking about?"

"What do you mean, what am I talking about?" Picard had never understood Calhoun's sense of humor, and this was clearly the latest example. "Jon Stephens. The transfer from your ship. Flight controller . . ."

Then he saw the look in Calhoun's face and realized that the captain of the *Excalibur* wasn't joking when he said, "Jean-Luc, I swear to you by all the gods of Xenex, I haven't the faintest idea what you're referring to. Whoever the hell you've got steering your ship, he isn't, and never has been, one of mine."

"Then who is he?"

Calhoun shrugged.

49

Somewhere

KATHRYN JANEWAY LOOKED AROUND AND SAW nothing. A lot of it.

Then she saw, or perhaps sensed, something near her. She looked at it without eyes and saw it clearly.

It was an odd-looking man with grayish hair and a slightly sad face.

"Who are you?"

"Jon Stephens. Former navigator of the *Enterprise.*" Then the form and substance of the man before her shifted . . .

. . . and Lady Q appeared.

"I don't understand," said Janeway. "What's happened? Why were you on the *Enterprise*?"

"Why do starships go to watch stars burn out?

Sometimes you just want a front-row seat when something great meets its end."

"Meets its . . ." Janeway's voice trailed off. "Am I . . . are you saying I'm . . . dead?"

Lady Q made a dismissive noise. "What a nonsensical term. You and your ilk, you're so locked into words. Words are useless. It's all about concepts. 'Dead' doesn't mean anything. Just like 'end' doesn't mean anything. I mentioned watching stars dying before. Except they collapse and form black holes. So do they die, or do they simply become something else?"

"And . . . what have I become?" Janeway asked slowly. "And why have you cared all this time?"

"I haven't," sighed Lady Q. "But Q has. And had. And did. And does. Which has, and had, and did, and does, made, make, and make you of interest."

"To whom?"

"To me. To him. To . . . others."

"But . . . what if I want to go back?"

"You can't." She said it not unkindly. "The universe never goes back. It's all about moving forward, evolving, the call of destiny."

"I don't believe in destiny," Janeway said firmly.

"That's all right," said Lady Q, and she extended a hand. "Fortunately, it believes in you. Come and I'll show you."

She considered the offer. "I seem to recall that at least once the universe 'went back.' Ambassador Spock. Dead and buried. Yet, he is alive and well."

Lady Q looked annoyed. She extended her hand once again.

Janeway decided to acquiesce. As a wise Vulcan had once said, *There are always possibilities.*

"Is there coffee where we're going?" she asked.

"Bottomless cups of it."

"Thank God."

"You're welcome."

Kathryn Janeway took her hand . . .

. . . and was gone.

50

The *Einstein*

CUT OFF FROM THE COLLECTIVE, CAST ADRIFT from the Borg queen, devoid of any purpose or mission, Number Two and the scattered remains of the Borg drones had piloted their science and exploration vessel far out of the solar system.

When the Borg cube detonated, they should have shut down.

They should have been helpless.

They should have died.

But the Borg queen had crafted them to remain a part of her . . . but also separate from her . . .

. . . just in case.

The Borg did not used to plan for "just in case." But their experience with the deceitful and resourceful humans had proved the wisdom of doing so. And so they had evolved in their thinking.

The *Einstein* headed off into deep space, propelled by the recollected shreds of the oath that every individual on the ship had—in another life—sworn.

To explore strange new worlds . . . and assimilate them.

To seek out new life-forms . . . and new civilizations . . . and assimilate them.

To boldly go where no Borg had gone before . . .

. . . and assimilate them.